The Mayor's Daughter

Other works by James Hoggard:

FICTION

Trotter Ross
Elevator Man
Riding the Wind and Other Tales
Patterns of Illusion

POETRY

Eyesigns
The Shaper Poems
Two Gulls, One Hawk
Breaking an Indelicate Statue
Medea in Taos
Rain in a Sunlit Sky
Wearing the River
Triangles of Light: The Edward Hopper Poems

TRANSLATION

The Art of Dying, poems by Oscar Hahn
Love Breaks, poems by Oscar Hahn
Chronicle of My Worst Years, poems by Tino Villanueva
Alone Against the Sea: Poems from Cuba, by Raúl Mesa
Splintered Silences, poems by Greta de León
Stolen Verses & Other Poems, by Oscar Hahn
Ashes In Love, poems by Oscar Hahn

The Mayor's Daughter

a novel by

James Hoggard

WingsPress
San Antonio, Texas
2011

The Mayor's Daughter © 2011 by James Hoggard
Cover art: Untitled watercolor,
© 2010 by Barbara Whitehead, used by permission.

First Edition

Print Edition ISBN: 978-0-916727-72-7
ePub ISBN: 978-1-60940-093-4
Kindle ISBN: 978-1-60940-094-1
Library PDF ISBN: 978-1-60940-095-8

Wings Press
627 E. Guenther
San Antonio, Texas 78210
Phone/fax: (210) 271-7805

On-line catalogue and ordering:
www.wingspress.com
All Wings Press titles are distributed to the trade by
Independent Publishers Group
www.ipgbook.com

Library of Congress Cataloging-in-Publication Data:

Hoggard, James.
 The mayor's daughter : a novel / by James Hoggard. -- 1st ed.
       p. cm.
  ISBN 978-0-916727-72-7 (pbk. : alk. paper) -- ISBN 978-1-60940-093-4 (ebk.) -- ISBN 978-1-60940-094-1 (Kindle ebk.) -- ISBN 978-1-60940-095-8 (library pdf. ebk.)
 1. Texas--Fiction. I. Title.
 PS3558.O34752M39 2011
 813'.54--dc22
                                    2011007195

Except for fair use in reviews and/or scholarly considerations, no portion of this book may be reproduced in any form without the written permission of the author or the publisher.

Again for Lynn

The Mayor's Daughter

CHAPTER 1

Dear John Evening,

I know the greeting sounds awkward. It does to me, too. But I feel too close to you to use "Mr." before your name. I know we've talked many times, but this is one of the only letters I think I've written you. You get my age, and some things start blurring.

I started to call you. I even picked up the phone, then something told me I needed greater distance if we were to talk more about that time—1924/25—so far from where we both are now—and you not even close to being born then. Still, what I've realized is not a truth but a sensation that periodically sweeps over me. It frightens me. I don't understand it. But for heavensakes, don't worry. You don't have an old woman on your hands about to do a king hell nervous breakdown. I wouldn't do that to you, or to me either, especially since it's your job to find the shape of this story. I also don't know how much you've already written—or even if you've written anything at all. But that's not the problem.

It's not old age that's frightening me. It's a feeling of disorientation. That's why I'm writing this letter. If I talked it out with you, I'd likely break down, and if I did that, I'd still be in this noisome fog, and you wouldn't have anything to work with.

What I'm referring to has happened before. But two weeks ago the sensation was especially strong when I was driving back from the library: since childhood that place has been my fortress and palace. Memories struck me, and I've avoided telling you about them. I didn't want to bother you. The images might not be pertinent, so if you don't need them, junk them.

As I said, I was coming back from town when it happened. I was driving up 9th Street, just as I've done a thousand times before—back when it was two-way all the way, back when it had a street car line, and now that it's just one way part of the way. For some reason I started noticing street numbers: 1300 block, 1400, 1500. I was ticking them off as if I were a fool thinking I was going somewhere. That's when it slapped me. Where 1601 used to be was a parking lot. Nothing rare about that. It's been years since that part of 9th has been anything at all like a neighborhood. I think, in fact, I got alerted to all this by realizing there's only (I think) one house left in that area—1407, where two lawyers have their offices.

Then there's a parking lot a bit farther down where 1601 used to be, and next to it a small office building where some doctors work, some medical testing facility. So what happened there that threatened to undo me? I didn't even know the people, but I did know of them, and what happened there occurred so long ago, on a Sunday afternoon in 1924.

The man's name was Daniel Rogers. He was in the dairy business, and about forty or so years old. His business, I gather, was doing well. But things like that, I learned, were beside the point. I got most of the tale from the newspaper. I know, too, that my parents and people they knew—surely a crowd of others, too—talked about it for awhile. Then they likely forgot about it, and I forgot about it myself until the other day when I noticed that parking lot where Mr. and Mrs. Rogers used to live.

Both of them out in their front yard, Mr. Rogers was begging his wife to come back. She kept saying no. From what I gathered Mr. Rogers was bawling at her that she had to, he couldn't stand it, couldn't live if she didn't, that everything with them could be good again, he knew that. I remember reading, too, that Mrs. Rogers never really said much that afternoon. This next was not in the papers, but I heard from some others that Mrs. Rogers—often a bit wild in the eye herself—was calm, as calm as you could be in a situation like that. Then her husband started yelling again that she had to, she had to come back. "Please!" he pleaded. "Please!" he screamed.

When she simply said, "I can't," he just looked at her, stunned, one of our neighbors said (we lived near there ourselves back then); and again, almost whispering this time, Mrs. Rogers coolly said, "I can't."

Mr. Rogers then reached back and pulled a .45 pistol from the top of his waist band, and looked coldly at his wife. Our neighbor who was actually there said suddenly there came the look of a terrible question on Mr. Rogers' face. Then without making a big to-do about it, he put the barrel up against his own right temple and squeezed the trigger. The explosion, I heard, nearly blew his head off.

As I remember it, there was no sign of great scandal that rushed through town about them. I don't even remember much wonderment beyond that article in the paper, and some talk, but not much more than the mentioning of a few facts. The paper called Mr. Rogers "a well-known dairyman," and that was about the extent of personal concerns in the article, except that he had a wife who wouldn't come back.

I don't have any idea what drove her away—whether she had fallen for someone else, the way people sometimes do, or her husband had somehow driven her off. I don't even have any idea why he had brought a gun with him out in the front yard on a Sunday afternoon. That always seemed odd to me. And if his wife had already left, why did she come back? No one ever said anything about her trying to retrieve her clothes or other objects. Besides, in cases like that, it's usually the man who leaves.

But I do know this. The other day I was driving up that street and suddenly gasped. There at the place I had just passed, something big had happened. For at least two people it was big, but there was no sign of it now, except for my own accident of memory.

After that, I noticed other places I had associations with, but nothing from the past remained there either. I admit it. I'd been struck by something I know full well is commonplace. But it struck me nonetheless.

Telling you this—though it's not helping me understand a thing—is bringing back some matters that, odd as they are, I need to travel to.

What I have in mind is a small painting, a portrait I did of Buster. I have no idea where it is, or even if it is. I gave it to him after I had finished it then later saw it on the wall at his mother's boarding house where he lived.

I liked that painting. In fact, it was probably the first one I had done that I really did like, yet all it was was a portrait. Buster called it his "blurry portrait," and when he said that, he and I laughed till both of us were crying, Buster all the while accusing himself of being ignorant, but having a fine time myself, I kept blaming him for being falsely modest because anyone could tell he had a great future as an art critic.

I liked his calling the piece "blurry." And when I was doing it, I don't think I was flirting with Impressionism. I didn't know enough to do anything like that, not then. I just had a yen to blur up his likeness. It made me think of him moving fast—little small-hipped, fast-legged perpetual motion machine that had the sweetest, most unselfconscious look in his eyes you'd likely ever see.

Then another memory came into view, but it was nowhere close to being personal—or so I assume. I've been shaken out of so many assumptions through the years that I'm not sure I can even depend on the truth of the obvious. It was about the same time as the Daniel Rogers disaster, but in Amarillo.

A woman—call her A—went into a café where another woman was having lunch. Finding her sitting in a booth, A immediately shot Woman B. Woman B, of course, had been carrying on—sparking we used to say—with Woman A's man. So B died and A was arrested, tried and convicted, and given a five-year sentence. Then immediately after pronouncing the sentence, the judge suspended the sentence; but what really struck me was the next item in the report: Woman A said she was glad to be going away to spend some time at her brother's ranch in northern New Mexico where she planned, she said, "to rest up awhile because all this has flat worn me out." That's what sent me spinning. You shoot somebody, get off scot free, but your main inclination is to whine about needing a nap.

The world here back then, Mr. John, was weird, just as weird as it was raw, but maybe the weirdest thing is that, of all people, Buster—happy-go-lucky as he often seemed—knew it better than the rest of us, though, lord knows, he was no great student, except in Chemistry, which got him a job at the refinery when he wasn't much more than a boy.

But saying that throws me back against myself, and I wonder how dependable the mystery of memory really is. Or is it a need, a chance to revise the past to make it make sense? I say that because—in December 1924—Buster quit school and went to work for the Texas Refinery. Thinking about that, even now sometimes, I feel like screaming, he and his fool notion that he needed to be able to support me.

Ru-Marie

CHAPTER 2

What often passed for lawns back then were strawlike runners of Bermuda grass that spread so thinly the red clay hardpan showed through. Except for flowers that determined women planted, the only color in yards was usually short-lived: yellow dandelions and spots of purple from henbit and wild verbena in spring—or what passed for spring in that wind- and heat-scorched place near the Red River. Tiny circles of white with tinier yellow centers came from asters. The soil was nitrogen-poor. Other meager points of yellow came from burr clover before it turned to grassburrs wheeling off a central root.

Settled for scarcely two generations, the town was growing, parts of it thrilling with bootleg saloons and the frenzy of the oil business. There was drilling to do, pumping, refining—and before all that, exploding formations with nitroglycerin that sometimes seemed to blow up at a glance so the wagons that carried the rope-cushioned cylinders periodically turned into bombs. In spite of all that—maybe because of all that—the place was growing. There was even a truck manufacturing plant in the city.

Some of the citizens, especially those who had come from wretched or legally questionable circumstances themselves, but had gotten, for a time, lucky, started affecting airs of superiority toward others who were still in or near those awful conditions and points of privation the others never wanted to see again. But even the gestures of snobbery and arrogance were often handled indirectly, though commonly with a certain air of belligerence—or was it really fawning?—toward those who presumed themselves better than the recently wretched wanted them to be. Some even assumed the public high school—there was no other—was too damn democratic. That was not an idle thought. This attitude would have serious consequences, namely murder, the crime taking place in front of witnesses at a lighted streetcar stop. Arrests would follow, even convictions. That does not say that justice was done. Some—those condemned to remember what they had seen or come to understand— would seethe, even rage; but there was little they could do. How could they? The judge himself—one of the judges; there were two trials—had been driven from North Carolina years ago because he had shot someone. Most people back then, however, did not know that. Then several months later the recently elected governor would take what many came to say was a curiously active interest in the crime.

Even the name of the place, Kiowa Falls, was illusory, some might even say fraudulent. There were no falls. Of course, there had been one at first: a little one, barely a foot high on the clay-red, gypsum-salted Kiowa River. In the early days, after finding the site, a man had laid a line of big rocks across the current at that spot to dam the flow enough to deepen the pool, at best another foot deep. Full of enterprise, he strung a rope across the river to pull his flat-bottomed barge back and forth. But the business quickly foundered. A big rain came, and with it a flood, and the slippery wall of rocks washed away; and there was no indication of where the falls had been. Soon, when the people there mentioned the name of their town, then city, they often dropped the word *Falls*, so the landmark, not even that anymore, became no more than a ghost in that wind-whipped, drought-prone place.

Winter northers also came with a troubling, terrible chill that, without much warning, roared through the area and turned the sky slate-blue. Terrible winds throttled the place with so much force the temperature might drop forty degrees in an hour. Who knew what to wear outside? Anarchy lived there. Viciousness lay beneath calm, but a cool air of indifference sometimes appeared beneath wild rage, even supplanting the rage, and spasms of passion were often short-lived gestures that would never take root, though even that assumption was undependable. Churches and whorehouses flourished, though the churches had greater staying power.

The place had another side, one that was often driven by women: the desire for culture at a community-wide level. Barely ten years before, the most prominent man in town had asked his wife what she wanted for her birthday. A city library, she said; and he had it built and stocked for her. She refused, though, to have it named after herself. She told her husband it would be more fitting to use only their last name. This is a gift to our place, she said: Not a monument to me or even you: we ought never be desperate for vanity.

There was a price—or benefit—one paid, the story went, for getting married to a good Presbyterian, especially a prominent one. The sister-in-law of the man who would turn murderer lived next door to the town's main benefactors. Some would soon say that the murder weapon came from the sister-in-law's home. Then counter-testimony came, others saying the murderer had had his own pistol. And hadn't his wife been armed, too? There was debate on that point, but that did not mean the accusers were wrong. Ownership of a pistol did not seem pertinent. So many had them; homicide, however, was worth notice, and during the trial, one of the trials, the rumor about the source of the murder weapon was proved wrong. The gun in question had not come from the in-laws of the man known as the Capitalist, but from the murderer's own sister-in-law. Two thousand years before, and more, the Romans had been right: rumor was indeed a creature with a thousand tongues; and in Kiowa the high school Latin teacher told her classes that each year.

But the murder had not yet occurred. When it did, a woman would sail wildly into grief, into rage, though in time she would learn—in odd turns of mood—how well acclimated she was to the changeable place she had been born to; and her allegiance would shift, then shift in time again, the alliances appearing to have been proven temporary.

As if she could have stopped the disaster, as if she were even responsible for it, she accused herself of having been too easily thrilled by her love's sweetly swiveling hips. He wasn't even taller than she was. He was just, some would say, a slip of a boy, but oh how she loved him, and his kisses were as dizzying as those impossibly swift moves he made on the dance floor, the new jazz numbers a celebration that had recently blown in on new winds.

Her parents—and others—told her that love was an odd little matter—certainly nothing for the young—and often anyone else—to depend on. It was best to leave it alone, at least for now. That's what they said.

During the middle of the night once, she woke up and found herself smiling. She had heard awhile back that her father had threatened her friend, had even driven him to run away into darkness. She was not, however, disappointed that Buster had not stood up to her father, the great *side-armer mayor*, she sometimes called him. He had played semiprofessional baseball, and he had been a good pitcher, but one without range, one limited to an insufficiently tutored side-winding pitch that, after a few years, threw his arm away, and with that the notion of anything more in the game. That's when he became a store owner. Then other possibilities announced themselves to him.

Ru-Marie rather liked the great drama she was becoming a part of; and, of course, nothing bad would really happen. Buster had escaped being clobbered by a tire tool—or so the story said. She wasn't even sure that he had truly been threatened, the tales people told so often undependable. She did, though, love the image of his quickness, and the way, when they danced, he made her feel silly in the belly.

Drifting in and out of sleep that night, she saw his lean legs and swiftly trimmed hips flying across yards then around the corner out of sight, but he would not be gone forever. She would see him in the morning, before the sun rose, at that lyrical point when in the hush a gesture of light appears, a subtle spread of a blush in the lower rim of the sky. That was the time when Ru-Marie would slip out of the house to give her friend a good morning kiss as she rubbed her fingers and palms over his back, and up under his shirt, then after a moment her fingertips would trail around his waist then slip behind his belt buckle and down, slowly down, and he, too, would slide his hands from the back of her head to the small of her back, then lower, inside her own waist band then onto her hips, though shyly at first, forward, and suddenly—she told Ima Jean, her best friend: *It's like the morning star singing*. Breath left her and she gasped. When she anticipated it, she said, that was the time a rush of blood thrilled her thighs. She was going to see her sweet love soon.

CHAPTER 3

"It's ridiculous," he told her. "Absolutely ridiculous."

"Don't worry about it," she told him. "They'll come around."

"No, they won't," he said. "They'll never come around. Not with me. They'll do what they do now—see me as trash, some idiot trashy creature who'll never be good enough for you."

"That's ridiculous," she insisted.

"I know."

"I mean," she added, poking her knuckles at his ribs to tease him, "they'll come around. It's ridiculous to think they won't."

They had had this conversation before, but its subject kept rising in an odd way that seemed independent of them. They were, though, aware of the fact that every time they talked about the crazed class system in their place—they even agreed it really wasn't a system—they ended up feeling awkward, the often open liveliness of their conversation disappearing. A sense of distance wedged between them, as if Buster knew that he could not let the subject fade, could not ignore the fact that the Colemans were pretenders. At some level they were, but that notion did not sit well with him either. He just could not leave the subject alone.

"Hey!" Ru-Marie said. "Are we walking together or not?"

"What do you mean?" he asked, tangled up, she thought, in his inability to think or talk his way into any sense. He had not even realized that he had begun walking faster. He had not even realized he had gotten ahead of her, she thought.

"Hey!" she said again and began laughing. "I'd like to walk *with* you—though there is some small advantage in being the required ten steps behind you."

"What?" he asked, sounding agitated.

She knew, in fact, that he was agitated, but she also knew his anger was not directed toward her. She knew, too, that her awareness of that was what let her play with him during times like this. She had no idea why she felt so close to him, but she did. Something about him let her feel freer with him than her girlfriends seemed to feel with their own boyfriends. She knew, too—but maybe this was just hope, she thought—he was wonderfully nuts about her, and she felt the same about him. She liked the fact, too, that neither one had any idea where they were going. She meant on this walk. That's all she meant, she reminded herself.

School was out for the day and she liked being thrilled by a fantasy she had been having—sleeping out on the second story sunporch and having him quietly leaning the ladder—stashed behind the garage, it stayed easily available, wonderfully alien to locks and doors—up against the house, quietly against the house. She could see him in the moonlit darkness. A breeze, a soft cool breath through the screen, was kissing her in all the places his lips and hands needed to be. She would have left the latch unfastened. She wanted him with her in bed. And she would have him again with her in bed. Their bodies would sing to each other. In the freedom of the night she'd be thrilled to have him in her arms.

"Okay," he said, still tense. "What's so good about walking behind me? And don't make fun of me either," he told her.

Eyes shining toward him, she could not keep from laughing. "You're really a delight," she said. "In fact, I'm thinking of you right now as an ice cream cone. I'm gonna lick you good—munch you up all over the place till there's not a thing left, except a big smile rummaging around all through me."

He was grinning now and hugging her to him as they started walking again, their hips brushing up against each other.

"So tell me," he insisted, "what's so wonderful about being behind me?"

Beaming at him, she quickly kissed his cheek and said, "I get to watch your hurdies sashaying all over the place."

"What are hurdies?"

"It's Scot for hiney. You have a cute bottom, Buster—so slappable and pinchable both."

"Where did you ever hear a word like *hurdies*?"

"Listen, sweet, you'd be surprised what'll turn up for you in the library."

"Which one? The school's or the one downtown?"

"Both."

"You're not suggesting, are you, that if I started going there and checking out stuff, your parents would start thinking I'm better than trash, are you?"

"No," she said. "I know how stubborn they are." Still flirting with him, she said, "But they're not the ones who count. I'm the only one whose opinion counts with us, and as long as you've got cute hurdies, I'll be your love slave."

"You'll never be able—or inclined either," he said, "to be anyone's slave, love or otherwise."

"I might. We might even want to tie each other up sometime and whip each other, too. There are people, you know, who go for that."

"You're just playing with me," he told her.

"And I plan to keep on," she said.

One afternoon she found herself unable to tease him out of his sorrow. He had told her, "It's not fair. I know what they think. They think I'm a bastard because my father's not around. I'm no bastard. Things just didn't work out between them," then he laughed as he added, "Of course, she did shoot at him one day, but that was a long time ago."

"He likely deserved it. A lot of people do."

"They think Mama's trash, too, because she runs a boarding house. They think we're both trash because we don't have a car while your own folks have that big, closed-in Franklin and don't even need streetcars. They even think, I'm sure, I live in a whorehouse—just because Mama's got men and women both boarding with us. I've heard what the rumors are. And your dad—Mr. Big Deal Mayor—doesn't want his little girl hanging out with poor wicked white trash like me."

"Hush, Buster. Just hush. There's something I'm going to tell you, so hush. Just listen."

"What?"

"Settle down," she said, "settle down. How many times have you heard me talk about my grandparents?"

"Why? I don't think ever."

"And there's a good reason."

"Like what?" he asked.

"In the first place, I don't have any grandparents—but I don't think that's unusual either. The wrong kind of toothache or cold hits and you're dead. But let's just narrow things down a bit. You're right. We do have a big car, and my father's business is doing much better than well, especially since the school system started getting all its sports equipment through him. And yes, he's mayor, too—and probably will be again after the upcoming election. And that's not all. He's Potentate of the Maskat Temple. He's a hotshot and that makes us, his family, hotshots, too. At least that's what my parents hope has happened. But there's something you don't know. Like you, my dad grew up in a boarding house. He didn't have a father either. Fact is, he and his mother were as poor as you and your own mother. And that's why you scare him to death. He won't ever say it—I don't even think he dares think it—but it crazes him no end to think if I keep going around with you, I'll end up p.g.—their damn silly term—and me somehow his surrogate, back in the same impossible poverty he thinks he grew up in.

"There's something else you need to keep in mind. The notion of class around here sometimes seems pitiful—though I ought to hush. If I don't, I'm going to get myself so worked up I'll start chattering nonsense. Still, about a generation or so ago, a lot of the people here—and the generation before them, too—were among and of the humble—some of them not even that impressive—living out in sod huts with the wind and buzzing rattlers driving them nuts. You don't have a damn thing to apologize for. And don't ever forget what an advantage you have in having the mother you do. A lot of the women—and men, too—who hang around with my parents are sometimes so stiff you'd think their circulation systems had been pinched off."

"Oh, Ru, I don't know," he said. "Don't get so rough on your own folks that you end up making yourself all miserable."

"I'm sorry. You're likely right," and she put her arm up around him and hugged him to her.

"You're such a love," he said, and both of them were now walking comfortably together again.

"I really ought to be careful," she told him.

"How's that?"

"Heavens! If I start criticizing the Presbyterians, I'll have to include myself and mine. We are, after all, a part of them, too—and have been, I'll admit, for awhile. So maybe I ought to lighten up on that crew called *God's frozen people*."

"That's funny," he said, laughing, "though I do have to confess I don't have any idea at all what the saying means."

"That's okay, too," she told him. "I know where I can get labels for pretty near everyone."

She patted his back affectionately.

"You're such a love," he told her.

"So are you," she said, squeezing him to her.

CHAPTER 4

She needed to talk to Ima Jean. She had been waking up in the middle of the night about to scream. There was not any mystery in what was bothering her. She was afraid of what her father might do. More and more—though mostly in her sleep at night—the world appeared to have turned into a violent dream. Days, though, were good. Buster still made her laugh. Just being with him made her sing, and he never seemed to have any trouble listening either. But he was not the one she needed to talk to. She needed Ima Jean who had been her best friend for years, ever since they had gone to Alamo together, luckily in the same homeroom from fifth grade on.

Ima Jean, in fact, just two years before, had mentioned how much fun she thought Buster was. "Try talking to him," she had told Ru-Marie. "You'll see what I mean."

At first she had wondered why Ima Jean had not staked her own claim on him, but she hadn't, and at the same time did not act as if she had done her best friend a favor. Her sweetness came naturally, it seemed, and so did her dry, often caustic wit.

Tucking her chin now and biting her upper lip, Ru-Marie felt lost in some unreachable, distant place. She also reminded herself that the notion itself, her own notion, was foolish, nothing even beyond silly. She also knew that upbraiding herself now was just as foolish. She had a friend and she needed to talk to her. She also had a boyfriend—he was so much more than that—and she was afraid about what her father might do to him. She could not shake the horror of the image one of her friends had given her: her father and another man walking up to the house where Buster was, where she was supposed to be, too, but wasn't, where all the kids there were partying in ways that Mr. Mayor Jeff Coleman simply was not going to tolerate. Or so he tried at first to suggest. He was really there to get Buster. That's who he asked for. It was not the stiffness of his disapproval that bothered her. She imagined that most parents went hysterical now and then. Everything she had heard from her friends indicated they did. That fact of mood-shift—unruly though it was—did not really bother her. What did upset her was the fact that there in late afternoon's clear light, her father had walked up to the house carrying a tire tool and not doing much of a job of hiding it behind his back.

During the day—even at night before she went to sleep—the image would fade, the absurdity of it dimming it to fog. But in the middle of the night, during sleep, the image of her father with the tire tool in his terrible grip turned so vivid she would flinch, feeling terrified that she had barely avoided being clubbed by it herself.

She had to talk to Ima Jean.

Spreads of dirt were showing through the yellowing grass. Wheels of burrclover had dried out so much that now they were nothing more than thready straw, and soon they would be dust holding briefly onto their old form. The stickers still left on the plants would blow away or sink just below ground—no deeper, the clay thick and hard—if rain ever came or mud ever formed. Sometimes the burrs would get tangled in the furry footpads and flanks and belly areas of dogs and cats or other creatures like possum, raccoons, and skunks that wandered the night. Only Buster, she thought, could run barefooted with impunity over this thorny ground. She wished that were so, and pleasant though the image was—Buster sailing painlessly across this little portion of oddly threatening earth—she knew how fanciful her daydream was.

"You don't really think he would've used that tire tool, do you?" Ima Jean asked.

"I don't know. I can't even imagine him having it in his hand—walking up to someone's house with it."

"He's never done anything like that before, has he?"

"Not that I know of—but that doesn't mean anything. I just can't comprehend it—his acting like—like those oil field and electric company guys in the bootleg bars downtown on Saturday after payday—fighting each other bloody for the crazy pleasure of it."

"Well, Ru, some people do like mayhem. And it doesn't much matter if we don't."

"Yeah, but not your own father going after your boyfriend."

"I don't know," Ima Jean said, then took a deep breath. "I don't even know what to say—I don't even know what to think about what he did. I mean, you'd think he'd be worried about his own reputation. I mean, who in the world goes after a kid with a damn tire tool?"

"My father," Ru-Marie said. Her legs going weak, she was feeling that—although she did not understand the sensation—she had just made a strange confession. Not an accusation, she reminded herself, a confession.

"Who knows?" Ima Jean asked. "Maybe someday we'll laugh at all this."

"I doubt it," Ru-Marie said.

"So do I," Ima Jean admitted. "Have you talked to Buster yet about all this?"

"For just awhile."

"What did he think?"

"I'm not really sure. He just basically laughed and said

how good it was to know he was fast on his feet. Then he laughed again and said it was like that story we had to read in class last year. His eyes oddly a-sparkle, he said, *I gave that booger a clean set of heels, didn't I?*"

"What did you feel when he said that?"

"Not really much at all. I just found myself laughing with him. It was only later that I realized how ridiculous I was being."

"You mean, getting upset about your father?"

"No. Thinking I could laugh the danger away."

Ima Jean reached out and squeezed her friend's hand.

"Thanks," Ru-Marie said, hugging her.

As they pulled back away from each other, Ima Jean said, "This isn't going to help explain anything—and it's certainly not going to help you feel better, but I can't help remembering what Buster did last spring."

"Which time?" Ru-Marie asked. Her lips suggested the beginning of a laugh, but her eyes, piercing and hazel, were glazed with a film of tears.

Hugging her friend, Ima Jean told her, "That time my cat got up on the roof and couldn't get down."

"I remember," Ru-Marie said, a smile finally forming.

"All of us standing around like idiots wondering what to do, all of us goofuses trying to call the creature down, then all of a sudden here comes Buster—we hadn't even known he'd gone—but there he was, walking up out of the alley carrying a long ladder. Then marching right up through us, he plants the ladder at the angle he wants and zips up it then over the second story's roof line, then onto the roof, and he's chasing the dumb cat around till it finally, going stiff, gives up, and Buster, just as sweet as could be, picks it up and starts talking to it as he strokes the poor thing's back.

"Then all of a sudden Buster's opened his shirt, stuffed the little creature inside it, then swings onto the ladder, goes one or two rungs down, then scaring us all, he whips around to the back of it and, holding on with nothing more than his hands, he climbs all the way down, saying *O goodness, if the beast starts clawin' or bitin', I'm dead.*

"And all of us standing there, stupid and helpless both while he turns himself into an acrobat. Then we got even dumber and someone asked him where he'd found the ladder. Then flashing that big grin of his, he said, *Oh, things like that aren't really hard to find.* Then after awhile he told one of the guys where to take it back, and like a good little soldier, whoever it was hustled it away, just like he was told."

"But what do we do?" Ru-Marie asked. "What do *I* do?"

"I'm not sure," Ima Jean told her. "I'm not sure there's anything to do except hope your father starts feeling embarrassed and ashamed of the spectacle he made of himself. Other than that, I don't know what to say—except to hope that he's got enough sense to be horrified by what he looked ready to do."

"But what if he's not?"

CHAPTER 5

RM told me:

I couldn't believe he did it—at first I couldn't, then it made sense, all kinds of sense for him. It was the craziest and sweetest thing he could have done. We weren't even close to running off and getting married then—well, actually we were, we just didn't know it yet.

My parents already disliked him. That happened the first time they saw him with me, there at our house. It wasn't him by himself so much that bothered them, it was what they thought he meant. Of course, what he meant to me didn't count. But it counted for everything to them. Just the same old trashy story, and nothing new or fresh about it. I could say it all simply, the same way my father put it: the sonofabitch wasn't good enough for me. And all that meant was there wasn't any advantage or land or lucre they could get hooked up with from his mother—no father around—and all she did was run a boarding house and go to one of those athletic shoutin' churches when she went at all, which was seldom. Something about the preacher she didn't like. I don't think she caught him doing anything; I just think she found out about something he had done. So I guess we all have our limits—an unbendable line of suspicion or severe limits on tolerance. But I never saw her bitter or full of rant either. I guess I'd put it this way: if she got down on you, Annie Lopreis would just get scarce, and she'd likely never bother trying to persuade anyone else to her conclusion either. She might not have had any money, and certainly nothing close to anything like position; but she did have dignity—at least the way I saw her—and she was always a delight to be around.

I got the idea early on—and this surprised me because of what my parents and the ones in their circles touched. I got the idea that it never occurred to Mrs. Lopreis that she had anything to prove to anyone. She wasn't defiant, I think, about anything—till there at the end, during the trials—but before that I just don't think she ever got bothered by notions of rank. In fact, I still think if there was anyone I ever knew who was grateful and satisfied with her morsel of daily bread, she was, in spite of the fact that she had to hustle hard to get that morsel. That's probably where Buster got his sweetness. Of course, I didn't think about that either back then.

I was about to tell you about Buster, what he did. As I've said, he knew my parents didn't approve of him, and they certainly didn't approve of my being with him as anything more than a classmate. They were scared about what might happen with Buster and me; and it turned out, too, they were right. It's just that they were likely a lot more instrumental in the match-making than they ever realized. And even if they were, that didn't lessen a bit what Buster and I were to each other.

What frightened them was that we might run off and get married—or I might get pregnant and we'd *have* to run off and get married. That's pretty much what people did back then, at least here that's what they did. The girls got nubile—and all that means is marriageable, and all marriageable meant was that we had breasts and periods and were little machines capable of having babies—or a family if you want to be a bit more delicate about the situation. So girls became nubile. I never learned what the term was for guys—other than something like perpetually horny, which wasn't a term that sounded anything near official. It certainly didn't have the—I'll call it—cachet that *nubile* did.

What was different about Buster from what I picked up about most of the other guys—and who knows how he got this way?—was that he did not get—I guess I'd say—bogged down about sex. He was passionate, of course—good lord, he was passionate, just as I was with him—but I don't think I ever heard him say a word about *need*, though from what I gathered, that was pretty much the only thing guys back then were concerned about. I, of course, don't have any idea about now, but that's fine, too. There's a part of me that's adrift back there in the past, and sometimes what I remember seems as clear as can be, though a lot of times the past is all aswirl and I'm not sure what's altogether true and what's been colored by who knows what—fear, hope, wishes, or simply the trump of bad memory—or sometimes this: a kind of paralysis that comes when you're—I'm speaking of myself—face to face with memories that are so accurate you're stunned by them. Not horrified—stunned, the world inside you such a strange and wondrous mystery in spite of all the points of injustice that taint it. But that's just something I've had to work through myself, and I have to say, too, it's doable, even when you remember the grief and horror you were sure would undo you, grief and horror you even hoped would undo you, the pain so wrenching you didn't think you could take it. That's when somehow another mystery kicks in and you find yourself, in waves, standing a bit outside yourself.

But what Buster never was able to lock himself into—or just admit—was the fact that my parents were *never* going to approve of him—no matter what he did or how deeply I felt about him. He'd always be forbidden, and it was all because of some notion of status they had, and these two people who never came close to finishing high school themselves—much less college or junior college—and if their parents didn't crawl out of sod huts or—sometimes I got the idea, though they wouldn't talk about it, sometimes I got the idea they might've slid out from under rocks like snakes—I just don't know who their parents were and who the parents of the parents were. To this day I don't know. That's probably why genealogy never drew me toward it. How could it if you were pretty sure you could come close to completing the known terms of the project in about ten seconds? I don't know why, but I was curious—then and later, too, about all sorts of things, but somehow genealogy never was one of them.

I found sportswriting interesting and read that section as much as I read any other section. I just never really cared much about how any of the teams or athletes did. I liked the energetic strangeness in the writing, the high energy that drove it. I think—it even seems likely—sportswriting did as much for me in helping me understand what a lot of people were starting to call modern art as anything else. Just think about it. The sports writers were calling boxing "the cauliflower art." You wrap your head around that and something like cubism seems easy, plus you realize you had already started playing with surrealism long before you had even learned the term. And, yes, Buster actually seemed interested when I'd get wound up and start in on the wonderful strangeness of this and that. I guess I somehow knew how different he was from the rest—or maybe I felt about him things none of the others ever stirred in me. I just know that if I started singing my head off about how funny and wonderfully weird phrases like *cauliflower art* were, he'd start beaming and listen whereas, from what I gathered, the other guys would prefer you shut up so they could get some of your buttons undone without all the unnecessary noise and distraction.

I warned Buster about my parents, about how they didn't approve of the two of us together, and how it was unlikely they'd ever change. He wasn't defiant about the fact. He just couldn't comprehend it, in spite of what he had said about knowing the fact. That's when he outdid himself. This was before he quit school and went to work the night shift at the refinery and, as I said, before we got married, but even more after we were married and they didn't know it.

One Saturday morning in the spring before we got married in June, he went down to the Kiowa River—nothing strange in that. He went down there fishing pretty regularly: helping make ends meet, as we used to say. But he went down there to the river—the moving clay pit I called it, though that really wasn't fair. Sometimes it cleared up enough so it just looked dirty rather than impenetrable. But he went down there and came back with a mess of catfish and perch. He cleaned and scaled the perch and even skinned the catfish, which is a lot more trouble than they're worth as far as I'm concerned. I don't mind eating them fried unless they come from still water and, if they do, their meat's mealy. I just don't want to have to get a pair of pliers and go to the trouble of pulling their skin off. But he did, and he got a rag sack, stuffed the fish in there with ice he'd chipped from the block in his mother's ice box then got on his bike—or the one at the boardinghouse he sometimes used—I never really knew whose it was—but he got on the bike, came over to the house. I saw him from upstairs—I was reading on the widow's walk above the front porch, but he didn't see me.

Then he knocked on the door, that rapping of his just as chipper as could be, and my mother answered. I couldn't see any of this from where I was, but I heard it all. As if she were some high class creature, my mother slowly said—even a bit nasally—"Yes?"—her voice rising as if she were using some kind of accent other than English, as if she were doing him a favor by even taking voice in his presence. But that didn't seem to miff him or rattle him either. He introduced himself as a friend of mine—as if she might have forgotten, though they hadn't actually met more than a couple of brief times. He told her he had brought our family a gift, a mess of fish he had caught. He said he thought we might like them.

Then along about that same time my father came to the door, obviously to see who this intruder was, and just as cruel and cold as could be, he said, "What do you want?"

And Buster, as if he might even be welcome, told him the same thing he had told Mother.

But my father said, "We can buy our own food."

"Oh I know that," Buster told him. "I just thought you might like some fresh fish. I've got perch and catfish both."

Still sounding gruff, my father said, "How much you asking?"

"Asking what?" Buster asked.

"How much are you trying to get out of me to buy them?"

"Oh, I'm not selling them," Buster said. "I'm not selling them at all. They're a gift. I had especially good luck this morning and thought you all might like them. I wouldn't think of putting a price on them—no price at all."

Then my father asked him, "What kind of fish you say they are?"

"Catfish and perch," Buster told him.

"Hell, son," my father said, "that's nigger fish."

Then came a silence that could not have been louder if it had exploded. And it did explode. It exploded all through me. I was horrified—and shocked. I had never heard my father speak like that. I had never heard him speak like that at all, and I never heard him speak like that again. And all I wanted to do—all I could think of doing was to fly down there where they were and scream in my father's face and scratch his face bloody, but I didn't. I didn't even move. You'd have thought I was paralyzed and mute. Then I heard Buster, and maybe his voice was a bit higher than it usually was, but it certainly wasn't quaking, and to hear him saying what he did made me want to throw my arms around him forever because—lord knows—that boy was as brave as he was good. I could even see him, his posture turning erect as he said, "Sir, I think you've given my fish a good compliment. The people you're referring to know where the best fish are, and some of them, sir, I'm glad to be able to call my teachers because, thanks to them, I know where the good places are, too."

Then growling like trash, my father told Buster we didn't need any of his fish, wherever they came from, and there wasn't any reason either for him to come back around here again, we didn't need him or his kind.

His voice low now, Buster said, "I see." But I gather he didn't turn away, not until I heard the front door slamming against the jamb. I was so ashamed—of my parents and me, too, for not interfering—that I just sat there, and though I was vowing never to let myself get paralyzed again, I didn't say a thing, and I certainly didn't stand up so Buster could see me. I didn't want him to see me. How could I? I didn't feel worthy enough for anyone to spit at.

CHAPTER 6

Dances at the Kreitz Hotel ballroom were held monthly, traveling jazz and dance bands playing for them. The music bouncy, sometimes witty in the face of mournful themes, the floor was usually busy and festive. In terms of age, the place had a democratic air, though no one had apparently planned that. The town's youth were as welcome as the adults. Bootleg beer and whiskey were usually available in several places: the hotel's parking lot and a rented room whose number made its way to those in the ballroom who wanted a drink, and nonalcoholic fare was readily available at the bar in the ballroom itself. The gatherings were also usually civil, the prevailing attitude being that all options were fine. The speakeasy bars were a different matter; fights there were common, the prevailing notion being that a lot of the oilfield workers would come to relax with a good fight after several unbroken days on rigs. But wherever one was downtown, the bars or the ballroom at the Kreitz, one's choice was readily available. If one wanted booze, no problem; if one preferred softer drink, that was fine, too. Many, of course, combined both, using the soft drinks to hide the smell of the stout fire-kicks the booze gave.

The so-called shakers of the community were often absent from the dances at the Kreitz. They seemed to prefer the Country Club and, especially when they rented it and made it exclusive, the Pavilion outside town by the city's nearest lake. The young people and a wide sweep of the city's residents felt welcome and charmed there, too; and a streetcar line made the journey as easy as the route downtown at night to the Kreitz.

Periodically some preacher—almost never from the larger churches—would get excited about the dances and exhort his congregation to avoid such places because all dancing really amounted to was license to prepare men and women and boys and girls to rub up against each other and lead each other to ruin. "The Devil, good friends," one of the preachers said, though others, too, in the smaller congregations would say the same thing, "the Devil is hard to resist. Believe me, Old Sin Death, the fallen and wicked angel of evil, is clever, and we're all carriers of Adam's stain, and though it's called original sin, believe me, there ain't anything original about it."

Buster told Ru-Marie and Ima Jean about hearing one of the exhorters a couple years back when his mother took him to a service in a small Baptist church. He said he thought it was Baptist but it might've been Pentecostal or an Assembly of one kind or another—maybe, he said, they were all the same, then he started laughing and told them he couldn't help it—"All that talk about energetic nastiness got me excited all to hell. Then when he started in about Old Sin Death I got tickled—half of me having no idea what he meant—that's one weird phrase when you think about it, and the other part of me liking the high energy of that guy getting all sweaty and worked up."

Ima Jean said she'd like to go herself. "What about you?" she asked Ru-Marie.

"I don't know. I've heard those services last a lot longer than I want to stay—and I don't want any callers coming around the house being a bother. You won't believe how many we already have. You two go on—you can have a good time for me."

"Frankly I'm surprised," Ima Jean said. "Is something wrong?"

"No. It's just that Holy Rollers aren't my brand of entertainment."

"No problem with me," Ima Jean said then told Buster he ought to take Ru-Marie onto the floor for a dance.

"No problem with that either," he said, extending his hand. The three of them, as they often did, had come to the Kreitz together; and sometimes there were more than the three of them.

Ru-Marie had mixed feelings about some of the new dances that had gotten popular: the Charleston, the Lindy Hop. She liked the energy of them, the pertness of the music that drove them, but she found the actual dances themselves unpleasantly jerky. What she especially disliked was what she thought was a self-conscious sense of happy posing in the dancers: their faces frozen in great smiles, their forearms scissoring ridiculously across their thighs as if everyone on the floor were declaiming the wonders of the great fun they were having.

From what she had gathered, and however vague and narrow her field of vision had been, she doubted that the attitudes behind the great phony grins and goofy whoops of joy were anywhere close to the sham exertions of spontaneity and happiness that the faces of the dancers aped.

When Ima Jean, egging her on one day—Buster was not around then—to confess what was bothering her, Ru-Marie said nothing was bothering her, then smoothly and with a wryly caustic air told her friend what she thought of the new dances.

"Land alive!" Ima Jean said, "but you're good at them, and here you are sounding like that Lord Byron we had to read last fall—how he went on and on about the immorality of the waltz when all the trouble was nothing but the fact the guy was clubfooted and couldn't do the dance well. So what's your excuse? Some nasty infirmity you're keeping from us? Hey, girl, listen—you're in bad company on this one," she said, beaming, suffering no fear at all that she might be driving her best friend angry; and, of course, there was no reason for her to fear the bruising of the friendship because Ru-Marie was laughing out loud and saying she guessed she really was sounding like a stuffed shirt, and Ima Jean, clapping the side of her friend's arm, told her, "No doubt about it—stuffed shirt's right. But, lord! The stuffing's supposed to come from your bosom, not from a bunch of damn hot air."

Feigning shock and severe disapproval, Ru-Marie looked at her friend behind a sham of severity and said, "I wish you wouldn't use foul language. Cursing is so unbecoming, especially in a young Christian lady like yourself."

"So it is, dear friend." Then aping a look of severity herself, Ima Jean said, "I just hope you'll be careful to keep those knobby knees of yours together. You can't be too careful. You let those two things drift apart, and not even very far, no telling what'll come up between them. Who knows? Maybe even a good-sized bitable snake."

"Okay, love bunny," Ru-Marie said, laughing, "you win."

The long streetcar rides to the Pavilion on the lake in the evening seemed like adventure itself. The line went far past the range of lights in town, though one never lost sight of those lights; and though they were scattered and few, farmhouse lights lit the way; and the Pavilion itself often seemed like a celebration of light. Breezes would play through the window openings on the sides of the streetcar. This, too, was part of the celebration. Men and women, youths and those well past that stage, huddled and snuggled together to keep chilliness off the flesh. Sometimes, too, there would be a quarrelsome couple on the ride. Some pique of jealousy, some spasm of mood, an accidental slight, even intended disgruntlement would make a couple sit stiffly apart or, to pretend one was above the partner's inexcusable, so terribly immature behavior, one curled up into one's own defiant embrace and mimicked the look of one so relaxed one had drifted off to sleep.

Then on the way back, that quarreling couple had obviously made up for now—though sometimes they would go back with someone other than the one they had traveled to the Pavilion with—but if they had made up they went on the ride back locked together and sweetly wiggling up against each other in a constant embrace, their voices full of whispers stirring up secrets in the brisk night air. The mayhem of love might also have settled during the evening on another couple and left this one bitterly stiff, this one not even a couple anymore. Only rarely, at least on the streetcar, did the tensions in couples turn rowdy. There was even a soothing effect in the lightly rocking progress of the streetcar, and with it came the gently comic sound of rattles in the chassis of the machine. Sometimes one even saw a coyote hustling over the track bed ahead. There might even appear a bobcat pretending it was safe—and defiant—though wickedly alert in the brush, or a raccoon would come into view. Sometimes one would swear a wolf had just crossed the tracks—"I mean a wolf, too, not a coyote"—but someone else would pipe in to say, "Only an idiot can't tell a wolf from a dog," then someone else would say, "Meanest looking cocker spaniel I ever saw," the streetcar itself having turned into a small community on a journey through the changeably dim and mysterious images of night.

Out on the edge of the Pavilion, the supporting wooden piers visible through cracks in the floor planking, there came, if the breeze were right, the mildly hypnotic smell of mud off the lightly lapping water, and even sometimes, seeming to use the watersounds as harmonic devices, the music from the dance band would range out to the edges of the pier where, though not always, there would be couples in boats rocking the water, couples whose darkness was far enough below the height of the pier that the people down there, waves lapping the sides of the hulls, were unidentifiable, and the same was true about what they were doing, the dance music a spell itself that lived in the weekend drifts of musky night air.

She leaned up against his ear and, taking his arm, whispered, "Let's go. Outside," she added.

They had been drinking soda water with some of their friends, Ima Jean and her date among them. "We'll be back," she told them, and before long they had left the Pavilion and were walking in a field past the range of the Pavilion's lights. Their arms around each other, they were ambling to find a good space to sit down, then to lie down. Comfortable together, they were in no great hurry. Even their half-aimless walking was playful.

They finally found the smooth place they wanted. Buster swept it clear with the sides of his shoes. He made long swipes over the ground, then taking off his jacket, he spread it out as a pallet for her to lie down on. No clouds about overhead, the sky was busy with stars.

Both of them were sitting on the jacket now, their arms full of each other, their hands and lips at home with each other. She was rubbing his chest, first over his shirt then soon she slid her fingers between the buttons then unclasped those so her palm could slide freely over his skin, first his chest and thin belly then over the muscle and bone patterns of his back, his fingertips now inside her blouse. She had helped him free it from her waist band, then he pulled her up closer to him, and bending down over her, he began kissing her throat, from one side to the other, and moving lower, he began kissing the tops of her breasts, the way she had told him she liked him to do, and pressing herself tightly against him, she ran her hands up under his shirt, then again up his back, her fingernails pricking his skin, and kissing her breasts again, he ran his hands up under her skirt as they lay down, the pads of their fingers moving up and over each other in waves, and he told her the little crying sounds she was making came to him like music.

"I want you inside me," she told him.
"Is the time right?" he asked.
"Yes," she said.
"You have the sweetest legs in the world," he told her.
"Kiss them," she said.

After awhile they were moving to lie on their sides facing each other. It would soon be time, they knew, to start putting themselves back together. He sat up and pulled his jacket up from behind her as she sat up with him, and he dusted it off with the back of his hand. While he was doing that, she unsnapped her purse, pulled a small piece of cloth from it, whipped it open from its fold and, pressing it up between her legs, she patted herself dry. Then finished with herself, she took another portion of the cloth and wiped and stroked him dry.

"Goodness," she said, squeezing him as he swelled in the grip of her hand. "You're coming back alive."

"How can I help it," he said, "with you?"

"Yes," she said, laughing as she stroked him once more, "this is the lever I'll use to crank the world into place."

"I like—that," he said, his voice a bit halting and weak.

Before long they were up again and brushing themselves off and helping each other dust off their backs, and the fleeting, light kisses they gave each other were continuing delights; and now, having walked back across the field in the dimness, the shapes of them more and more visible, they were going up the steps to the entrance to the Pavilion, and soon they were again mingling with their friends then going back out on the dance floor one more time for the evening. Then when they were all together again, Ima Jean reached over and flicked away a midge of something that only she had apparently noticed.

"Gotta keep you neat," she said, smiling.

"Thanks."

"What time is it?" Ima Jean asked, turning her attention back to her date.

He pulled out his pocket watch and told her, "Ten-thirty—close to it."

"Guess we'd better head back," and before long there was a group of eight of them again—they had all come out here together—but after they had been on the streetcar awhile, the group became, with the others in the dimly lighted vehicle, a series of couples once more. Some of them huddled together for warmth and pleasure. Others were animated and talkative; and again the car became a community, the lovers after a time—some of them—moving away from their guises of privacy into the company of acquaintances and friends.

As they had, a good time back, agreed that this made sense, Buster pulled away from the cluster of friends before they saw Ru-Marie home. So when she walked up on the porch, Ru-Marie told Ima Jean and the others that she had had a good time, and she and they all spoke in their normal conversational levels, all of them careful not to whisper. For Ru-Marie's sake especially, they needed to convey an attitude of openness. This is no secretive crew, they were in effect saying to the presence of the lights inside that were conveying a message that likely there were people inside still up and, like bird dogs, on point.

"See you Monday," she said.

"Till Monday," they told her, then Ima Jean said she'd

likely drop by the next afternoon.

As it turned out, her parents were not waiting up for her. After turning off the downstairs lights, she went upstairs to her room. She heard a noise in her parents' bedroom and went stiff, alert to the possibility of someone coming out to run her through a drill of accusatory questions. Even the possibility of that made her angry. *What do you want me to do*, she silently spewed toward the closed door she was facing, *pull up my dress and let you sniff around to see who's come for a visit?* But no one came out, and whatever the noise was died away. She went into the bathroom and began washing up.

She had assumed she would drift sweetly off to sleep the way she often did, maybe even more quickly. She was restless, however, for most of the night, at least till some unknown point when she fell deeply asleep, or discovered she had some time back. It even confused her that she had not dozed off easily, with waves of light sleep sweetly interrupting her memories of the evening, the projection of other images from times that had not yet kissed her flesh. That often happened, but it didn't tonight. Tossing in her bed, she tangled the covers. Tossing in bed, she felt worn and exhausted. Tossing in bed, she felt hot, then cold. Tossing in bed, she resented her parents for imposing their own bitterness and suspicions on her. Tossing in bed, she felt herself a fool because half the things driving her now were mad inventions. All she wanted was to be unconscious. Something was pounding loudly on a wall, or was it a door? Her door, or the wall again, and a shout exploded through the night, then the pounding began again, and she realized—as she held herself still and listened—that she had actually been asleep and had dreamed the angry pounding, the big fist banging against the wall then the door. Her head was throbbing, then she was fitfully yawning, a shiver going through her, she wondered if she had only been hearing the throbbing pulsing of blood in her temples and there had been no dream at all. It shocked her to realize that notion, too, had been a dream, that she had been moving through layers of dreams, that her hand was pressing between her legs and it must have been there for some time, she had no idea how long, but the rhythm of her breathing was tight and short and the heat from some fire was burning within her, voluptuously within her, then biting her lower lip, she muffled a cry that was rising into voice, a loud and piercing cry that she managed to push back, and as she pushed the cry back again, the burning inside her became a shudder, a flowering convulsion that made her begin to feel that she was floating into a gently rocking world she was barely conscious that she had reached. She cupped her hand, first one then the other, up under her breasts, now one and now the other again. They were exquisitely tender, and suddenly she was shuddering again, her spreading toes tight in the thrill of tension she was moving through, then a gasp of a yawn burst from within her, and she sighed as she stretched her arms and legs out as far as she could push them then found herself curling tightly into herself. It was then that she realized she was weeping but did not know why, the tears moist on her cheeks and briny on her tongue.

CHAPTER 7

Documenting grief, the papers documented hope as well, and the worlds—so often separated in kind and value—the material world and the spiritual world—seemed to blend easily, though in fact they stayed in the papers fragmentary blocks of print in the mid-decade ferment. The minister of First Christian Kiowa, the church summaries showed, was not the only one praying for prosperity, for a continuation of financial well-being. In Washington, Secretary of Commerce Herbert Hoover had his own pulpit that he was using to deliver a stern message to industry: the American people were demanding better radio programs. Industry needs to take heed, he insisted. That other world, the small and erratically personal local world, had serious plans, too. A man in Electra—a village burst into size because of oil—announced he was giving a scholarship to the boy with the highest standing in the town's senior class. The honor was a memorial to his own son, killed two years before in an automobile wreck. "I expect great things from our men," he said, revealing that the yearly scholarship would include one year at prep school followed by three years at Princeton. Reading about the opportunity, some gasped over their morning coffee.

Other reversals brought commentary, too: the son of Leonard Wood, governor-general of the Philippines, was having to resign his commission in the Army. News reports said that Lt. Osborne Cutler Wood had pyramided $25,000 into $800,000 in only a few months. "He did it all by cable," the news source said. Then another controversy struck the movies—numerous theaters announcing they were barring the showing of Mabel Norman's films. Famous as Charlie Chaplin's leading lady, she was guilty of employing a chauffeur who had shot a man in Denver on New Year's night.

"What do you think of that, Mr. Mayor?" asked one of the men at Jeff Coleman's table in the Kreitz Hotel coffee shop.

"As little as possible," he dryly replied.

"I think it's good," another man excitedly broke in. "We have some leaders here, business though they are—and they're insisting on morality. And it's high time, too, if you ask me. Don't you think so?"

"Didn't say I didn't," Coleman said. "I'm just not inclined to think of theater folk as leaders. Who knows?" he said drolly. "Whoever it was got shot might've deserved it. Some do."

"Hah!" one of the men said. "Pretty good."

"On the other hand," Coleman said, "the trouble might've been a mistake. It's sometimes," he added without expression, "hard to tell."

The senior man of the group, the one who never listed his profession as anything but "Capitalist," allowed himself a slight smile.

"Mr. Mayor's pretty slick, don't you think?"

"How's that?" the Capitalist asked, as if he were subtly testing whoever answered, and to some it was clear he did not expect to be impressed.

"What I mean is—always keeping himself covered."

"Perhaps that's why he's mayor."

Another article they remarked on was the news that Senator Frank Green of Connecticut had been shot by a bootlegger.

"No question," another place at the table said. "That's a case—if I ever saw one—of not keeping yourself covered."

"What do you think about that?" another man asked Coleman.

"Which issue?" Coleman asked. "Bootlegging or shooting a politician?" The table laughed.

"Take your pick," one of the men said.

"No, I'm serious," insisted the man who had brought the subject up. "Don't you think Prohibition's gotten out of hand? I mean I don't approve of anyone shooting anyone, but that's not exactly the issue. What I'm saying is I think Prohibition might be causing a lot more trouble than it's solving. That's what I was getting at. I just wanted to know what you thought."

"I never have used whiskey myself much," Coleman said. "I suppose it's capable of doing for men what Lydia Pinkham claims she does for women—makes a sick fellow happy," and the table laughed again.

As the group broke up to go to their various offices or stores, one of the men said there was going to be a twenty-piece orchestra at the Palace to play alongside the new Ramon Navarro movie—"*Scaramouche* it's called. Can you believe that? A twenty-piece orchestra! Sounds to me someone's got a lot more money than sense. You don't think they're just donating their services, do you?"

"I don't have any idea," Coleman said. "That's probably something else I'll choose to miss." Pushing his chair up under the table, he glanced at the Capitalist who gave him back a small nod of approval.

"I believe my wife," the Capitalist said when they were walking toward the outside door together, "is planning to call your wife—the four of us plus a few more for dinner tomorrow night at the club."

"I appreciate that," Coleman said, a leader's look of comfort in his manner.

As the two walked out toward the street together, the Capitalist said he was glad that some of their friends this morning "didn't get into that other big story."

"Which one was that?"

"The best one I've heard yet."

"I must've missed it."

"The man-eating mermaids in the Amazon jungle."

Coleman chuckled and said, "I think somehow I find a story like that comforting."

"I thought you would," the Capitalist said, smiling. "So do I." Then he added, "Today or tomorrow you might drop by Perkins. There's a suit there for you. Their new tailor's especially good."

Coleman nodded his thanks, and the two men, compatible in their inclinations toward restraint, turned in separate directions.

The sky, he thought, said trouble was about, the high cirrus clouds auguring snow, the wispy crystalline formation appearing so early in the day. Usually, he thought, cirrus clouds didn't appear till mid-afternoon, but this morning they had formed early and were clearly indicating a cold storm was on the way. Maybe it won't develop, he hoped, heavy snow such trouble for people here, a number of streets still unpaved. Then for a moment he noted the absence of harshness in the air. Maybe the storm was farther off than he had thought. No harshness was marking the air, not even here, in this low-lying downtown area where the wind often swirled. But it was not swirling now, and he found that odd. After all, the cirrus formation said a cold storm was on the way. But not knowing what to do with his reading of the sky, he dropped the notion, though he did keep glancing upward as if there were something else he might see and interpret, though he did not know what it was. He also did not know that he had been wrong in reading what the formation itself was saying. Skies here were undependable, but that was not the problem. The cirrus formation often suggested the possibility of snow in the air, but a notion like that was different from a storm; and winds which no one at ground level could register often dissipated formations, often altered their shapes, and the weather's rhythms changed and then changed again, a chaos of possibilities so often available here. Although he did not know this, Coleman was reading things in the sky that simply were not there.

He did know, however, that storms might blow in with few indicators hailing their arrival, and he knew, too, that sometimes clearly defined late-arriving signals blew away to invisibility themselves. Reversals occurred all the time. Summer skies were often full of huge billowy thunderheads that never dropped rain, that never even yielded a sprinkling of rain or any gesture toward any level of wetness and cooling beyond a thick and massive cumulonimbus organization of vapor. Usually the gigantic thunderheads did not relieve the terrible weight of summer scorch at all. Coleman had been here long enough to know that, though today he had forgotten, something similar happened in winter as well. Sometimes the sky said things that meant nothing or little at all.

"Morning," a man walking by said chipperly.

"To you as well," the mayor replied. The people here were friendly. He knew that, but he also knew that his office was what was being greeted, and such was fine with him. He had, after all, never been bothered by the nagging inclinations toward reflection he had heard agitated certain others he had heard about.

He glanced again at the sky then turned his attention to the sidewalk. Concrete needed his attention more than the sky. An unevenly settled spot could stub the toe of a shoe and send one sprawling. Wouldn't want to do that, he chatted idly with himself. Besides there's nothing up there to read anyway, he reminded himself, having forgotten the flurry of interest he had shown a moment ago. Not knowing he had over-read what he had seen in the cloud formation, he had no inclination to warn himself that he ought to be careful, that he ought to insist on being accurate when he made claims, that one might drift into a danger far worse than a passing snowstorm if one pretended to read evidence that was not really before one. Maybe what was before one was unreadable. All sorts of possibilities about. Ghosts of these thoughts came to him but soon faded and, leaving no aftersigns, they caused no bother. Out of habit he glanced at the sky again and this time, with not even a passing flurry of concern, was content to note that image of trouble up there, the cirrus cloud formation, though it actually was not an image of trouble at all. In some areas at least, Jeff Coleman did not know how to read signs as well as he thought he did.

CHAPTER 8

Ru-Marie had not been able to sleep. But then she hadn't wanted to. Sleep was what one could do tomorrow night, or the one after that, any night that Buster wasn't able to see her. Her mother, however, did not have that level of flexibility; and this November night, curiously restless—her husband had gone down to Austin on city business—Mrs. Coleman woke up in the middle of the night. She never knew why, she said—even when later she was grilled on the subject—and she never, ever, attributed her waking to maternal instinct. "I don't even like that kind of language," she had said. "We are not," she insisted, "an assortment of instincts."

At some juncture of thought or dream or, even more likely, unexplainable restiveness with a desire for oblivion, she heard noises. Getting up, she slipped her robe on and went out to the back sunporch on her home's second floor. Ru-Marie had been sleeping there for weeks—or was it months now? The girl had somehow changed. She had become both sullen and flighty. Eileen had even confided that fact to a friend, but the friend had said, "Oh, for heavensakes, those two things don't even go together."

"Maybe so, but something's gotten into her that makes no sense."

Tightening the cinch of her robe, Mrs. Coleman strode out onto the night-darkened sunporch. What she had expected to find, she later told herself, was an unconscious daughter and a tangle of covers. That's what she wished she had found. Instead, what she saw was Buster hightailing it down a ladder in his undershorts. All she could do was scream, then she was rushing back to her bedroom to get the gun in her nightstand. Startled, Ru-Marie had bolted upright in bed, but darkness covered her face, and Buster was already past the bottom rung of the ladder when Mrs. Coleman came back into the room and, slapping Ru-Marie out of her way, she fired into the darkness. The shot from the .45 sounded like a bomb going off.

Ru-Marie screamed, "No! Damn you! No!"

"I will! I'll kill him, where is he?" Mrs. Coleman screamed as she waved the barrel of the pistol at all the directions of the darkness.

Ru-Marie flailed at her mother but her hands kept missing, then suddenly Mrs. Coleman slapped her daughter, the blow catching her shoulder. "Don't ever do this again! I could've shot you instead of him. Oh!" she screamed, a sob catching in her throat, "what did he do to you?"

"Nothing, Mother, nothing! I love him."

"Oh for heavensakes, don't ever talk like that. You sound like trash, which is all that creature is himself. He's trash, Ru-Marie, just trash, and what will people think?"

"Think about what?" Ru-Marie asked coldly.

At first her mother, as if shocked, said nothing, and Ru-Marie let the awkward silence hang. She did not care how long it lasted. She had already known she would probably get caught, she just had not known when.

Out of breath, Mrs. Coleman began heaving. Desperately she yanked the belt of her robe tighter till it bit into her stoutness. "I can't believe," she said, "what you've become—caught about to do who knows what, and you don't even have an ounce of shame."

"Why should I?"

"Oh my God, how can you say something so shameful? Listen here—don't you dare talk to me about love. I don't want to hear anything about such nasty nonsense. Just look at you!"

"What?"

"You're dressed like you know what!"

"What do you mean? You're sounding like a crazed somebody. It's the middle of the night. I'm in my nightgown. What else would you have me have on—a concrete truss?"

"But he was here!"

"Who?"

"I don't even know his name and I hope I never find out. But I do, young lady, need to know something."

"What?"

"Has this kind of thing ever happened before?"

"No," Ru-Marie coolly lied. "And besides, it wasn't what it looked like."

"Thank heavens," Mrs. Coleman said, "thank heavens. And I trust it never will again." Then, as if in a spasm, she reached out to hug her daughter, and the girl submitted to the momentary crushing press of flesh.

Thank goodness, Ru-Marie told herself, using a variant phrase of her mother's, *thank goodness gestures of affection around here never last long*. She did not even like the idea of her mother and father near naked in bed. She had heard them, several times, and their carrying on sounded awful, so different from the way it was with Buster and her.

"A promise then?" Mrs. Coleman asked. "A mistake like this won't happen again?"

"No, Mother," the girl said wearily. "You know that. Besides, everything was a lot more innocent than you think. He's a dear friend and he's been having trouble and we were talking. And he wasn't in his underwear either. I'd have probably died of embarrassment if he had been. It's been hot lately. For heavensakes, Mother, that was a swimming suit he was wearing."

"I'm so glad," Mrs. Coleman sighed. "So now that things are back to normal, let's try to get back to bed. And, too," she added, "there's no reason to say anything to your father about this. He'd just get upset and probably not understand."

"Good night, Mother," Ru-Marie said, and waving her hand—the gun still grotesquely in her hand—Mrs. Coleman looked as if she were brushing gnats away with a short club. The image of her mother with the pistol disturbed Ru-Marie, but it didn't seem altogether freakish. Ru-Marie had never touched a gun in her life, but her mother obviously had. But when? And why? And how had her mother so quickly accepted what she had seen tonight as an odd dream, so different finally from what it really was: there for awhile the nicest lovemaking she and Buster had ever had.

Reliving the sweet sensations, she gathered up his shirt and socks and shoes and stuffed them into a trouserleg of his pants and dropped them into the back yard. Then she struck a kitchen match to let him know what she had done, that his clothes were ready for him to run and pick up near the foot of the ladder.

CHAPTER 9

RM told me:

It took a long time for me to understand how the University of Chicago put its imprint so vividly on the new junior college here. But it did and it had its effects in ways that Ima Jean and I never expected. The curious thing about the matter was that the point of influence simply made sense, once you understood a piece of background information. In fact, Ima Jean's boyfriend—not exactly the term I'd have used back then when we were in high school and college—went to the University of Chicago for his undergraduate degree before he came back to Texas then went to law school at what a number had begun calling *The University*. Of course, a lot of others among those who went to other colleges, any college, and there weren't that many of us—SMU, Rice Institute, TCU, Baylor, OU—found the phrase pretentious—*uppity*, we said, *prissy* so to speak—so to level the devotees of the University of Texas, people began calling them "tea-sippers." Of course, a term like that might have been applied to anyone in college, enrollment among us so rare back then.

As close as we were to the frontier—something that took me a fair time to realize—one of the worst things you could accuse a person of—especially if you were talking about a guy—was being a sissy, and that was certainly the impression one was giving when someone called someone a tea-sipper—whiskey, of course, bootleg or not, being a real man's drink, tea supposedly incapable of putting hair on your chest, or wherever else a guy might think he needed it. But since the notion of "tea-sipper" primarily implied inadequacy in the readiness department, the insult applied whether one was male or female. What was even clearer was that none of this bandying about had much seriousness in it, insults being a common and friendly way of chatting. Most of us had grown up in the area, so nothing like that—being insulted—was a problem or surprise, though it was, I admit, with a few. But those were the kind the more informal among us might catch one afternoon and run their britches up a flag pole—the guys, I mean, not the girls. And no, I was not a part of that crew, though I think I came to know somehow early on that, except for some individual oddities, abilities maybe, none of us was really much different from the rest. We were, curiously, pretty democratic in our tastes. The pretense that we were at a seriously different level from the rest was a parental sort of idiot enthusiasm much more than ours. But in spite of its foolishness, that was what introduced me to grief.

Maybe a part of me has always been slow, but I didn't really think about grief till it slapped me senseless. Sometimes I wonder whether, if I had been more alert, I might have been able to stop the terrible and unfair disaster. What I think drove me—and what I think walled me off from seeing any portion of the world clearly—was a quality of defensiveness that masqueraded as independence—or, to put it another way, a glorious feeling of comfort in the presence of irreverence. That's why I liked Ima Jean so much. We each had points that helped the other—she certainly did me—but in one key area we were radically different from each other, but that was likely because of an accident of association. I guess what I'm saying as much as anything is that I'm not even sure the world we were in back then was capable of making sense. I still don't know why, but cynical as I was I danced into love. Maybe if Buster had not been around—if I simply hadn't known him—maybe I'd have had that sensible sense of distance from intimacy that Ima Jean seemed to have come by naturally—or so I foolishly thought.

The summer after our friend David Webber graduated from Chicago then three years later from UT's law school, he came back home and a cannon couldn't have blown Ima Jean and him apart, though they never even seemed to have carried on a hot correspondence when they were apart. From the time they got together you couldn't think of one without the other, and I mean for decades till death broke them apart. Lord knows, nothing else could, and I loved them both, though I do admit they had as much grief with their own kids as anyone did. But even now, because I saw them a lot through the years, I still think of the two of them together. And I think sometimes that confuses me. I've loved two men deeply, but for some reason I don't see myself with them with that natural intimacy I associate with Ima Jean and David. Of course, if you had asked me back then—that moving field called *then*—I'd likely have described things differently. Who knows? Maybe a part of me came to discover I was my parents' daughter a lot more than I thought I was. But thank God, that's another thing I'm unsure of. I don't think I was, and I certainly hope I wasn't.

But let me get back to Chicago, to something you need to know. The junior college was established in 1922, and classes were held in the high school building for the first several years. Some of the teachers taught in both programs. The business community—at least some of the more notable ones—were strongly supportive of the college, and with all the growth going on here there was nothing surprising in that. I kept noticing in the newspapers references to several of the major officers of the junior college having University of Chicago backgrounds. They hadn't, as far as I could tell, gone there for undergraduate work. They had been in one of the graduate programs. There were references, too, to quotations from professors there about the program here. I kept wondering why a big established place like Chicago had an interest in a little half-wild place like Kiowa. I don't even know why the question gripped me—passing curiosity, I assumed—but I finally found out what Chicago's interest was, and it didn't stop at our place. There were junior colleges popping up all over the state—all over a number of states, I discovered—and Chicago was behind a good percentage of them. The university, in fact, had a driving theory in their Education wing that regional junior colleges needed to be pushed. Students all across the country ought to go there for their first two years, their theory went, then if they wanted or needed further study or additional programs, they could go for advanced work at the major universities. That's where the research took place. So the junior college was seen as both prep school and finishing school. And some of the business people here saw that as a good way to develop well-trained employees and keep the population growing. The Capitalist and his friends wanted to import workers and families, not export them. I think, too, I began seeing connections between things through the new school, even before I went there myself. I didn't think anything in particular about the junior college students themselves as pioneers or anything dramatic like that. But I was beginning to see how one thing might be connected with something else—like Chicago and Kiowa, though on the surface there wasn't any image of connection at all.

Then the next year—after all the horror occurred—I was still in town, still in the same school building but part of a college now, the junior college that had Chicago—a big driving place—essentially behind it. In effect, that's how I think I ended up going to Pratt. And yes, I did think about the Chicago Art Institute—I just kept thinking—and this will undoubtedly sound nutty—I'd be distracted there by connections with home.

In its own way Chicago had given me the idea to go somewhere that was—I'll go ahead and say it: *grand*—a place that was bigger than what I had known, and, lord, I hoped, different from what I had known.

CHAPTER 10

She knew well enough what a norther could mean. Almost everyone now in her Solid Geometry class was watching it. She had happened to notice the low slate-colored wall of the wide cloudmass in Latin 4, her previous class, and now that she was one floor higher in the building she was keeping her eyes fixed on it. The storm was driving toward her, toward all of them in the school, in the town, in the sprawling and sectioned masses of farmland out of town in all directions, and already the wind was high. The sky was darkening rapidly. A thrill rushed through her, and even the building seemed to shake. At this point the quaking, she suspected, was primarily in herself. The time of separation between building and self was narrowing. The explosive drive in the sky would not be as powerful as it would have been in a tornado, but the rush of the wind would be far broader and would last a lot longer, and tomorrow she would learn in the newspaper she faithfully read each day that in not much more than two hours the temperature would drop forty-eight degrees. The day after that she would learn that the storm had killed several people as it swept down from the Panhandle, hard flurries of hail and frozen rain, then a blizzard, slamming into Amarillo with such force that it would come close to immobilizing the place for three days. And not even two hours from now she would be out in the terrible wind herself, but that did not frighten her. Somehow, she imagined, she and Buster would turn the time into an adventure. To get her home as fast as he could, he would make her run fast, and as miserable as the cold bluster of sky would be—they really would, she knew, be running through the sky—a thrill would swell through her, as it was doing now, when their slender bodies ran together for cover through this explosion of wind and cold.

It would be so nice to bring Buster into the house with her and out of the fierce weather, if just for a time, the two of them getting warm together, but that was not yet possible. Both of them knew that. It still surprised her that he never seemed bitter about the fact—angry sometimes but not bitter, never really resentful about the unfair limit, and sometimes that mystified her. She knew good and well he wasn't satisfied, or in a state of humble acceptance of his "place," as some called it. His attention simply seemed elsewhere, and she often knew where elsewhere was. She would love to invite him in, to ask him into her place that was walled away from the jagged ice of the wind that was trying to tear to pieces everything in its way. She would love, too, to invite him upstairs and into her bed. She had even done a sketch of them in bed, though she didn't think it was very good. Daydreaming about him, she had put another part of her attention into capturing their likenesses together in just a few lines. She would try again, try this time to capture just him, and she already thought she knew how to do that. She would have to test the idea, and if it did not work, she would try another way. She would go back to the library and look again at what others had done, and as much as she could she would draw their ideas and techniques deeply into herself, after she had practiced with them, but that would happen later. Now it was time to meet this wild norther directly.

Meeting Buster in the school's big foyer, she broke into smiles when she heard him tell her that she wasn't even dressed close to right for a walk in this weather. No one was, but they all would have to go out in it.

As much as they could they ran the mile and a half to her house, but their running involved as much stumbling as anything else. The wind kept knocking them both off balance. Her blouse and his shirt were ballooning, swells of icy air against their skin, and more startling swells stormed chaotically up her skirt. Chills swept through her. Her teeth were chattering even before they had gone barely three blocks. Both of them were shivering, but there was no way to get warm. If they tried keeping their arms around each other, they would stumble again, and several times one luckily kept the other from falling. They could not even chatter at each other. The simultaneous high pitch and low thunder of the wind made it impossible for one to understand what the other had tried to say, and their mouths, so clumsy now with cold, their face muscles so stiff in the cold, they could form no coherent speech, and if they tried—which they did—they would have to stop and repeat to the other what one had just tried to say. All kinds of sounds rushed through the wild mood of this icy, tossed part of the world they were in. Even breathing was hard, and the freezing air burned their throats and lungs when they had to breathe it in.

For a moment the wild rush of wind seemed to stop then immediately it was back, shoving them off-course as they tried to cross the street. There were flurries, too, of others trying to get home—anyone's home would do—except hers. Even the automobiles—all of them stuffed with a chaos of passengers—seemed to have trouble staying in motion, and each time one turned a corner, the chassis seemed to tilt, sometimes so much that Ru-Marie was surprised one didn't turn over.

They were finally getting near her place. Only now did she realize they had been holding hands, or in some way touching each other, the whole time.

"Hurry on fast home," she said shivering, grabbing his other hand and, bringing it to her lips, she kissed it quickly again and again. "Hurry!" she said. "Hurry home fast!"

"You're such a love," he cried out so she could hear him.

"Oh, my dear," she said, thrilled, "oh, my dear, my dear."

"Run!" he told her. "You've got to get inside fast! We're both gonna freeze."

"Yes!" she yelled against the wind, and instantly both of them were running in different directions, she to the front porch of her own house, he to the corner then he would have to turn east then at the end of that block turn back right and run three-quarters of a mile to his own place.

On the covered front porch now, she turned around, expecting to see him from the back, his thrilling, quick body somehow able to maneuver directly through the wind, but that was not what she saw at all. What she saw made her shake her head and laugh out loud. He was running backwards, not at all concerned about the cold or the wind, and waving at her, just wanting, she knew, to see her face him at least one more time before he really started sailing through the storm.

"Run!" she cried, waving in wild joy at him. "Run, sweet, run!" And oh how he did, she thought, staying out on the porch in the cold, amazed that anyone could run so fast and look so effortless doing it. Then his right fist sailed quickly upward, and she thought she saw him doing a little quick-skip, a bit of a gift just for her pleasure, but she really wasn't sure she hadn't just invented that notion to reprise her own pleasure. Then she saw that he did not even glance back around to make sure she had noticed the little laugh he had made with his feet. *You don't need to*, she told him, but made no sound saying that. *You don't need to check at all.*

"That's awful!" her mother said. "Both of you! Out in the middle of the street hugging and rubbing each other all over the place. What in the world were you thinking?"

"Awful? Good gosh, I was colder than I've ever been. I'd have done anything to get warm."

"Well, you didn't have to do it in full view of the neighbors and anyone else who might happen by. We do, you know, have a reputation to keep up."

"Just hush about your damn reputation," Ru-Marie told her.

"You don't talk to me that way."

"Well, I am—and I intend to keep on, if you don't settle down and start making sense."

"I never—"

"Well, you'd better start now. So hush, damnit! Hush!"

Her mother jerked backwards a step, Ru-Marie's rage swarming all over her, the room itself turning electric, and the icy wind outside howling, as if Ru-Marie herself were a part of the storm. Windows were rattling. The afternoon sky was now the frightening color of slate, only darker than it had been before.

"I mean it," Ru-Marie said. "Just hush," and when her mother took a deep breath but did not try to say anything, Ru-Marie said, "All right. That's better."

Her mother lifted her right hand in a tentative gesture of protest.

"Don't even move!" Ru-Marie told her. "In the first place, damnit, we weren't even in the street, except when we had to cross it. And we weren't all over each other either. Do you have any idea at all how much the temperature dropped—and just the early part of this afternoon? Here it is, early December, and for three days straight it's been weirdly warm. You couldn't have even found one coat in the school, and there was no reason you should have. Then the north wind hit. What did you want—for us all to get pneumonia?"

Pursing her lips, her mother said, "I'm not talking about *all* of you. Your father and I just wish you'd be with more people. I don't think that boy is at your level. There are appearances after all. And they're to be kept up. I know it's not his fault, but he doesn't really come from a healthy environment. There's a certain atmosphere that his mother's house gives off, and a number of people have noticed it, and not just us. I'm not criticizing those people—neither him nor his mother. I'm not criticizing anyone else either. That's not my way. It's just that they're not our kind."

Ru-Marie kept her icy stare fixed on her mother. She thought there was something gross about the slackness of the doughy flesh of her mother's arms. Her mother glanced down, her hands now protectively fixed below her waist, her fingertips picking at each other.

"So what is our kind?" Ru-Marie asked. "I wasn't aware that you and Dad grew up in French chateaux. Or were you two the traveling wing of the Medici clan?"

"I didn't mean that," her mother said. "I'm not praising myself. That's not my way either. But there are differences that need to be respected. You do have, you know, a reputation to keep up."

"Like what? A little cold-natured shivery slut? Little lady with fire in her bloomers? Or just some girl who wants to pitch a lot of good *nekkid* woo in the middle of town—to celebrate the year's first blue norther."

"No!" her mother said. "I don't want to hear you talk like that. There's just no excuse to use that kind of language."

"There's no excuse either to wish your daughter would get a death of cold."

"Now wait just a minute. I never said—never even meant to say or imply anything like that. So don't go twisting my words."

"I doubt I'd have the chance if you weren't so inarticulate."

"You're mean!" her mother told her. "There's something about you that's mean. I don't know what it is, and I don't know where you got it, but there's something in you that's mean. And I think this conversation needs to stop."

The air of her voice suddenly light, and her features relaxing happily—or at least seeming to—Ru-Marie started toward the stairs.

"Where do you think you're going?" her mother called after her.

"Up to my room. You did say we're done with our little parlor talk. Besides, it's cold down here, so I'm going up to where the heat rises. I've got lessons to do—for tomorrow. And I also have some new ideas I want to play around with and sketch."

"Like what?" her mother asked, full of suspicion.

"I've told you before, and I meant it. I never really know till I get the pencil or brush in my hand."

"You're not talking about doing those nudes again, are you?"

Laughing, though her eyes looked both hot and icy, she glared at her mother, but her voice stayed oddly calm when she asked, "So what have you been doing? Sneaking looks through my sketchbooks? And if you have, I hope you're smart enough to realize that I'm really pretty good."

"You've always been good," her mother said in a rush. "Your father and I have always said you have a gift. I've never had any doubt about that. Never! It's just that you might start turning your attention toward other things."

"You mean things that aren't *nekkid*?"

"Yes! That's exactly it. I don't want you to get one of those things called obsessions."

"That's good," Ru-Marie said. "I like that a lot. And if I do get one of those things, and if one of those things starts causing a rash, no telling where the thing'll start itching. Then I'd have to make a choice. Do I scratch the unmentionable—or just squirm around on it? Boy! That'd make the town sing, wouldn't it?"

"Now, now," her mother said. "I wasn't prying. I wouldn't do that. It was just an accident, so don't go accusing me of snooping, doing something I didn't do. I was dusting and accidentally knocked some things off the nightstand. The book just happened to fall open. Good heavens! Anyone can see what a talent you have. We all—all of us—just need to be careful about directions we take."

"As well as be mindful of the fact," Ru-Marie told her, "that I don't keep my sketchbooks on the nightstand."

Blanching, her mother took a quick breath, cleared her throat, then started chattering rapidly, but Ru-Marie was no longer listening, and only odd fragments of her mother's palaver registered as she went up the stairs, her right palm cupping the long smooth flow of the mahogany-stained banister. The wind was still loud and branches of the yard's one tree, a pecan, scratched the side of the house. The irregular but insistent pace of the noise sounded as if a huge rat were trying to bite through the wall.

CHAPTER 11

Another cold front was predicted for New Year's Day, this one due to drop temperatures well below 20, maybe even to near 10, the paper said. But the cold front, and with it a long freezing rain, hit at suppertime the day before. The city was suddenly immobile.

The winter had been particularly harsh. Waves of cold fronts had moved in since mid-November. The same had also been true across the country—New York City, New England, and major sections of the Midwest coming close to being immobilized themselves several times. Other outbursts as well made the news. The new governor of the state would be a woman, Miriam "Ma" Ferguson. Her husband Jim had been impeached from his own position as governor, but his removal from office did not shame either his wife or their supporters. Capitalizing on the debacle, Ma's campaign had emphasized that the citizens would get two governors for the price of one, and the promise of that carried the day. Ma's victory would have a major effect on the lives of Ru-Marie's mother and father, though they did not know that when the new year came.

Wyoming's new governor was also a woman, the paper noted: Mrs. Nellie Taylor Ross. Changes were occurring throughout the land. Again and again political parties and other groups had clamored to expose the Ku Klux Klan for corruption and vicious outlawry. *We Don't Need Such Trash!* numerous posters said, though many throughout the country still held to the notion that many upstanding men had been and still were members of this citizens' group called the Klan, but those voices were fading, though there was a group rumored to be getting ready to organize a Klavern in Kiowa. Some were afraid of what might happen, but those fears and the group's plans were short-lived. The young District Attorney—he would turn out in several years to be the youngest governor in the nation, though no one knew that now either—and a young oilman and rancher who had decided to stay here years before after getting tired of waiting for a late train—got together and decided over a cup of coffee—they rarely ate lunch because it wasted good time—to have a meeting with the men who were setting out plans to bring the Klan here. The young oilman and increasingly land-rich rancher, J.S. Bridwell, suggested they meet in his office, and the young DA, James Allred, agreed, saying, "They might get shy if they had to come to my place."

The meeting was held and, for those who knew the two, characteristically short. Mr. Bridwell told them that he understood they—there were six of them there in his City National Bank office—were interested in starting a Klan group here. He said he thought it wonderful that people gathered to improve the community they lived in. He told them he thought that was an honorable thing to do, to think beyond oneself, to lift the community to what it could be, not leave it near the slough pit where it had been. The six seemed to swell then with pride. Everyone knew how productive Mr. Bridwell already was. Everyone in town also seemed to know, too, what his posture was when he walked: a forwardleaning briskly paced stride directly into the wind that did not dare try to slow him down, the story said.

Then standing behind his desk, he said, "Gentlemen, I have a hobby. I've had it since I was a boy, and that's to read history, and in most of what I've read there has—again and again—been a truth that shines through, sometimes tragically, sometimes bitterly, sometimes justly, often justly. That truth—and it has been with us since ancient times—suggests—and often demonstrates—that one of the greatest, most defining facts of life is a pattern called the reversal of fortune." Eying them intensely now, he told them, "What that means is that a man can never tell what might happen—to himself, to his family, to his business. He might be comfortable today, but tomorrow might bring unspeakable misery and loss—all kinds of loss. Fortune and respect," he told them, "can turn, sometimes overnight, into poverty and shame, and with no one around to listen to one's tale of woe and ruin." He stopped, then nodding toward the District Attorney, said, "Mr. Allred, is there something you might like to say?"

"Yes, sir, there is. Gentlemen, what Mr. Bridwell says is true. There are even in prison people who have learned how true such reversals can be. But prison is not the real threat. That's not really a likely destination for most of us, so we should not dwell on it, not here, not today, since prison is a relatively rare turn of fate. And often, when one goes there, one's life turns out to be something other than long. Health and position and financial stability are more precarious than we sometimes think, and our fortunes are more fragilely set than we sometimes think. As you have just heard, one's fortunes can be easily reversed. One might never even know exactly how one was blown into what the ancients called oblivion. That turn of fate, that reversal of fortune we've mentioned, can happen overnight, or even just minutes after breakfast. Mr. Bridwell?" he said, turning toward his friend who was still standing comfortably in the erectness of his posture.

"Thank you," he told his friend. "Gentlemen," he said to the six, "what we have been suggesting is that you think carefully and deeply about your plans. And after you have done that, proceed to do what's right, with honor and with courage and with full awareness of what might happen." Then with no gesture toward humor, he looked at them, each one in turn, and said rather slowly, "I believe this meeting is over. It's time for you to leave."

And they did. Some of them were shaking, bumping against each other as they hurried clumsily through the doorway. And they apparently never brought up their plans again. Ru-Marie would not hear that story till years later, but when she did hear it, from the young DA's son who was in the state legislature, she began trembling, her vision blurred by tears. When asked what was wrong, she said, "It's hard for me to say. It seems so strange, that level of clarity and strength so present during the same year when things went so crazed with Buster and me. I feel as if I had been living in two different worlds then, and one of them I didn't even know was there."

That New Year's morning, another story, a column, in the newspaper that Ru-Marie read reminded readers of what had been front-page news two weeks before. A white man had been sentenced to five years in the penitentiary for killing a black man. He had claimed the gun had gone off accidentally in what he had testified was "a struggle between us." The column said, *We're on our way to justice*, then reminded readers that a conviction like that had never before been given in the county. Other wrapup stories used lighter tones and made fun of those predicting doom. A solar eclipse (*Relax*, the column said, *it'll just be a partial one*) was due in less than three weeks. The same columnist was openly skeptical of a wealthy Chicago family's response to their son, the infamous Richard Loeb, who had been convicted with his best friend, the equally infamous Nathan Leopold, for murdering Loeb's fourteen-year-old cousin Bobby Franks. The two young men, sons of prominent families and students at the University of Chicago, confessed that they had wanted to study their own reactions to murder. Each one an *Übermensch*, they claimed, they were supposed to be able to handle complexity well. *Supposedly brilliant,* the column said, *the two had been caught quickly. Maybe criminals aren't so bright after all.* The columnist reminded readers that one of the two had left his glasses where they had dumped their prey. The frames turned out to be rare. Only six people in the greater Chicago area were known to have bought them. Day after day during the previous summer, stories about the trial had run on the front page of the two Kiowa papers, and countless others across the country. In the fall, more than a month after the conviction—Clarence Darrow saving them from execution—Loeb's parents said they had given their elder son too much leisure. Idleness, they said, had allowed their son to stray. *Don't start nodding your agreement too quickly,* the columnist said then reported how the Loebs had said things would be different with Richard's younger brother. From now on, they announced, the boy would rise at six a.m., even on weekends, "and be put to regular work."

The columnist said he had nothing against Loeb's parents, that he was comfortable thinking of them as good people who were undergoing levels of guilt and grief that would never leave them. *But I'd be mindful,* he wrote, *of the temptation to say that all that's needed to correct our own flaws and those of others is "good common sense." That and the virtues of what's now being called "boosterism" are sometimes as threatening as they are silly.* He went on to say, *There seem to have been an inordinate number of murders—suicides, too—in our own community. Our country's problems aren't north and east or even west of us. The potential for explosion lives near us and with us.*

The columnist's other reflections touched on the rise in the price of crude oil in *what we now call Texoma. Just last week,* he wrote, *it was selling for $1.60 per barrel and now the price is already up to $1.75. But before you get comfortable,* he added, *there's a woman in California saying the Earth's going* to die on Feb. 6—not much more than a month from now. She, who calls herself Mrs. Margaret Rowen—her official title is "Prophetess"—has 1,000 followers, including a doctor described as her "Chief Disciple," a one Dr. F.E. Fulmer. Members of what's called the Reformed 7th Day Adventist sect, she and her people are not planning any celebration or precautionary rite to commemorate or honor the planet's forthcoming demise. I will add, though, that the "unreformed" branch of the denomination excommunicated her last year for "pretentiousness." That and the fact that this story was filed in Hollywood, California, give me comfort. I like the fact that she's been sent into exile for "pretentiousness." I'd even be glad to send them a list of folks from nearby and beyond who also might qualify for their wrath.

In other realms, I'm happy to report that in our own town Packards are now available for $2,960, down from $3,925. I refuse, however, to link these curiosities. But now for one more item before I wish all Happy New Year. A new garment's become available to the distaff crew: the "Jop-Cape." One can wear it to the waist line or even slightly below over frocks made of soft, clingy material. No doubt about it: one or two of these in your chifforobe will make your life even better than it already is.

Upstairs in her room, Ru-Marie was looking out the window at the gray sky. Evening had come and the world had turned to ice. Even last night's New Year's Eve celebration at the Pavilion on the lake had been canceled. There had been nothing for her to do—no way either for her to get to the dance at the Kreitz Hotel downtown. Or if she had gotten there, she was not sure she would have been able to get back home without freezing to death.

Her parents had gone next door to a gathering, and Buster was sick. He had come down with another cold. His night shift was wearing him out. She was worried about him.

She had been by herself all evening. Accepting what she jokingly called her fate, she recognized that she had neither hope nor need for company. The world was here with her.

She listened to the wind rattle the upstairs windows on the north side of the house. She found herself wishing a blast would smash its way through and freeze the place. More and more she was finding an odd but passing sense of comfort in images of destruction. Half-amused at her own foolishness, she reminded herself that she was only flirting with notions of destruction, that she was not exposed herself, she was well-protected by brick veneer, by shiplap walls and hardwood floors. She found herself glad for the presence of storms; and now, in numerous ways, she was in the middle of one. She was sorry that Buster was not here with her. If he had been, she would already have taken him to bed and told him what she had been feeling about the storms blowing through. If he were here with her, she knew, no clothes would separate their sweet-tasting flesh, and no cold draft would make them shiver miserably, as she was beginning to do.

Glad to have the house to herself, she went downstairs and poured herself a short glass of her father's bootleg whiskey. He rarely drank it but he liked for some reason to keep bottles of it around. Having tasted it before, she added a splash of water to soften its burn. She was not trying to get drunk. She was simply giving in to the impulse to have a bit of whiskey for the evening. This was New Year's Eve night, and she was husbandless for the evening. It hurt her that Buster probably did not have access to any celebratory drink. She wished he did. Some whiskey and honey might make him feel better. Whiskey tonight would be better, lots better, she thought, than Aspironal, a new product whose advertisements claimed it was "better than whiskey for colds and flu." But she was doubtful of that claim—studiously doubtful that it had any credence.

Allowing herself another drink, she laughed as she thought that what really might hit the spot—Buster's spot and later her own spot, too—was a snort of Lydia Pinkham's Vegetable Compound. "Oh hell, sweet one," she said out loud, "there's nothing to do this cold, lonely night but go back upstairs and draw and paint the wholeness of you nakeder than the world."

CHAPTER 12

JE: I keep wondering what your parents were like, especially together. When I try thinking about them, I keep coming up blank. I can't picture them together, and I'm not sure why. I started to say I've had some impressions, but I don't think I really have. I've had some assumptions. That's all. And I don't trust those.

RM: What kid ever knows what her parents are like? Or were like? I suppose if you've lived year after year in some extreme situation—which I never did, at least not for any sustained time—you might know, or at least think you do. Except in terms of Buster, as important, as big as that was, we passed *through* an extreme period. We just didn't live in it year after year. And in certain odd ways I'm not even sure how revealing that awful time really was. You'd think it would be, but the way things turned out, I'm not sure it really was.

JE: You don't have any impressions of them?

RM: Oh, sure, of course, I do. You know that very well, just like you know that sometimes I start stalling, keep trying to push you back a bit, pretty much the way I'm doing now. So let me try to slide into the subject. With all that went on—and *didn't go on*—the latter as important in my case, as I've already told you—I don't think I can even conjure them up, except singly, unless I go toward them sideways. I'm not even sure what there is to reveal.

JE: Is that because of the pain, the horror you went through?

RM: No, though there was that. But my hesitance to approach them doesn't have anything to do with pain, at least with my pain, then or now. Let me try putting it this way. They—my mother and father—were not especially affectionate with each other. Of course, they weren't especially affectionate with anyone else I know of either. I ought to say, too—and this is just my own impression—the little world we lived in wasn't especially a loving place. At the same time, it never seemed driven by hatred either, except in individual cases. Even the kids—with all our congenital silliness—didn't seem much inclined toward love. It may be different today, I don't know. I've been out of circulation for awhile. Maybe if I traipsed around town more regularly—had a zippier level of night life than I have—I might be able to answer what you want with more authority than I can, or at least with more precision. But I can't.

JE: Now don't try to pull that stay-at-home wallflower pose on me.

RM: (*smiling*) I won't—unless the urge gets too great to resist.

JE: Okay, we'll come back to your parents later. What I've wondered about—more than anything else perhaps—is your marriage—you and Buster running off to Grandfield with your friends. That happened a number of times with kids when I was in high school. I even remember a girl I'd known in junior high breaking up with her boyfriend in the tenth grade, just a couple weeks after school started, then a couple weeks later she was going steady with someone else. Of course, no one found any of that much more than a little surprising. People were often breaking up or making up or shifting over to new steadies. Just a part of growing up, most of us thought, and only a few, I suppose, were truly bashful about what I'd call strong sensations. Most of us seemed happy enough to dive back in the water.

RM: (*laughing*) As we both know, it's the same with grown-ups, too. I don't think I'd ever call fickleness—or flightiness, folks used to call it—anything close to rare, and it doesn't make much difference what age you're talking about. Life in the nursing home, I've heard, even gets torrid, though I hope to hell I don't ever have to find out directly.

JE: Let me be blunt. Do you think that you and Buster—running off and getting married, the way so many around here have done through the years—primarily happened because you thought you needed to legitimize your sex life?

RM: I've thought about that. I even thought about it back then. Everyone has thoughts like that. You can't help it. But before we get into that, I want to go back to that tenth grade girl you mentioned. I know you well enough to know you had something else in mind than a dippy little tale about someone swapping steadies. What were you getting at?

JE: Sorry. I got distracted. I have a tendency toward what the Aussies call walkabouts.

RM: It's a common disease, but not much more than a mild form of senile dementia. It's amazing how screwy a lot of people's wiring is. So tell me now about that flighty young tart you knew.

JE: Near the end of the spring semester we found that she and Andy—the longtime boyfriend she'd broken up with in September—had been married since a couple weeks before the breakup. They didn't want anyone to suspect they'd gotten married, and everyone—including what I'll call their new steadies, now rather longtime steadies—was shocked. Especially the steadies. They both thought they had a hot thing going, and apparently, in terms of emotions—and *motions*—they did.

RM: (*laughing*) Folks do have their charm, don't they? So why did Andy and what's-her-name finally announce their marriage? She was pregnant, wasn't she?

JE: Yes, and as we all found out, they'd never really broken up either. They just went through the motions—even saying nasty things about each other—to keep their marriage a secret. They did a good job, too, because the ruse lasted about eight months.

RM: (*smiling*) I think I'd say those two were a little more advanced than we were. Some of my friends might've stayed up with them, though, given them a run in terms of style and daring. Still, I don't really think getting married had as much to do with sex, or legitimizing sex, as you might think. A lot of kids had sex. A lot of their parents did, too—and not necessarily with each other. You might be surprised at how many shootings took place—men and women both, and the lot of them not at all afraid of the trigger—even to the point of turning the gun on themselves, but usually not until they had already done some mayhem to others. You might consider this. The option for most kids back then, there in the twenties, was pretty limited—graduation from high school, maybe, then going to work. Most kids around here—and other places, too, it seems—didn't have as long a transition into adulthood as a lot do now. We—and not just Buster and me—we knew the parents wouldn't approve of the marriage, but Grandfield was such an easy option. Oklahoma didn't have a waiting period, and a preacher there was usually pretty casual about details—just slip him a couple of bucks and the Lord was already smiling at what you had just done. In fact, on the drive back, all four of us started laughing because Buster's friend Roy had gotten the marriage license himself, but in Buster's name. And we all agreed because Buster did look awfully young, so to make sure there wasn't any trouble, Roy stepped in for him.

JE: Why didn't you just keep seeing Buster on the sly? That's what you did anyway. Even after you got married, your situation wasn't any better. So why the trouble of marriage? Are you sure you didn't simply want to make yourself think you were still—what I'll call—*good*?

RM: Oh sure, there was some of that. I'd never argue there wasn't. I do know, though, that sex wasn't our primary concern. Let's face it. It's not a really complicated enterprise—unless you've got some kinks that need straightening, and of course some do. But worrying about sex wasn't my problem, and I don't think it was the driving issue of most of the others I knew who made the little trip to Walters and Grandfield. In fact, you might even be surprised at how many who drove across the river and got married later split with their spouses then married someone else without even bothering to get a divorce or annulment.

JE: You're saying you know some people here in town now who are, technically speaking, bigamists?

RM: Sure. You've probably run across some of them yourself. To put this another way, there are a lot of people, now and long ago, too, who never were real formal—about a lot of things.

JE: So what was the driving concern that made you take that trip across the river?

RM: I don't know, I really don't. I just know it wasn't sex, but it wasn't clearheadedness either. But let's back off me awhile and get back to my parents. You wanted to know what they were like. And I think I'd put it this way: pretty unreflective and naturally stiff.

JE: Did they love each other?

RM: I'm not sure that's the kind of language that touched them. I did, though, hear them making love. I heard them a number of times, though frankly I don't think they were anywhere near as regular about it as Buster and I might've been, or wanted to be.

JE: Did their passion surprise you?

RM: I don't think passion is the word I'd use. The noise I heard sounded more like work.

JE: For both of them?

RM: That's where things go strange. That's where I'm blank. I never was certain who I was hearing. Sometimes I thought him, sometimes her, but I never was sure. The image, the images that came to me—the two of them together—weren't vivid, and my impression of them—in every way possible—was that neither one of them wanted anything more than they had, or anything different from what they had.

JE: So you think they were satisfied with each other?

RM: I don't think they even thought in terms of satisfaction.

I think if you'd gone up to either one of them and asked if they'd like a more fulfilling life, they'd have looked at you and asked, *What kind of fool question is that?*—only they probably wouldn't actually have said anything. They'd likely have just stared at you—and pretty blankly—for awhile, but with no look of hostility in their eyes—or curiosity either.

JE: Were they that inarticulate?

RM: Maybe. But what I'm getting at is the possibility that there might not have been any real complication deep inside them that they struggled to express.

JE: Is that why both of them were so comfortable with violence?

After awhile she looked at him softly, her eyes sweet but penetrating. She said that instead of following the impulse to joke she ought to confess she didn't know how to answer his question. She said there were numerous things that seemed to have no valid reasons behind them—that is, she added, if you make a distinction between impulse and reason. And keeping her gaze on him, she said she did, she made a distinction between the two.

JE: Do you believe in love? Or is that just impulse, too?

RM: Yes, of course, I believe in love. No question about it. I've known love. I've known it deeply.

JE: You've made it clear a number of times how rich your thirty-seven years with Grover was. But what I really want to know is this: Was what you and Buster had something you'd include in what you now consider love? Or was it primarily something else—something you came to realize you outgrew?

RM: John! Good heavens! You sound as if you're playing with a tiny little adding machine. You know better than that. What in the world are you thinking?

JE: (*holding out his hands, palms up, to confess his guilt*) Okay, I'll try again. Did you really love Buster?

RM: Of course, I loved Buster. Surely you don't think I'm one of those saps who tries to tidy up the damn past by pretending that what really happened didn't happen. Do you?

JE: No.

RM: Good. So what are you driving at?

JE: Clarity. I want to know what you see when you look back now at what happened.

RM: John, my love (*reaching out to take his note-taking hand in hers*), have you already forgotten one of the first things I told you, that I felt awful about the fact that as far as this damn place goes Buster quickly passed into what doesn't even come close to qualifying as memory? That it's not enough for just me to remember. I've never pretended I've ever thought of myself as clearheaded—then or now either. But what I felt back then is not the issue. You ought to know me well enough by now to know I never have gone around trying to examine myself, and that's not because I'm trying to hide or avoid anything. Look, love, I didn't even keep a diary growing up. I didn't then—and probably don't even now—care much about what I already knew. What I really cared about—and do care about—was and still is learning how to draw and paint better than before—that and camping out in the library to learn what I could about whatever I came upon or got curious about. Listen—I even knew a girl once—a classmate of mine from grade school through high school—who kept better than a diary. I've seen the big book. She recorded each date she ever had and stuck on the page her movie ticket stub or dance card for the night, plus newspaper clippings identifying the movies she saw. She even stuck on the page the chewing gum wad she had worked in her mouth that night. And if she's still alive, she likely still has it. I didn't even learn about all that till she showed it to me and a few others who got together one night some thirty-odd years after we had graduated from high school.

JE: Was that Ima Jean?

RM: Good heavens, no. But Ima Jean was there that night when Patsy brought it out.

JE: How did she react? Ima Jean I mean.

RM: (*laughing*) She just looked at Patsy for awhile then said, "Goddamn, lady, you either need a counselor—or a dog." Then Patsy went into something like shock while the others had trouble trying to quit laughing.

JE: How did you feel?

RM: Oh, I was trying to quit laughing myself, but what I really felt was envy—just crippled with envy, because I hadn't made the remark myself.

JE: Did Patsy still live here then?

RM: Oh no, and hadn't for years. That was part of what was so funny. She lugged that damn scrapbook halfway across the country just in case we got anxious for some documentation of her early social life. The compassionate part of me, though, was glad she had left her cheerleading outfit at home.

JE: Why?

RM: Because I know what Ima Jean would have said.

JE: What's that?

RM: The same thing she said when one of the other cheerleaders wore her outfit to the thirtieth or something high school reunion. "I'll be damn," Ima Jean said, "tummy tuck and boob job, too. How much them things cost these days?"

CHAPTER 13

She knew the meal was going to be awful. Standing by the stove, wooden spoon in hand, her mother kept taking deep breaths. Her father was in the living room reading the paper, or pretending to. Sensing the tension when she came downstairs to help her mother finish preparing the meal, she asked her father how his world had been today.

"Fine," he said flatly.

She whistled and left the room. In the kitchen now, she told her mother, "Your husband's just dazzling with charm."

"I suppose," her mother said.

"And so are you—both of you: Jesus's little sunbeams fluttering through the air."

"I'd prefer you not talk that way. I don't like hearing people take the Lord's name in vain."

"So what should I do?" Ru-Marie asked. "Get down on my knees and mumble the mass?"

"Just hush! I don't want to hear any more of your smart mouth—and neither does your father—so hush, just hush."

"No problem," she said, running her thumb and index finger together across her lips. "I gonna stitch my mouth clean shut."

"I'm warning you," her mother said.

"I am," Ru-Marie said. "I'm gonna even contract that condition called aphasia. I gonna paralyze my mouth clean shut."

"I'm warning you—one more smart-mouth remark—"

"And you'll do what? Clobber my head with the skillet? I doubt it, so you might think of hushing yourself. I came down in a good humor—at least a good enough one for you.

I don't know why you're so pissy, but—"

"Young lady, you clean up your language. We don't talk like trash in this house."

"I do," Ru-Marie said cheerfully. "I talk whatever way I want. I'd also suggest you stir the blackeyes a bit. They're about to get scorched."

Her mother sucked in a deep breath.

"Here, give me the spoon," Ru-Marie said. "You might want to sit down a moment and relax. Go on," she said, taking the spoon from her mother's hand. "I'll finish up," then opening the oven, she bent over and said how fine the roast looked. "Smells delicious, too," Ru-Marie said, affecting a lightness in her voice. "You just sit down and relax. Sometimes it does one good to simply sit down with nothing more than your teeth in your mouth."

Angry but apparently realizing momentary defeat, Eileen whipped off her apron, tossed it on its hook, sat down and loudly huffed out another breath.

Getting a serving dish from the cabinet, Ru-Marie took a hotpad off the hook on the wall by the stove, clamped it over the skillet's handle and spooned out the blackeyes.

"Dad," she called, "supper's ready."

Without responding, he came sullenly into the kitchen and took his seat at the table. He and his wife looked at each other sourly. What Ru-Marie realized surprised her at first. They were not feeling bitter about each other. Whatever the source of their anger was, it went beyond themselves, and likely, she thought, directly at her.

Oh god, she thought, not the same damn subject again. She was prepared to wait them out. She would not address the matter herself. If they wanted to bring it up, fine; she would deal with it then, but she was not going to help them. If the three of them passed the meal in silence, that was fine with her, too. As sour as they seemed tonight, she wasn't much interested in hearing their palaver anyway.

Setting the blackeyes on the table, she saw that a trivet for the roast was already there. She went back and got the pot with the roast in it then put it in its place. She took her seat. Everyone kept looking at their plates, no one breaking the silence until her mother, getting up, said that with all the hoorah going on here she had forgotten to get the diced tomatoes and onions from the ice box.

"I'll get them," Ru-Marie said.

"No, you won't," her mother insisted. "I'm already up."

After Eileen had set the bowl on the table and taken her seat, all three, as their custom was, bowed their heads and Jeff said the blessing, the same one he always said: "Thanks, Father God, for the food set before us. Bless, Father God, the family, the city, the nation. In Jesus' name, amen."

He then began slicing the roast. Eileen's expression stayed grim, while Ru-Marie wondered why, whatever the words were, so many people sounded cranky when they prayed, a strange, rough stiffness in their speech. Of course, some, she knew—girls and women especially—sometimes got so wound up and chummy about sweet wonderful Jesus that she often thought that the language of romantic love that got appropriated in prayer and certain hymns made her think that soon one of the more fluid exhorters was going to get carried away to the point of trying to stick her tongue in Jesus' ear. The image made her grin.

"What's so funny?" Eileen asked.

"Nothing. Just a silly thought passing through."

"You want to share it?" her father asked.

"No, it doesn't amount to anything. Just something one of the girls said at school," she lied. "Remembering it amused me for a moment."

"It wasn't that boy we've warned you about?" her father asked, his phrasing clipped.

"No. I told you—it was something a girl said. Just chatter-in-the-hall kind of talk that I overheard."

"That's acceptable," her mother said. "I've gotten amused like that myself."

Ru-Marie quickly decided not to ask when.

"But as we were saying," her mother continued, Ru-Marie knowing that whatever her mother was referring to was something no one had just mentioned. "I said, as we were saying, that boy's just not in your league. I'm sure it's not his fault, but his background is awfully common."

The subject had, of course, come up before, but this time Ru-Marie was determined not to fall into their trap. She was not going to help further the conversation. Her style of reply was to fork a few blackeyes. Bringing the food to her mouth, she noticed her mother's gaze was fixed on her, the woman obviously expecting some reply. Ru-Marie, however, looking back at her plate, began chewing the bite of food she had taken. Her mother looked ready to explode. Out of the corner of her eye she noticed how tense her father looked. He was staring at her, too. Taking another bite, a bit of tomato this time, she kept refusing to say what they were inviting her to say, even insisting that she say. For a moment she wondered how long they would keep sitting here motionless, their dinner getting cold. If this ridiculous, paralyzing obsession kept on long enough, she thought, she would finish her meal well before they had even started theirs; and that would be fine. She would go up to her room and set about her evening's tasks. She still had work to do in Latin and Solid Geometry, the latter a subject—she cut off a bite of roast this time—that was much harder for her than Plane Geometry. She had whizzed through that with no trouble at all, but the demands of depth complicated matters. She smiled again, this time amused by the notion that a number of people she knew weren't afflicted at all by problems of depth—mainly because they didn't seem to have any.

"Your mother," her father said, "asked you a question.

Are you going to give her an answer—or are you going to keep sitting here grinning like an idiot?"

"Oh, I'm sorry," she said, pretending to submit to him, then turning toward her mother, she calmly said, "There's a wonderful crunch in the food tonight. It's just amazing, I think, how a bit of charring really brings out the flavor."

"Damn!" her mother shouted, and storming up off her seat, she grabbed the table's edge and screamed, "I've had enough of you! And I'm not putting up with it anymore! I'm not putting up with any more of your sass! You're mean! You're just mean, and I'm through!" Throwing her napkin down on the table, she muffled a high cry, and thwarting a scream, she rushed from the room.

Maintaining a guise of calm, Ru-Marie asked her father if he would like another serving of something. "Perhaps some more tomatoes? They've been awfully good lately."

"No," he said bluntly. "I don't want anything. Like your mother, I think I've had enough—except I'm not getting up and leaving. You and I, young lady, are going to have a talk."

"I'm sure," Ru-Marie said, "it's one we've had before."

"I'm telling you," he threatened her. "You just sit where you are and listen. And don't try smartmouthing me back. I won't tolerate that—not at all. And after we finish, you're going to give your mother an apology. She and I had planned to have our talk with you in a civilized, dignified way. But apparently you can't accept that. You've made that impossible. So it's up to me now to tell you what's what. And this time you're listening. There are going to be changes. There are some things we're not going to put up with anymore. From now on we're not putting up with them at all."

"Don't you think we should finish our meal first?"

"Not tonight. We can both go hungry, though I've noticed you've never even stopped eating. So there's little chance you're going to go faint."

"But what about you?"

"We're not worrying about me. Just don't try to turn things light."

"I wouldn't even pretend I could."

"Good. And what I have to say is simple. Your mother and I don't want you going around with that boy anymore. He's not up to your level."

"Good heavens, Dad! It's not like we're Vanderbilts or Astors. Lord! And it's not like he and I are going steady or trying to get married either."

"I'm glad to know that. That shows some judgment. We just don't want you with him."

"Why not? He's fun and he's sweet."

"He's not the right kind. He doesn't even have a father."

"Did you?"

"It was different with me."

"Some day, if you don't mind, I'd like to hear more details. You have a knack for going vague when things start getting close."

"All right, I'll level with you a bit more directly. Buster's not the only problem. He may not even be the primary problem. What we're concerned with is the fact that the circumstances he's grown up in, or with, aren't good. If you don't mind, I'll even get blunt. The story goes, his mother—this was a good while back, some years back—his mother tried to shoot his father. In fact, she did shoot at him."

"For heavensakes, Dad, he probably deserved it. Haven't you known folks who might've improved if someone could shoot them now and then?"

"Listen, girl, I'm not joking. This is no laughing matter. This is serious. Do you know anything about his mother's reputation?"

"Like what?"

"That it's not just a boarding house she's running. There are other things going on there."

"Like what?"

"I'd rather not say—at least not to you."

"Why? You afraid I'd be shocked? Or afraid I'd get some new ideas?"

"You just settle down now. I don't want any more talk out of you. The situation that boy's grown up in is not healthy—not at all healthy."

"All right," Ru-Marie said, "I'm getting damn tired of you beating around the bush—and implying nonsense here and nonsense there. You're sounding like nothing more than a niggling little gossip. What do you think? That Buster's mother's running a whorehouse?"

"Hush! I don't want to ever hear any more talk like that from you. Where'd you pick up such language?"

"From Buster," she told him coolly. "Pretty often after school we have little sessions. That's when he teaches me how to talk dirty. I even think I have a talent for it."

"Listen—I'm not putting up with this smartmouth talk."

"That's what's bothering you, isn't it? That she's keeping a kind of brothel, a little House of the Rising Sun place of ill repute."

"Yes," he said, his fist tapping the table. "That's it exactly."

"Would you mind telling me where you picked up such hooey?"

"There's talk, there's plenty of talk—and it's not new either."

"Fine! Now let me tell *you* something. I've been there. I've been there a bunch of times. And I know his mother, too—and there's nothing like what you're saying going on there."

"Then I'll tell you something. I grew up poor, too, and my mother ran a boarding house, but mark my word! It wasn't anything like the one Annie Lopreis runs."

"What was the difference? As if I couldn't guess."

"There wasn't any mixing going on—that's what!"

"Mixing? What the devil does *mixing* mean?"

"Men and women staying at the same place."

"Good Lord!" she said, "I'm shocked. You're just old-fashioned—you and Mother both. That's all there is to it. You're just a prune-sucking, old-fashioned prude." He raised his hand to stop her, but she told him it was his time to hush. "Do you really think if you put a bunch of people in the same place—men and women both, too poor to have their own places—that all they're going to think about through the night or in the parlor is going down the hall and getting as much good grubbing in as they can?"

"What do you mean *grubbing*?"

"Lord! You're even more out of date than I thought."

"I know what you mean. I just don't like you obsessed about these things."

"Obsessed?"

"Yes—obsessed! You've got a reputation to uphold. All three of us do. And I won't have you compromising that or your own well-being just because—for who knows why—you've started feeling sorry for a trashy poor boy like Annie Lopreis's son. He can't help the situation he got given, but I can, and I'm not allowing you to go down, to sink into that level. I've been in the poor life and you're not going to sink into that yourself. I'm seeing to it—you're not to carry on with that boy—not any more you're not."

"Would you care to define *carry on*?"

"You know what I mean."

"If you mean what I think you mean, I'm insulted. No one I know has ever accused me of anything like that. I guess it's come clear what you really think—at least about me."

"I didn't mean it that way."

"Well, that's what you said. And I frankly don't care if you're my father or not—and I'm not smartmouthing you either—but I'm not going to stay here and listen to you tell me how nasty you think I am." Rising, she carefully folded her napkin and laid it beside her plate.

"Where do you think you're going?"

"Up to my room. I have lessons and new drawings to do."

"Look! You misunderstood. I didn't mean what you think."

"I'm glad to hear that," she said. "But right now I'm too upset to listen to *you* carry on. And since Mother's upset, too, you can do the dishes yourself—and while you're at it, you might try to swallow some of the soap—swish it around that trashy mouth of yours. And don't you ever forget it either—no one ever talks to me that way, and nobody ever will. And I'd suggest you remember that next time—or I may end up, and not too long from now either, being somewhere else."

"Please," he said, standing, the gesture looking like a confused attempt to show respect. "Please," he said, "please."

"Not tonight," she told him. "There's already been enough talk," she said, walking toward the door.

"Please," he said again, "we just want you to be careful."

Stopping, she turned around abruptly. Pointing her finger at him, she seethed, "You're the one who needs to be careful. You don't even have any idea what you're saying, so I'd suggest you stitch up your own mouth. And I'll say one more thing, too, and it's making me sick to say it, but I'm going to and you might think about it, too. I wonder how many people here in town—since we're talking about reputations—I wonder how many people realize—or how long it will take them to realize—that just awhile back they re-elected an idiot for mayor."

Running now to keep herself from throwing up, she ran from the kitchen and flew up the stairs.

CHAPTER 14

RM told me:

My father did not come up to my room that night to apologize to me or to even try to smooth out the raggedness our tempers had caused. He did not, in fact, come to my room at all. He didn't do things like that. Apologizing was just not something he did. And the same was true with Mother. Sometimes I thought—*hoped* would be more accurate—that they were simply too proud or too inwardly bound or, for whatever reason, too helplessly overbearing to relax enough to allow themselves to make an effort to make sure that I—no—I started to say *felt loved*, but I had learned long before that night not to worry my young self over foolishness like that. Soft talk with them simply never seemed to be a possibility. And I have to add this, too: for whatever reason I don't think that fact scared or scarred me. Who knows? Maybe I ought to admit what I've thought now and then—though I never have even come close to knowing if it's true. As different from them as I was, there might well have been a dimension of me that was like them. Oh, I'm sure there was—no doubt about that, but I have in mind here something more precise than odd or passing points of similarity. Let me put it this way: I'd hate to have to own up to having in me their own level of hardness, what Mother that night called my *meanness*.

Let me for now just say this: My father did not come up to my room that night, and maybe I should simply leave it at that. And maybe I did, who knows? And my mother didn't come to my room either. But then I didn't go to them myself. I also don't think they expected or even hoped that I'd come to them. And whether this next is due credit or blame I don't know, but the next morning, at breakfast, no one even mentioned the previous night's—let's be diplomatic and call it—unpleasantness. At the same time I didn't get the impression that any one of us—and I'm including myself in this—was really having to work to avoid the subject. To some that might have been disconcerting—to be face to face with someone who simply felt no need to work through—or even yearn for—clarity. I say that because that's exactly what Ima Jean told me—and she told me a number of times that she'd have gone mad long ago if she had had to live in a situation like mine. She actually called it *a condition*. It wasn't that the air was always sweet in her own home— they had their set-to's, too. The difference was that Ima Jean said she always knew she was loved. She even said that was the secret to her playfulness—irreverence some called it. She said she felt secure enough to make a fool of herself, though it's doubtful she ever did.

I know, too, you're skeptical about my reading of the matter, my reaction to the explosion that occurred that night at supper which, as you also know, echoed the weather in the house a number of other times, too. But I did not go up to my room that night full of hope that Mother or Dad— either one or both—would, in whatever way they could, take me in their arms. I don't know why I didn't hope for that. Lord knows I'd have certainly loved it. But I didn't. I don't even think I wished they would come to me. I guess I knew pretty well that hugging wasn't a big part of their style.

As I indicated a moment ago, I might have been as unreflective as they were. On the other hand, I'm not going to pretend that I was indifferent to their absence. I wasn't. And I certainly didn't simply dismiss them and slide into my own work—studying and drawing. For awhile that night I didn't—I *couldn't* do anything more than piddle. I tried reading but had no idea what I was reading. I couldn't even sketch anything. I usually had no trouble doing that.

I'd start scribbling and almost instantly a shape would start forming, usually crudely at first, but I'd keep up the incessant scratching as I began to see the shape becoming more precisely defined through the scribbling, and before long I'd feel fine, and sometimes would even have some imagery worth developing later. But that didn't happen that night. I think, for the longest time, I couldn't think about anything with any kind of coherence, other than to recognize an absurd wish that started surfacing—that I, of all things, was doing Plane Geometry again. I didn't and don't know what that meant—if it even meant anything—but periodically—and who knows what usually prompted it?—that same wish, or urge, often returned—and even still does sometimes—when I've gotten upset about something. I'll go to a world that's workably flat.

 I did, though, calm down—finally. One thing especially helped. And I know you've picked up on this before, but one part of what I told Dad was a lie, my down-pedaling what the situation was with Buster and me. I didn't feel guilty about doing that either. And I wasn't lying to Dad to be vindictive. Sometimes I think the truth doesn't need to be fixed. I don't mean that I approve of unreliability either. You might have picked up on this, too: my husband Grover being the most reliable man I've ever known. I know I have in mind primarily myself, the relationship between us, Grover and me. And he could count on me, too. And though we were young—so awfully young—I think Buster and I could be sure (or were sure) about each other, too. It's just that we didn't have much authority over our own situations.

 Let me put this another way: There are numerous shapes the truth can take. I think, too—and I was even beginning to notice this back then—that the more rigid or doctrinaire one was, the more prone to violence one was, even if what one was loyal to counseled peace. My father and mother were horrid examples of this. They were bound and determined that Buster symbolized some kind of leper, though of course neither one of them ever really knew him. But they typed him as something I had to avoid, that they would make me avoid. And they did. And I still shiver and want to scream every time I think about it. They shot that poor boy to death, and goddamnit they got away with it, too.

I'm sorry. I need to hush. That was so long ago. And here all I set out to do was tell you what happened after supper one night—part of me lying my head off to my father and another part of me nothing but screamingly gutsick because the world I knew was turning toward war.

JE:

I saw tears beginning to purl down her cheeks. She daubed them away with a tissue she drew from a side pocket of her light blue housedress. I wanted to comfort her, but something was holding me back. I wanted to get up out of my thickly cushioned armchair and go to her, to put my arm around her, but I didn't. My resolve to sustain a guise of objectivity was fading however.

Finally, after realizing how awkward I felt staying seated, I got up and walked toward her and laid my palm against the back of her neck to support her. She said, "Thank you" then reached back and patted my hand. Then squeezing it, she told me, "Hon, don't you worry, I'll be fine. You just go back to your chair and take more notes because, Mr. John, I have a lot more to tell you."

CHAPTER 15

On the way to Grandfield, the four seemed more determined than joyous. They wanted to make sure nothing interfered with what they were doing, though they were not talking about that. For awhile they were not talking at all. Buster and Ru-Marie were in the back seat, leaning casually into each other; and in the front seat were Ima Jean and Roy DeMent. Roy was driving his father's car. There was no romance stirring between the two, but they had always gotten along well, since early childhood, and both were usually good for adventure. They had lived on the same block almost all their lives, and through most of those years, until recently, little foliage had shielded one lot from the other.

In numerous areas of town when the four were children, it was common for several undeveloped lots to be between houses. Because of the rural backgrounds of so many in town, the open quality of the land in town seemed normal, and the transition from what sometimes looked like randomly placed houses to neighborhoods with few empty lots on the streets was gradual. Growth, however, was coming in faster spurts as new oil fields were discovered and new businesses opened in town. Ru-Marie's father even had three other sporting goods stores he had to compete with.

Because trees tended to be scarce or small, a visual spareness prevailed except on the north side of town where, near the river, shrubbery and brush were often thick. There was also a curious air of tolerance in the town that included many things: yard conditions, economic level, religious affiliation. Certain families, of course, had distinct reputations—some for generosity, some for roughhewnness, others for a casual attitude about their own involvement in what some called noncriminal violence, what others called fighting; but often those reputations seemed handier or just more quotable than accurate, the actions or tempers of one or two family members gradually coloring the way the other families' members were perceived.

Substantial fortunes had already been made by a fair number of families, but no rigid social strata had been set. The world here was too fluid and hot for business to bother with things like that. Dry holes also ruined fortunes, and already there were a few men in town—people of flair and nerve and an ability to draw other people's money their way—whose fortunes would rise and fall dramatically a number of times, but ordinarily not as rapidly as the folklore in later years would indicate. Ruin in one day, however, was a threat.

Ima Jean's father was a doctor and Roy's father a grocer, and though the two vacant lots between their houses now had homes on them, the two still considered themselves next door neighbors. Churches were spreading throughout the community, too. Numerous denominations had revivals that began and often ended with dinner-on-the-grounds, a congregation-wide picnic that welcomed all. A vigorous sense of community was forming, and with it came grief as well as hope and murder as well as life, and with a world of adventure and opportunity about there were also the often-realized threats of fatal accidents. A slight misstep atop an oil derrick—all the pipes and braces slick—or a hand caught between a twirling pipe and chain often stopped the world for some; at the same time the work brought new produce and energy and wealth into the place.

Several years before, the Sunday School class taught by Judge John Kay for men at First Methodist Church downtown had had to move to the Strand Theater several blocks away. Sunday after Sunday more than seven hundred men would come, from numerous congregations and denominations (except Baptist) to listen to him tell Bible stories and discuss the lessons in them. The man had a learned air about him and an easy sense of friendliness modified by a clear quality of authority. Alien to shouting and clearly disapproving of fanatical claims, he preferred information to exhortation.

More and more people came to his talks. Each Saturday the two newspapers would include lengthy articles about the next day's topic. The papers also included précis of the upcoming sermons of many of the ministers—at least those who planned rather than improvised their talks. There were, of course, the shouters and exhorters, but those ministers were even more itinerant than those like the Methodists who seemed to move their pastors around from town to town every two years. The Presbyterians were more stable in that regard, and the expository style of the minister at First Presbyterian gave a tone of stability—some called it dignity—that numerous prominent families in town seemed to favor. The fact, too, that the Church Session, made up of Elders, had to interview prospective members before accepting them into official fellowship increased the air of stability in the church. The Methodists, too, were strong, their congregation having been first in town. Most of the congregations were growing, though periodically there would be splits, sometimes due to the congregation outgrowing their facility, other times because of politics—a cadre of families gathering others around them and starting a new church up the street that they would have better control of than they had had with the one they had just left. The Methodists' vigor and emphasis on inclusiveness appeared appealing to many who, becoming established in the community, were deepening that tie by joining churches. Many in town had grown up churchless on the frontier, but the tone of community was developing as fast as the population was increasing.

Ima Jean's family were Methodists. Her paternal and maternal grandfathers had both been ministers. Ru-Marie's family was Presbyterian, and she gathered that her parents had not had any church affiliation as children, their going to church having begun, she remembered, with her father's sporting goods business beginning to flourish. She even told herself she remembered that happening. She said she had been about five then, but whenever she and Ima Jean discussed the subject, which was rare, she had no trouble admitting, after she had been goaded a bit by Ima Jean, that she might only be remembering thoughts she had developed, and not actual events themselves. Ima Jean had the ability to challenge her without agitating her. Temper was never a factor in their friendship, but play often was.

A lot of groups were flourishing in town. In fact, it sometimes seemed that the only one unable to generate any interest was the Ku Klux Klan. Across the nation the Klan was going into schisms itself and being faced with an increasing level of criticism, a lot of it baldly insulting. Looking for votes, politicians often made fun of the Klan outfits. Few seemed horrified by or even respectful of the organization anymore; it apparently seemed beside the point to many communities. The young District Attorney, on his way to becoming the youngest governor in the nation, had put a stop to that in one short meeting.

Beth Israel, the Jewish congregation in town, was flourishing, too. One of the town's newest and already most successful jewelers had moved to Kiowa from Graham, a town less than sixty miles away. The story went that, strong there, the Klan had run the Zales out of town, but Kiowa had welcomed them. The rabbi in the community was even active in the Ministerial Alliance, a group of Protestant ministers who wanted to give a sense of coherence and responsibility to the religious life of the community. Now and then a

Catholic priest became part of the group as well. The Baptist ministers almost never did.

His sense of hospitality burgeoning, Ru-Marie's father invited the rabbi to play handball with him at the Y, but the rabbi turned down the offer, saying, "We'd both likely be happier if I taught you Torah."

"You don't like athletics?" Jeff had asked.

"I love athletics," Rabbi Goodman said. "But think of what would happen to your chances for re-election if the story got out that I beat you."

"Oh that would never happen."

"Don't be so sure. In Brooklyn I took a good number of medals."

"So let's play," Jeff insisted.

"Maybe later. In the meantime I'll teach you Torah."

"What're you trying to do—convert me?"

"Oh no, I'd never do that."

"Why not?"

"Jeff, my friend, it's simple. Grown men like you aren't usually brave enough to get circumcised," he said, his smile light on his lips, and Jeff laughed out loud. "Am I right?"

"No question at all," Jeff said. "You're as right as can be."

"I figured I was. That's probably why we're not much good at proselytizing. You Christians have the great advantage. All you need is a bit of water, unless you're in a group that insists on dunking. Give me a call," the Rabbi said dryly, "if you ever get brave enough to take the knife."

As they crossed the Red River bridge into Oklahoma, Roy glanced back at Buster and Ru-Marie. He said he had an idea.

"What is it?" Buster asked.

"What about me applying for the marriage license for you?"

"Good lord, Roy," Ru-Marie said, learning forward. "You're turning out to be a lot more forward than I thought. You haven't even asked if I'd rather marry you than Buster."

"No no no," Roy said as they all laughed. "What I had in mind was the possibility we might have less trouble if I applied for the license but did it in Buster's name. My beard's darker and I'm taller, too. I'm just trying to avoid any complications. The guy we talk to, I've heard, sometimes gets contrary. He's probably trying to keep his operation respectable, and he probably wouldn't ask any questions if I made the application myself. What do you think?"

"Fine with me," Buster said, then Ima Jean said she thought it might be a good idea, too.

"You've heard things?" Ru-Marie asked.

Ima Jean said no, she hadn't heard anything, "But Roy's got a point. There's no way anyone could tell who's who anyway."

"Sounds good to me," Buster said. "We're going to the Baptist preacher for the ceremony, and if what I've heard is right, he'd never turn down a two-dollar fee from anybody. Then he asked Ru-Marie what she thought, and she said she couldn't see any problem with anything they were talking about.

"The sun's even shining," she said.

So they followed the change of plan. Roy and Ru-Marie bought the license, then, as many others had done, they found the preacher's parsonage next door to his little church, and five minutes later the ceremony was over. The preacher said his wife, for just a token extra, would be honored to provide a short reception so they could celebrate. "The lemonade's already made," he said, "and I think we have some cookies."

"Thanks," Buster told him, "but we have to go on to Oklahoma City and catch a train for St. Louis."

"That's where you all are from?"

"Oh no," Buster said, "that's where we're going. I've got a job waiting there, but before too long, you know, that's where we will be from. You ought to come visit us sometime," and Ru-Marie tried to keep herself from laughing when Buster told the preacher, "I understand they have a great zoo there."

"I appreciate the offer," the preacher said. "Sure you all wouldn't like a little reception—just put a bit of icing on the cake, so to speak. It's just a bit extra and wouldn't take any time at all."

"Thanks," Ru-Marie said. "Maybe next time."

"Next time?" the preacher asked. "What do you mean *next time*?"

"Oh in case this one doesn't work out," Ru-Marie said, putting her arm around Buster and hugging him to her. "Say in case he turns out to be some kind of ne'er-do-well monster, I'll have to come back with someone else and let you do another service."

"I appreciate that," the preacher said. "I appreciate that a lot. But you might call ahead if you'd like something other than lemonade and cookies for the reception."

"Thank you so much," Buster said, reaching out to shake the man's hand and palming two one-dollar bills his way.

The four of them told the man goodbye and went back to the car for the drive home. There would be no wedding night in a hotel or tourist court, but that didn't seem to be a problem with either Buster or Ru-Marie. As they had before, they would find times and ways to be alone, and though they would keep their marriage secret for however long a time it seemed wise to do so, knowing they were now married was all that counted. No one could split them up, no one, no matter how angry they got.

Quiet in the back seat, they sat snuggled together. Now and then they looked at each other and broke into smiles, then both of them, focusing their gazes on each other's lips, silently mouthed their love, and in the front seat Ima Jean and Roy talked a bit, but mostly they were silent during the drive.

Later Ima Jean told Ru-Marie she had stayed quiet primarily because, for the first time in her life, she found herself—"Who knows why?" she asked—"peacefully awash in a deep state of incuriosity."

"Is what you're really getting at the suggestion that you felt like an intruder?" Ru-Marie asked.

"No, that's what I found so curious. I expected to feel like an intruder, but I didn't."

"So why didn't you turn around and talk with us? We wouldn't have minded."

"I don't know that either. I think on the ride back I was primarily thinking."

"About what?"

"I think I was trying to figure out what we four had all really been a part of."

"Did you come to any conclusion?"

"No," Ima Jean said, reaching over and squeezing her friend's hand. "I didn't figure out a blessed thing. What about you?"

"I think I'd done all my thinking for that day sometime before. I knew what we had just done, and I'm glad you were with us."

"What's that?"

"I knew very clearly there wasn't anything we needed to do to prove our love. But we did need protection, and that's what the trip to Grandfield meant. We got our protection."

"I hope so," Ima Jean said. "I really do."

"You're worried, aren't you?"

"I guess I probably am—but I'm not sure what it really is that's bothering me. After all, your father's already in effect threatened Buster with a tire tool. What else could he do?

And even if he tried to do something—he doesn't know what the situation really is, and you do, so maybe everything's okay. You might, though, wait awhile before turning up pregnant."

Giving her friend a little laugh, Ru-Marie said she didn't need any advice on that, she'd try to keep everything pretty much the way it already was.

"What about Buster?"

"He's talking about leaving school to get a job."

"Do you think that's wise?"

"That's what I really don't know. Part of me thinks it won't make much difference—except we might end up able to buy a bit of freedom. On the other hand, part of me thinks his quitting school would amount pretty much to confession about what our situation really is. And it might not be the right time for that."

"Are you scared?"

"No, though I probably would be if we hadn't already made such good love together. I can't tell you how much his sweetness thrills me. And I don't know why but it's unbelievable how easily he makes me laugh. I think sometimes he could simply announce the temperature and I'd break into stitches. Have you ever felt anything like that?"

"No—except maybe accidentally a time or two. But there is a possibility you haven't yet mentioned."

"What's that?"

Ima Jean laughed out loud before she slapped Ru-Marie on the leg and told her, "That you've turned into a lunatic," and Ru-Marie laughed with her, both of them hugging each other.

CHAPTER 16

Another City Council meeting over, he walked briskly in the wind to check on his store six blocks away on Scott then met some friends for lunch at the Petroleum Club atop the new eight-story Kiowa Hotel, just finished the year before. He had been having these lunches for three years now. At one of the early ones he had been approached to run for mayor. His sporting goods business, one of four in town, had recently gotten contracts from four more school districts in the area to provide uniforms for their athletic and cheering teams. So things were going well. He had come to understand, too, that those first lunches several years before had taken place to test him, and the men had obviously seen what they had hoped to see. Such was fine with Jeff Coleman.

He felt at ease with these men. They were friendly enough and obviously well-meaning in their concern for the community. Jeff had been at first amused, too, that the senior one of the group always listed his profession as "Capitalist." And so he was, as his holdings indicated.

When, still in those early days, Coleman's wife had asked him if he felt nervous being around these important figures—"They do control so much, you know"—he had simply looked at her, nothing fiery in his gaze at all, as if he not only did not know what the source of her troublement was but that he was not at all curious either about finding out why she seemed concerned.

"I'm sure they're good people," his wife said. She sounded defensive, a ghost of a threat moving within her.

Briefly touching her shoulder, he simply said, "They seem so."

When they proposed that he run for mayor, he received the offer with cool-eyed quietness. In measured tones that suggested alertness more than humility, he told them he appreciated their confidence and would give serious thought to their offer. Their own manner of response mirrored his. None of them approached the work of their days and nights with flamboyance. They all maintained a uniform quality of restraint that seemed to be a fundamental part of their nature. They did not seem suspicious of the world or the people they met, but they also did not appear to assume that fate was inclined to favor them or anyone else. They, in spite of their primarily Presbyterian association, did not see the world as depraved but as a place where one should never act like a fool. Officially Calvinist through church membership, though these lunches often included prominent Methodists as well, these men were not inclined to study theology, nor were they inclined to maneuver their thoughts—according to the turns of their conversation—into deep reflection of any kind. The oldest among them, the man who called himself a Capitalist—he and his brother-in-law (their wives sisters)—had come to the area some six years before the century turned and was often considered the town's father, though there was another prominent family who had arrived in 1881, as the community was forming.

The Capitalist, though not altogether by himself, had arranged for the town to become a railroad stop. Folklore said that the stop, a conjunction of stops, was to have been in Henrietta, some twenty miles southeast of Kiowa, but plans had somehow gotten modified. Kiowa then began growing quickly into a shipping center, and the subsequent power of rich oil fields stirred a building boom. The area itself, for years even, seemed to be balancing easily on a sprawling lake of oil. The population shot up from 5,000 in 1910 to 20,000 ten years later. Prosperity itself seemed to be a powerful, generative force. Just twenty miles away, Henrietta, however, was doomed to stay a small town with a short-lived colorful ranching history. Nostalgia for the rip-roaring past would soon be institutionalized into a three-day festival called Pioneer Days, and each year, as if in defiance of the country's cult of youth, one of the oldest women in town would be named Queen of the festivities.

Year after year tales were told in Henrietta about how on Saturdays—pay day—cowboys would ride their horses into town and, exuberant in their drunken joy, fire their pistols up in the air then ride on through the doors of Alcorn's Dry Goods Store. Or so the stories said.

Kiowa was not looking back, partly because so many in it, in their own brazen or hapless ways—losses could be as sudden as gains—were moving ahead as well as they could; and partly because they were stirred by what was often an amorphous sense of vitality in their environment, they had no inclination to look back, to analyze what they had come from, or the nature of what they had passed through.

His assets nowhere as ample as the wealthy men who lunched with him, who insisted they lunch with him, Jeff Coleman had his own level of authority: an abruptly fit sense of body and what seemed like a natural sense of restraint that pulled people toward him. He never seemed to make an effort to get anyone's attention. He did not go to them, they came to him. His strong features were finely defined, his body still fit from the years he had played semi-pro baseball fifteen years ago for the Spudders, the team so-named to celebrate the numerous oil strikes in the area.

At the lunches talk often came around to Coleman's baseball days, the men around him curious about a world they had never had the ability to come close to entering. Although he had pitched his last game more than a decade before, his reputation was still strong in the area. He had never, people heard, been shy about spitballing a batter away from home plate. As calm as he seemed, he had given the impression that he was, of course, comfortable in terrifying an opponent.

With some regularity some new lunch companion would ask if he had ever considered the major leagues. His body gracefully still, though the look in his eye flinty, Coleman would say, "The majors aren't something you get into through consideration."

"Yeah, I know, but do you think you could've made it at that level—I mean if you'd gotten a break?"

"Yes," he said.

"So what happened?"

"I wasn't playing the right position."

"What do you mean? I've heard all sorts of people talk about what a good pitcher you were."

"Maybe so. But I should've played shortstop."

"Why?"

"Because I'm a natural side-armer."

"But there've been a lot of good side-arm pitchers."

"Some," Coleman said. "Not many." Maintaining his steady but unreadable look, he said, "Side-armers throw their arms out." Then he turned to the others as if to ask them in silence if they had further questions for him, yet he did so with no suggestion of impatience or irritation. It was this trait, this imposing restraint in his manner, that made a number of people refer to him as the Country Club set's golden boy, though there was nothing boyish about him at all. Some important people seemed to like being around him just as he felt comfortable being with them.

There was, however, no suggestion—except from some supporters of the two men who had been unlucky enough to run against him—that he was in thrall to his wealthy supporters, some of whom were rumored to be thinking that he might later on be suitable for bigger political positions.

That kind of talk, though, never became much more than a flurry of chatter. There were numerous people who the town's influential cadres said might be suitable for elective office, especially the young District Attorney who had gone away to a nine-month law school program in Cumberland, Tennessee, then come back home and, barely twenty-one, sailed through the state bar exam. He was a "comer," people said. But so were others. In fact, about a decade later, two of the three top Democrat candidates for governor lived in the same precinct, and the Republican candidate lived in town, too. The young District Attorney had an advantage that few others could have. He had two brothers who were also District Attorneys. People joked sometimes that the Allreds might just take over the law.

Jeff Coleman seemed indifferent to the notion of a higher office, though some tried for awhile to think he was just holding back, disciplining himself not to seem hungry. Others would argue that they were sure he was pretty much what he seemed: "Someone," they would laugh, "you can't read." Then someone else would likely say:

"I just never want to get in a fight with him."

"Why? Afraid he'll spitball you?"

"No, not that. I don't even know why—I just think about him fighting now and then. Maybe it's his eyes—the sonofabitch sometimes looks as unreadable as a rattlesnake."

"Hell!" another said. "What are you two doing—worrying yourself into some kind of conflict?"

"Naw—just passing notions around. Who knows? Coleman's cool manner—that damn distance he gives off—might be why everybody and his dog keeps voting for him."

"That and his well-heeled supporters."

"There are those, but there's nothing wrong with that either. In fact, I'll likely vote for him, too, if I get another chance. You know I didn't last time. I'm just not offering to fight him. I have a feeling about that, too—fighting with Jeff

Coleman would likely be as bad as tangling with Ty Cobb—one way or another, you're gonna get spikes dug in you. Hell, I even think they favor each other. You ever notice that?"

"Nope. Nothing like that ever came to mind."

"Did to me. Both of them spitballers, too."

"What do you mean? Cobb's not a damn pitcher."

"I know. I didn't mean spitballer literally. I think it takes a certain type to be something like that. I still think Coleman and Cobb look alike."

"How'd the Council meeting go?" his wife asked when he got home that evening.

"Went well," he said.

"You did remember we're invited out tonight for dinner at the Club, didn't you?"

"I did. Is Ruthie going with us?"

"No. They invited her but she asked if she could stay home, and I said, *Sure*. She's got a lot of homework and some project for her art class to finish. She said she'd fix her own supper, so I'm ready whenever you're ready to go."

"She'll probably make somebody a good wife one day," Coleman said, his wife looking at him full of questions, as if she were asking *What's this all about?* "At least she might if the guy doesn't crowd her too much."

"I think what you're saying is she's just like you."

"I didn't mean that at all. In fact, I don't think she is. It's probably better, though—her staying here."

"That's what she seemed to want to do, and frankly it made fair sense to me."

"Ima Jean coming over to be with her?"

"Not that I know. She didn't indicate anything like that. Why?"

"Nothing. Just a notion. Let me shave and change collars and I'll be ready," he said, loosening his tie as he went toward the bathroom. Then turning back around, he said,

"You don't think anyone's coming over, do you?"

"Like who?"

"Never mind. We'll take care of that later—if we have to."

"What do you mean?"

"Shotgun or axe," he said. "Whichever's more handy."

"Jeff?" she said, staring at him. "Are you making some strange kind of joke?"

"No," he said coolly, "not at all."

Upstairs, Ru-Marie had been listening to her parents. She was finding her father's new turn of attention irritating. Smiling, she thought that he found her own turn of attention irritating, too. We're a happy family, she thought, all of us irritated together. She glanced back out the window, the sky already dark. She was ready for her parents to leave. Such a shame, she thought, their dinner party didn't start sooner.

CHAPTER 17

She turned the lights in her bedroom off and on twice to give him the signal that her parents were gone, and though she was listening for the sound she could barely hear the top of the ladder touching the house on the wall of the sun porch in back. He was always so careful, so remarkably able to control the lowering of the heavy wooden ladder her father kept behind the garage.

Excited, she met him at the screendoor and immediately they were in each other's arms.

A chill had settled in during the afternoon when another cold front had blown in. Snuggling against him, a cold breeze all around them, she said, "I wish we could stay out here—especially if they come home earlier than I expect."

"It's too cold," he told her, "but don't worry. Everything will be all right."

"I'm so glad you're here," she said, squeezing him tightly and loving the thrill of his hands rubbing her shoulders then sliding zigzaggedly down her back to the hollow just below her waist, a mere hand's width before her rump's slight swell, the side of his hand at home upon it.

They were kissing now, but after awhile he began mumbling that he was glad, too, that he was here, but he sounded as if he were mumbling through mush, and they both started laughing.

"Been talking long?" she perkily asked.

"Three months," he said, "right after I learned to walk."

"You're such a honey," she told him, moving her hands down now below the press of their bellies, her palms gripping his thighs.

"My god," he said, then his own hands moved to her thighs, then on back around, they were finding and cupping each other's buttocks now to press, to pull the two of them, pushing pelvically now, together, more tightly together, the spread of their flesh a field of moving delight that stirred them to kiss again, and not stopping the rhythms of their open-palmed rubbing of each other's backs and legs, the sweetness of her breasts soft upon his chest, they were soon in her room and stretched out, the lengths of their bodies together, they embraced on her bed.

Sometimes, though their touching of each other was constant, they would talk, or one of them would, then after awhile he was telling her to go on and say what she needed to say, "But if you don't mind, sweet one," he would add, "I'll speak to you in another way," his hands already cupping her breasts, gently pushing her breasts slightly upward, he slid down to kiss her throat, then lower to kiss the top spread of her chest, and he was now unbuttoning her blouse while kissing her breasts, now one, now the other, through the thin covering of cloth that veiled them, then she gasped, rising up against him she gasped again, there being no cloth now between her breasts and the movements of his lips loving them. She slid her hands between his legs and pressed. She slid her hand up and down, and up and down again, she pressed her palm hard against him, and now he was the one gasping for breath.

After awhile, both of them still breathing deeply, they lay on their sides facing each other. She was telling him what a delight he was and he was murmuring that what she was saying was music. She told him she would love to devour him. Then his look, not immediately but after awhile, turned sober as he told her he knew there was something she needed to say, and still murmuring, and moving in rhythm with her rhythm against him, he encouraged her to say it.

"How did you know?" she asked, a look of startlement in her eyes.

"I just did. But everything's okay, so tell me." He kissed her. "Tell me when you will."

At first she was hesitant but he didn't press her. He kept his fingertips lightly dancing over different parts of her: hips, thighs, belly, temples, the nape of her neck, the sides of her breasts, her nipples, her lips, her temples again, and when his fingertips grazed her throat, he smiled broadly and told her that her whole body was a world of toys, and she threw her arms tightly around him and kissed him, then kissed him again and again.

After awhile, and momentarily calm now, they were looking directly at each other.

"What is it?" he asked.

She did not answer right away, just closed her eyes for a moment, as if the lids themselves were a gesture of modesty, then he told her he thought he knew but she shouldn't worry about it.

"It's all okay," he said, and sighing, she rolled over, her gaze on the ceiling.

Finally she told him, "The curse is back."

"Oh no," he said, "that's no curse at all—just a bit of news that we haven't gotten pregnant yet."

"I wanted to make love tonight," she told him, her eyes still on the ceiling, as if she were dreaming, or lounging now alert in a world of memories.

"We will," he told her. "No worry at all."

"But what about you?"

"What about me?"

"You got all worked up—and then now nothing."

"Hey, sweetheart, you seemed stirred yourself."

"You're not—frustrated?"

"No! At least not enough to jump off the sun porch. I still plan to use the ladder." She snuggled against him. "I am, though," he said, "as I think you can tell, still pretty notably at attention." Smiling mischievously, she kissed him then he told her, "But you don't have to salute me or anything formal like that."

Quietly laughing, she kissed him again and again.

"No worry at all," he said after checking his pocket watch. "They're probably not even into their dessert yet," he said as he embraced her. "There's plenty more time for hugging and kissing, sweet."

Pressing herself up against him, she sighed, then relaxing in his arms, she told him, "Yes, love, there's a lot more time."

CHAPTER 18

RM told me:

  I should have kept more of a scrapbook back then than I did. I've realized, though, especially lately, that I actually cobbled together more than I thought I had. I considered the notes pretty much the way I did sketches: something interesting but not important enough to organize and file. I know there was a lot of backwardness around me (and undoubtedly in and about me, too), but the entertainment was rich, and not just the dances at the Pavilion on the lake. I think, too, that if I hadn't read the paper(s) back then I'd have missed out on even getting a glimpse at the world I was in. Everything seemed to surface at once. King Tut's tomb was found, mummy and all, then what was often called an "important new scientific discovery" revealed that a girl dwarf had been cured of her affliction in just three months with sheep glands. I'm not sure which glands, but the plans there for awhile were to cure all pygmies and produce a race of giants.
  Then along came about that same time some notable medical figure who said laziness was a disease. We were going to cure that, too. I know a lot of what came out was silly, but I found the ferment stirring—even bus trips to football games, for even in that there was an odd level of equality. Kiowa's so much larger now than towns like Electra that you would never think of matching them up with the Kiowa teams, but with all the population shifts due to the oil boom, what are now the little dying places were comparable in size to our own place—and Lord knows the boys in those places were tough, scrappy and tough. Of course, ours were, too; and I found all the hoorah fun. I just

didn't get all aflutter about the school or the town being something to cherish, at least not on the level of an imprint of the Virgin Mary on a tortilla. I guess what I really came to like—though it would be years before the implications of this set in—was the fact that in the mid-twenties in our town a group of women met on Saturdays in the library to discuss the works of Sigmund Freud. I like that, and I frankly don't care how deep or how shallow those conversations were—if they were shallow. The fact that they took place notes something I value, something I think I need to remember about our place back then.

I ought to remember the churches, too, most of them in or close to downtown: First Methodist and First Christian across the street from each other; the Episcopal Church of the Good Shepherd and First Presbyterian just up the street, with First Baptist, Sacred Heart Catholic and Temple Beth Israel nearby, too, as was Grace, another Methodist church downtown. A lot of religion here, but that seemed true in much of the country. I remember, year after year, New Year's Day articles pointing out that New York City churches were often packed for the New Year's Eve services. I'm not saying the culture back then was better than it is now. I don't think it was. And sometimes I'm not altogether certain the textures were all that different, though in ways I know they were.

I remember a battle we had at home, one that I personally saw to it for awhile to keep going. I also still like the fact that by most people's standards the level of the controversy was minor; and even looking back at the crisis now, I'm not sure I can sort out whether I was driven by mischief or an exploration of taste. Likely both.

I'm not even sure how the hoorah really got started. Well, that's not quite true. I'll get back to the source later. But homes back then tended toward the dark. The woodwork was stained dark, deep mahogany, and the rather dim lighting emphasized the shadowy atmosphere of the place—

home or business, there wasn't much difference in either. Then a book I was skimming through in the library caught my attention. I saw some photographs of homes in some Greek island towns. They were bright white, and so were their interiors. I think I just stared half-stupefied and half-enraptured at the pictures. Then suddenly I thought, *Why can't we do that?* I kept thinking how the whiteness—inside as much as outside (though I'd have been willing to spread a world of white over either one of them)—would startle us all awake to a beautiful, vibrant world. And, as you'd expect, I brought the idea home. I suggested we redecorate our own place, paint all the walls white, floor to ceiling.

I was told, of course, my idea was crackpot. That's when I said, "The Greeks do it—and I'm learning, too, they're not the only ones."

I got told firmly—but, I also will admit, politely—that their way, the Greek way, was not our way. Then I sailed in and accused the whole country of trying to ape the English.

"Let's make sure the look is dark and heavy," I said and, because I liked the statement a lot, I said it again, then appealed to the Greeks once more, their ancient sense of authority, their ability to transform sculpture—I had recently been thrilled to find this out. Then I told my remarkably untutored audience—my parents—that my friends the Greeks had gone from Egyptian flatness and stiffness to heroic realism in close to two hundred years. Just think about that. The Egyptians had kept essentially the same style pretty much intact for three-thousand years, and the Chinese had left their own style alone for some five-thousand years."

Heady with that, I sailed into some other great Greek gifts then Mother held up her hand to hush me, and I relented—this was no war—though I was having myself a good time winding up my own enthusiasm to the point you'd have thought I was ready to take up religion and become a revivalist exhorter for all things Greek.

"Settle down," Mother said. "The Greeks don't even believe in God."

"Good heavens!" I told her, and my father, too, "they had scads of gods—Zeus, Apollo, Aphrodite—"

"Yes, but none of those are real. And another thing—that Zeus was not a nice man. I've heard about some of the stunts he pulled, and if a reprobate like that is going to inspire a bunch of depraved foreign people to paint their houses white, then I think that's a good indication their idea is not the way that people like us ought to go."

When I laughed out loud, Dad told me to hush, that Mother was right and he was not going to get suckered into any argument about decoration in the first place. I said I might just paint my own room white, but Mother jumped back into the fray and said there wasn't anybody in this family going to act like a pagan, and a foreign one at that.

Even then I thought that was one of our better conversations. I doubt, though, that they would have ever billed it so high. So now I was a pagan, but that wasn't anything I thought I ought to get congratulated for.

The more I thought about it, the more I realized I had another subject to explore. I soon found out, however, that this new subject I was interested in was harder to find out about than I had expected.

Years later—and who knows why?—I brought the subject up again, not that I was trying to persuade anyone to whitewash a home. I was well on my own by then. The memory was just a passing notion I gave voice to. My father walked out of the room—not stormed out, just walked out—and Mother let me know that she had not found anything amusing about what I had tried to push off on them.

"It upset me," she said, "to hear you sound as if you were trying to become an atheist."

I dropped the topic, and another memory passed before me, and immediately it wiped away any impulse I had to joke. Then shortly after that, I did what my father had done a few moments before: I left the room.

It—at least for awhile—was easier to laugh about dwarfism being cured by sheepstuff than it was to face the fact that the gulf between us was a fact of life, seemingly unimportant in itself, but devastating in terms of what it led to. The notion of the short folks' cure I had read about stirred another article into memory. This one was still another discovery that some said promised great things, the new insight of the day being that love and hate are caused by electricity in the body. I came to learn, of course, that all these notions—sheepstuff fixing short people, the havoc or glory of electricity within us—I current you, you current me, he she or it currents whoever or we all current each other—and the thousand other notions surfacing, all implying, as foolish as some of them were, important questions that were worth more than passing distractions. I wasn't ready, not then, to mull over the great (and lesser) worlds of conclusion.

A cloud had moved from the sky to somewhere within me, but sad as I suddenly was I couldn't tell if that cloud had covered the sun and brought a world of dimness to me or if it had moved on away from the sun and left a sweep of brightness that left me startled to the point that I was unable to turn my open-eyed face to it.

Maybe the headlines back then revealed more than I realized at the time. Here are two that I even want to say are emblematic: *Insane Asylum Spent $28.39 Per Capita In February*. And the other: *Ft. Worth Lawyer Shot, Wife Arrested*. And by the way, you could have bought yourself a good suit—Hart Schaffner & Marks—for thirty-five dollars, and if you had been around then and taken a turn toward sweetness, John Evening, you could have bought me a blouse for a quarter plus a dime.

CHAPTER 19

"We've got to do something," Jeff told her at the dinner table. "Trashy as his background is, there's no telling what kind of trouble he's going to get her in."

"Listen," Eileen said, "you don't have to convince me. I even wonder if she really is at the meeting tonight, the drama club."

"You must doubt her worse than I do. If she's not where she said she'd be, if he's twisted her to go do something with him, I'm gonna kill him. I am—I'll kill him!"

"She and the town both might be better off if you did," she told him, and he nodded: she was making good sense. "I gather," Eileen told him, "you know all about what they're saying about his mother."

"And have been saying—for years," Jeff said.

"Boarding house, my eye! And it's probably not even the kid's fault what he is."

"Hell, that's his problem—don't make any difference whose fault it is. No way we can fix what somebody else broke—no matter how long ago it was. Look—I'm not interested in how he got to where he is. He's poison for Ru-Marie. That's all I care about."

"And us," she said, "the whole family."

"I used to think she had—sense," he said, his voice falling.

"Lord, I quit thinking that a long time ago. Whatever caused it or whatever she's given in to, there's something coarse and mean about her. She is! She used not to be, but she's mean! And to tell you the truth, I don't care if she is our daughter—I wouldn't trust her for a moment anymore. I just don't trust her."

"It's that kid," Jeff told her. "I know she acts like there's nothing special between them—and I don't know what all you've seen when I've been gone—but something's happening. I know it. In fact—and tell me I'm wrong if I am because I'll take, goddamnit, any way out of this hell I can. Hell! I don't know what's railroading through this house— the potential for her to run off and get married or *having*, godforbid, to run off and marry that trashy little shit. Mark my word, he's going to drag her down. And I'm not standing by and letting that happen either. I'd rather bathe in a goddamn Kadane Corner slough pit than live with what we'd have to face if they—I don't even want to say it."

"It makes me sick, too," she told him. "He and his mother just disgusting. But what're we gonna do?" she asked. "You've already gone through the motions of threatening him once, but apparently that didn't work. Do you think he's simply too stupid to get scared?"

"I don't know," Jeff said, lowering his head. Then looking his wife straight in the eye, he told her, "Somehow we're gonna put a stop to whatever those two are about."

"You mean him and his mother?"

"No, goddamnit—Ru-Marie!"

"Look, damn yourself," she snapped at him, "you don't yell at me!"

"Goddamnit, I didn't mean to."

"Well, you did. You yelled right in my face and I'm telling you, buster, you don't ever do that again."

Lifting his gaze to meet hers, he said weakly, as if he'd been shocked, "What did you—you called me—his name— Buster—you called me his name."

"Oh good lord, I didn't mean anything by it, I didn't mean that at all. But I'm telling you—I don't care how upset you're getting—you don't ever yell at me again—*never!*"

"Okay," he said, "I'm sorry. I didn't mean to. I didn't mean to at all."

"That's better!" she spat back at him. "There's a way—believe me, there's a way. We'll find a way. We'll stop all this, I don't care how mean she thinks she can be. We'll find a way. We will."

Under his breath Jeff muttered, "A bullet between his eyes might be a good way. That'd make the trashy sonofabitch pay attention. Make him pay attention good and fast."

"Good and fast," she said. "Both of them. Him and his slut mother, they'll pay attention—and pay attention fast, real fast."

For awhile now they had tried to quit passing hints at their daughter to pull herself up out of this pit she was sinking into. But that had not worked—neither the passing of hints or their more recent attempts to be silent, at least with her, about the mess. Arguing with their daughter did not work. And their silence was not working either. They knew that. They simply did not know what to do. More and more all they talked about when they were together at home was what they often called "the problem," though both of them, in their own helpless ways, knew there were many problems, and they had no idea how to solve any of them.

Again and again they had said they wished this horror would all go away, but the unsolvable problem had worn away any sense of hope, but when they would use the term, they would find themselves knotting up even more tightly than they had been before uttering the word. Both of them had also said—they had blurted it out several times—that they could scream, but that had not helped either. Nothing seemed to help, neither rage nor absurd lunges toward hope. All they seemed to end up doing was to drive each other uncontrollably into new spasms of anger. But at least—and they reminded each other of this when they tried aping a calm they did not feel—both of them desperate for something, anything, unwrecked, unstained, barely coherent now, they would say, *We haven't—we haven't, have we—gone crazy and started blaming each other—we haven't, have we?*—though they usually would not express themselves so directly. Somehow they were able to ignore—or was it simply to pretend?—that they were not telling the truth either. When their voices turned harsh, when they blamed each other without saying so directly, they went into a league of silence, desperately trying this time to keep quiet when their daughter was around.

Sometimes the insouciant obliqueness of her manner—she could affect that mood in a moment—agitated them even more than her periodic inclinations to try to face them down while lying about what was going on between her and that creature who could only lower her pitifully to the point—and she had better be smart enough to be aware of this, they warned—that she was, *mark my word*, one of them would say, going to fall into a nastiness of ruin that she could not even fathom yet. And there will be no turning back, they would say, you'll turn into wet rank trash yourself.

"Oh my god," she once said when they were ranting, "you're making me hungry." Shocked, they both froze.

They had tried to stop the arguments. The arguments were not helping any of them. They told each other that, though their daughter was not a part of this turn of their conversation. Both said they agreed, this arguing was not helping anyone. Even when Ru-Marie was in the house at night, they sometimes ignored their resolutions, the cravings of their will to be quiet, to pretend at least an air of civility. Surfaces, after all—they both knew this and said so—meant a lot. Then before long they would begin making their complaints again, and though they worked hard to keep their voices low, Ru-Marie would sometimes hear them, overhear exactly what they were saying or trying to say in their own tangled ways. Other times there would drift through the air wretched sounds, sounds torqued by pain and confusion, with no coherence in the textures of the phrases drifting into earshot. The muttering itself seemed to move, to ooze through the house, and with that muttering came fragments of passing conversations, phrases independent of the three being battered by their own chaotic flurries of speech.

Awful as it was getting, the tension was not moving Ru-Marie toward tears but toward a quality of sullenness that made her unreachable, sometimes even to herself.

Almost always rising early, she would drift outside each morning to retrieve the newspaper from the front porch. Often she would be barefooted, even during the cold times of year. Seeing her with no slippers on, her mother or her father would say, as they nodded toward her feet, "Do you think that's wise?"

With a voice of unconcern, she would likely say, "No," then drift on to the breakfast table, either to scan the paper there or simply to lay it down on the table and drift back to her room to start preparing herself for the day. There seemed to be no drive in her for consistency. Her parents wanted to say their daughter was falling apart, but both of them knew that was not so. They just wished she would collapse.

Faced with her periodic air of vacantness, the parent who saw her this way would blow a small jet of air through pursed lips. Ru-Marie would notice, too, the sameness of their responses, but she never commented on the fact. She noticed, too—unlike the folklore she heard from her friends about their own fathers—her father did not rush up first in the morning to turn up the floor furnace during the cold times of year. Ru-Marie sometimes wondered if there were not something in her father that was unintentionally and unguiltily distant from the family, from his wife and his daughter both. He, too, often seemed unreachable to her.

There was no reason to ask, she reminded herself, but she wondered if her father were as indifferent to coldness as she sometimes pretended she herself was. But neither father nor daughter needed to bother about this small and passing matter because Eileen was as likely as anyone to be up in the mornings to turn the heat up herself.

Such a harmonious little crew, Ru-Marie would sometimes mutter as one of her parents drifted by on these cold, mostly silent mornings.

But mornings were not the most troublesome times. If a threat of war oppressed the air, that was no problem, not in the mornings. No one would have to be in the house for long. Ru-Marie would go to school, her father might well have already walked downtown for coffee, and her mother would soon have the house to herself, though likely she would be preparing for a meeting or a neighborhood visit with friends later in the morning.

They never spoke about their understanding that a truce was possible in the mornings, but all three seemed to know that. They were civil together and sometimes even friendly with each other. Evenings, however, were different. The sun having disappeared, the house would take on a dimness, an oppressive sense of shadow, even with the lights turned on. The woodwork was dark, as was customary in so many homes then, no one having taken Ru-Marie's idiotic notion of bright white walls into practice.

If they had not gone out, Jeff and Eileen would usually sit in the drawing room. Both might read or one would, magazines usually: stories in the *Saturday Evening Post*, enough variety in there for both of them; and unlike their daughter, they did not tend to devour, or even remember what they read. Each would often skim the fare before them. This let them go back and reread, as if for the first time, what they had already passed their eyes over. Some evenings they would turn the radio on and half-listen to dance music, but because the quality of reception was erratic, their listening had not become habitual, as it was with others they knew.

Both of them had also come to dread one of them bringing up *the problem*. Away from the chaotic stir of their conversation on the subject, they could even feel sensible while murderous notions passed through them, even exotic turns of mayhem they might inflict on what their daughter had once called "a sweet little dance machine." Taking the phrase innocently at first, they had even come close to finding the epithet and their daughter's witty enthusiasm amusing; but the phrase had an ominous air about it, as if their daughter were suggesting some shamelessly uninhibitedly lascivious drive the young man was trying to stir alive in her. To keep from fostering its development, they tried to avoid the subject, but sometimes something as trivial as a glance, a frown, an awkward insinuation of silence would stir them into talk and, before long, rage, and with it would come a wildness of speech that knotted up both of them, nothing ever seeming to get clarified or dismissed or even momentarily relieved when their voices rose.

One night Eileen asked her husband if he didn't think it might be a good idea to try talking through *the problem* with their minister at First Presbyterian, but Jeff wouldn't hear of that. He told his wife he knew what she was getting at but he did not want any more people than themselves knowing about the problem. "I just don't like talking about personal things outside the family," he said.

"Oh I understand," she said. "I just thought he might have a word of guidance."

"It's not guidance I want," Jeff said, "it's for the goddamn problem to be over. And the way things look, there's only one way I know that might happen."

"Oh, hon, no, please—don't get me started. Let's drop the talk for tonight, change the subject or I'll end up in worse shape than you'll be in. When I start thinking what I know you're thinking, the only thing that shocks me is that the idea of actually doing what I'm thinking about doing to him doesn't even horrify me."

"Horrify? Hell, I'd welcome it—blast the little sonofabitch till nothing was left—nothing left at all but smoke and blood."

"Careful now," she said, "careful. Please. Not tonight. Ru's up in her room and I'm sometimes afraid she's going to explode one day. Somehow she got a kink thrown in her that makes her nuts for the underdog. But it's more personal than that—at least it is now. So, please, not tonight."

"Okay," he said, agreeing.

The next morning, while they were still in bed, as he lightly, almost absentmindedly massaged her hip and thigh beneath the covers, he told her he was glad she had made him hush the night before.

"Good," she said and moved his hand to her breast. "Don't you feel better now?"

"That depends," he told her.

"On what?" she asked.

"I don't want to get into it—let's drop it," he said, moving his hand away from her breast. "I'm confused," he said. "I don't even know why I told you I'm glad you made me hush last night. That's not what I feel. That's not what I think. Nothing's even close to being solved."

Gently she pressed her index finger over his lips. "Hush," she said, "just hush," then moving her hand from his mouth, she moved her length against him, and embracing him, she rolled over on top of him, his arms going around her, he twisted his head to kiss the side of her neck, then down till he began munching her skin beneath the collar scoop of her nightgown.

"We should've done this last night," he said, "when we had more time."

"No," she said, lifting herself up then forward so her breast was lightly pressed against his lips, and she began to move side to side, slowly, her breasts back and forth across his face. "There's enough time now," she said, arching her hips to help him as he pushed the hem of her gown up until it was above her waist and she, reaching down to slide the hem of his nightshirt up as well, found the hem had already slid up and their flesh, moving deeply together, had little cloth between them.

CHAPTER 20

They had gone to his house, and they were visiting now in the small living room. She liked being there, but because the roomers often came and went, there was usually little privacy for them. That, however, never seemed to be a problem; and if Buster's mother was there, her presence was a boon. She was always nice to Ru-Marie. But Buster's mother had left to do an errand, and the two of them were alone. Buster was teasing her, telling her she *needed* to go swimming with him in the river. He said it would make her a better person, and laughing, and reminding him that the season was winter, she told him she had already gotten as close to that river as she needed to get—ever.

"When?" he asked.

"Years ago," she said. "Ima Jean and I went down there ourselves—when we were kids."

"But you didn't go swimming."

"We did," she told him. "That's why I'm not going down there again."

"What happened?"

"It was awful! That's what happened. The river's so muddy it looks half solid, and all that red clay in it dries on your skin. You can almost hear it cracking on you when it dries. There you are, walking back through the brush and hearing your skin cracking into something like a checkerboard. And it's almost impossible, too, washing it out of your clothes. Good lord! I'd be red all over if I went down there."

"I'd be glad to wash you off."

"I know you would. You're helpful that way," she said, taking his cheeks in her hands. "There's just no way I'm going to swim or wash or do anything else in that place. All I'd be doing is putting new dirt on me."

"Okay," he said, "I guess I have to give up. I was planning on giving you a tour of the place."

"Do you really like going down there?" she asked him.

"Sure," he told her. "There are mussels all over the place, and you can almost always see a crane—those huge wings lifting it slowly up off the earth. There's always something down there to amaze you. I even saw a roadrunner agitating a rattlesnake once."

"How?"

"The most amazing thing I've ever seen. It would make pecking motions at it—the roadrunner would—and the snake would strike but the roadrunner—fast as lightning—would dart its head back so the strike would miss. It kept doing that till the snake must've gotten tired because after a time there wasn't as much fire in its strikes as there had been. But that's when it really got wild. The moment the roadrunner pulled back, jerked back to make the snake miss it, it would then strike back at the snake itself—fast as could be—and drive its beak at the back of its head, even into the head. After that happened a couple times, the snake wasn't anything more than a thick hank of rope with a hole in it."

"You really saw that?"

"Yeah," he told her, "but just once. But that wasn't all that happened."

"What do you mean?"

"After pecking around at it a few more times—I guess to make sure it was dead—the roadrunner picked it up in its beak, and, I swear, struck a pose to show what a hotshot it was. I almost laughed out loud. I'd seen them do that with lizards—goofiest picture you've ever seen. But I had never seen one with a big snake in its mouth. I wish you could've seen it."

Smiling at him then squeezing his wrists, she told him, "You're almost making me wish I had. Did you ever eat the mussels you picked up down there?"

"Sure," he said, "though they've got a taste that's a bit muddier than I like. But finding the shells with the mussels still in them is tough. They're usually just open, empty shells, and I never have been able to figure out what might've gotten them—maybe raccoons."

Hugging him, she quickly kissed him on the cheek, and he glanced back at her, as if to ask what had brought that trick on, and she thought his eyes looked as if they were singing to her, and she thought that her own eyes must be looking that way, too.

"No doubt about it," she told him. "I'll go down there with you. I just don't want to go swimming."

"Do you think Ima Jean might like to go, too?"

"I bet she would," Ru-Marie told him. "She might even want to bring Roy, or David—or maybe someone else."

"Good. We'll get a little crew together," he said, "and have ourselves a cookout, a picnic. It's even warm enough, though it probably won't be for long."

"Sounds great," she said.

"I'll even show you some egrets."

"What's that?"

"Snow-colored birds. There's a herd of cattle near where we'll go, and a lot of times the egrets are with them. You'll usually see a bird for each cow. They'll be standing in the grass beside them, though sometimes you'll see a bird up on the cow's back. They're up there eating insects off the cattle. There's always something out there to entertain you," he told her. "I like it better than going to the show sometimes, unless it's a new Harold Lloyd. Something neat is always happening."

Laughing again, she threw her arms around him and kissed him, and soon they were curled up together, then as if trying to catch his breath, he quit munching the back of her neck and her ear lobes, but immediately she found he wasn't trying to get his breath back at all. He was asking her if they ought to put up a sign for anyone who might walk in on them and tell them, if they were going to stay and watch, that they ought to pay a fee—leave a good-will offering or such. She bit his nose in reply and told him, "No, I'm serious. We may even want to turn pro—be sideshow lovers in the circus." But now he couldn't say anything back to her at all because she was on top of him and joyously trying to smother him.

He managed to tell her, "You're probably right."

"About the circus?"

"No, about not worrying if someone walks in on us."

"I know I'm right," she said.

"You always are," he agreed, touching her cheek with the back of his hand. "I just wish I could charm your father."

"I know," she said, lowering her gaze. "I regret that." Then taking his hand in hers, she told him, "You don't know how much I regret that."

"Yes, I do," he told her. "I know very well. But we'll figure out something. Some day we'll figure out how, I know we will."

RM told me:

We tried but nothing worked. I doubt—no matter what we tried—that anything would have worked. I can still hear his voice—such a young voice but not so young that my own dreams can't reach it. The images, though, don't stay—except for one, and I guess that's really what made him different from everyone else.

I saw a lot of romances take shape then blow up, and a few just faded and were somehow over, and no one had to say anything for that to be known. We probably weren't any more fickle than any other group back then—or since then—or at any other time either, but there was a lot of romancing and a world of awkwardness with it. And, of course, marriage and motherhood and wifedom was right next door, so it wasn't as if we thought we had a world of time to play freely.

Still, I saw girls ruining their own interests because they'd get clutchy—grabbing the guy desperately and driving him away. Or the other way around—a guy going into some monumental jealous fit—and a fair amount of times even justified, but he'd be grabby, too, and drive his girl away if he didn't scare her half to death first. And though I wasn't as aware of it as I might have been, I don't think the adults were any better. Half the time—though mine didn't—they seemed as fickle as we were, but the price they had to pay was a lot more expensive then than what it usually was with us.

But, as I said, that was not the case with Buster. He was sweet and he was fun, and I never felt an urge in him to try to tie me down or make me prove how much I cared about him. There just wasn't anything like that in him. And back then I thought he simply had a gift, but now I'm not so sure that was the case. My attitudes started changing after I saw what Ima Jean and David were like together—years later, of course. And Buster had been gone some years by then, but seeing Ima Jean and David together, I couldn't help thinking about Buster—and me with him. That's when I found what his secret was. It wasn't some special gift he had, though he did have those, and I think sometimes I'd have been happy just being able to see him coming down, every day, the back side of a tall ladder, with him clowning around and having as good a time as the rest of us who got to see him do that.

But maybe what I thought back then was maturity was something else—maybe simply the fact that it never seemed to occur to him that he had anything to worry about with me. And he was right—if that's the way he thought—or maybe he didn't have to think because there *wasn't* anything for him to worry about—at least from me there wasn't. Lord knows, I was at least as nuts about him as he was about me.

CHAPTER 21

The street paving work was going well. There were few streets now in the residential areas that had not been paved, but the work still looked as if it would never be finished. The city limits were expanding; new acreage was regularly being brought into the city. Jeff Coleman had begun saying at Council meetings, "There's hustle in the air." He was saying that regularly now, and each time he did the Capitalist gave his chin a slight tuck to show his approval. It had become the Capitalist's custom years ago to attend the City Council meetings regularly. "Nothing notable," he'd say to brush off compliments about his civic dedication. "Just a convenient way to keep track of investments."

Business moving smoothly, the Council often adjourned before noon, as it had just done again. Before Jeff and some of his friends who had been in the audience left the building to go to lunch, the Capitalist motioned him over. Breaking momentarily away from his group, Jeff said for them to go on, "I'll catch up. I'll just be a moment."

He went to the corner where the Capitalist was standing. The two shook hands, but before Jeff said anything, the Capitalist quietly asked him if he were all right.

"Sure," Jeff said. "I thought the meeting went well."

"Of course, the meeting went well. I was asking, though, about you. You seem a bit tense. Anything wrong?"

"No, sir," Jeff said, "not a thing."

"That's good," the Capitalist said then nodded that he needed to go on.

It surprised Jeff that the man had noticed. Of course, he was tense. He just didn't think anyone except his wife knew it. It made sense for him to be tense, he told himself. Something, goddamnit, was going to have to be done to keep that little shit away from his daughter. Something was going to have to be done, too, to keep his mood in better control.

When he walked out the back door of the municipal building to catch up with his friends, a cold wind struck him. He had barely gotten his hand up in time to keep his hat from blowing away. Ahead of him, his friends were walking quickly to get out of the cold as fast as they could. Faster than they were to begin with, he caught up with them quickly.

"You up for handball later this afternoon?" Herb Solomon asked him.

"I'd like to," Jeff said, "but what about trying for Thursday? I'm tied up this afternoon."

"Sounds fine. Either one of you two sissies," he said, grinning, to the others, "want to join me at the Y?"

Friendly in the face of his banter, they said they'd better decline.

Jeff liked the game, though he had only taken it up two years before. The courts at the Y were often drafty, even cold in the winter, but it did not take long, he had quickly found out, for a player to warm up.

"No," Herb said, "you guys don't really have anything better to do. Come join me later this afternoon."

"That's a young man's game."

Laughing, Jeff jumped back in the conversation and told them, "You guys are young."

"May be. But I've already tried that game. And it winded me more than I like."

"Think about it," Herb said. "Jeff and I'll be glad to play you doubles. Better still, come down to the store. I'll give you a good deal on a chair. Got a new one in—comfortable enough to let you take a long nap in it. Fact, sitting in it guarantees a nap. Money back if it doesn't."

"Now I might take you up on that chair. I actually might. I'm just not going to play any more handball. Just count me retired from that sport."

"What about you?" Herb asked Will who hadn't said a word. He was a big man and usually quiet. "Hell," Herb said, "long as your arms are, you wouldn't even have to move."

Laughing, Will told him the offer was tempting, but he still preferred cards.

"You ought not to," Herb said, "you'll lose all your money you start playing cards."

"Not the way I play," Will said. "I don't gamble."

"Then why do you play?"

"To pass the time."

"Okay," Herb said to the wind. "Just you and me," he told Jeff. "All our friends here are sissying out."

After lunch, Jeff went back to his store. He hadn't said much during lunch. He was still bothered that his friend the Capitalist had been right. There *was* something bothering him. It upset him, too, that the man had noticed. He didn't want anyone to know how bothered he was. That wasn't because he had any desire for privacy. He didn't want anyone to know how he felt because if they did know then they also knew about Buster and Ru-Marie, and he did not want anyone at all to know about those two. His daughter, he thought, ought to have more sense than to hang around with a guy whose mother was a hooker—or a madam. Sometimes, when he wound himself up tightly, he actually started believing that was what she was—or had been. Now ugly and involuntarily retired, he told himself, she ran a boardinghouse, or so she called it, but talk said that was just a front, and talk was likely right. Ru didn't have any business or right either being around that kind of trash. What was just as bad and maybe even worse was that Buster now had money. The damn kid had quit school in December and was working the night shift at the refinery, and in the damn lab no less, and now that he had money he'd likely start trying to get Ru to settle in with him. Thinking about his daughter being tied up with a trashy family like that—and the rotten environment that came with it—repulsed him.

CHAPTER 22

Usually he was disciplined enough to drop any personal concerns when he played handball. He had learned to do that pitching. He had learned to distrust what his coach had called *private inspiration*. "That'll get you in trouble," the coach said, "at least as much as it might seem to help. Just don't trust the damn thing." Jeff at first didn't think the coach knew what he was talking about, but he quickly discovered he was right. He learned to distrust the idiocy of private inspiration one day when he got homered out of a game. He had blown three straight smokers past a batter while thinking about a problem he was having with another player, a sonofabitch he just didn't like. He had gotten excited then, thinking he had found a new trick—channeling hostility—then suddenly the next batter—the cut he was taking looking slow even, his swing so in control, so deliberate, no image of power at all in it—made what sounded like a mere clicking contact with the ball, but the ball sailed high and long, far above and beyond the fence. Almost the same thing happened with the next batter, too.

So Jeff knew if he didn't get Buster and his daughter out of his mind, the game with Herb would be horrible, and disgust at that would knot him up even worse than he was already tangled. During warmup, he felt off-balance, with no dependable sense of rhythm in his arms, his hands and his legs. The awkwardness came from stiffness. He knew that. And Herb, he found, knew it, too, Herb even heckling him about his natural penchant for clumsiness, but then Herb was good for heckling people most days.

"It's just like golf," Herb said. "Keep your eye on the little sphere and your feet on the big sphere. Nothing to it. Even a no-talent like you can master the move. You do look pretty bad. Ready to quit?"

"We haven't even gotten started."

"I can tell," Herb said, "but can you?" he added, sailing a low corner shot so it caromed directly toward Jeff, but Jeff caught it left-handed before it bounced off the floor; he sent it off the side wall, but the angle of impact made the shot die a fault. The ball never came close to touching the front wall. "No, no," Herb said, dipping low to sail the next shot ahead. "Always try to hit the front wall. Rule of the game, rule of the game."

They finally began rallying well.

"I thought you were smart enough to remember that," Herb said. "Front wall. Ball hits the front wall. But apparently not," he added. "I'll bet you'll be a gentleman, though, when you lose. No question about it," Herb said, sailing a shot high off the front wall so it drove Jeff back to the end of the court to slap the ball back before it hit the back wall and bounced out of reach. "Not bad," Herb said. "A good man like you gets used to losing—that's good." They were moving smoothly now, neither one trying for kills. "You lose enough, you learn not to cry."

"Damnit, Herb, don't you ever shut up?"

"Can't," he said, making a three-wall shot. "God tells me to talk."

"Good shot," Jeff said, and sailed the ball low against the front wall, but Herb was there in time to pick it up and sail it high off the front wall, and staying high, the ball sailed off the back wall, too, but his movements fast and powerful, Jeff got to the ball in time, and the rally kept on.

"Thought I had you," Herb said.

"So did I," Jeff told him, knowing full well that for now at least the force of Herb's chatter, infectious as it sometimes was, was stronger than his own inclination to sink back into bitter rage, and he was glad for that but realized, too, that his concentration had started flagging again, and if he didn't get it back, if he didn't sail back into that sweet condition of mindless attention, Herb would cream him mercilessly. He had done it before.

Suddenly Herb caught the ball in his fist. The rally was over. He had simply stopped it.

"You warm enough yet?" he asked, and Jeff said he was, knowing Herb would do anything to throw an opponent off rhythm. Ceremonially, Herb bounced the ball once then made his shot to see who would get to serve first. Bouncing off the wall, the ball hit the floor barely two inches from the service line. "I doubt you'll be able to beat that," Herb told him, catching the ball then tossing it to his friend who would win service honors if he placed his shot closer to the line than Herb had.

"I probably won't," Jeff said, bouncing the ball then catching it and bouncing it again to find the rhythm he wanted. Smiling, he dropped the ball, caught it off its bounce and after it hit the front wall, it landed directly on the service line. Honors were his.

"You sure you're up for the match?" he asked Herb. "A feller like you," he said, "might do well with a bit more practice."

"Highly possible," Herb said.

"Ready?" Jeff asked.

"Serve," Herb told him, and with his first return the ball caromed low off the front wall then sailed almost flatly off the side wall, breaking Jeff's serve.

"Sweet stroke of luck," Jeff said. "Sweet stroke of luck."

The match was going to be a good one. He was sure of that, and glad to be impressionable himself today, he did not regret at all that he had slipped into the bantering Herb offered him. Who knew who would win? They would both try hard, though they would both keep on with their chatter—Herb's motor mouth a good distraction from mayhem—try to throw off the other, try to make the other think he was thinking *I'm not trying at all—don't have to with a clumsy man like you.*

Off the handball court Jeff was not much of a chatterer at all; and if he were playing with anyone but Herb he was usually quiet, well-focused and quiet. He had started out playing well today—recovering quickly from losing his first serve so fast—but again and again he had to fight to keep his concentration. He even shocked himself to hear himself thinking that Herb—for a time at least—was saving his life. A thought like that was crazy, then he saw the ball as Buster's head and sailed it clean off his neck and shoulders and it struck the front wall hard but, making a kill, Herb drove it back so low and fast that the ball basically slid back on the floor, and once more Jeff had lost his serve then he thought of his wife and somehow knew when they were together tonight they would stir each other up again, even if they did not even bring up the problem they were both so desperate to solve. The ball was sailing toward the wall and if it hit the back wall—he had to get to it first—there would be no way for him to catch it and sail it back. Lunging, he made the shot and the moment he knew it was going to be easy for Herb to return it, he crashed into the wall and with fine control Herb sent the ball back softly against the front wall, low, so all it did was roll fast back toward them with little bounce even, and the point was Herb's and would have been Herb's, too, even if Jeff were not struggling to pick himself up off the floor.

"You all right?" Herb asked, coming to him and holding out his hand for Jeff to take.

"I think so," Jeff said. "Good kill."

"Thanks," Herb said. "How's your shoulder?"

Jeff heaved to catch his breath then blew hard. "I think," he said, puffing, "I'm okay."

"You're not dizzy, are you? You didn't hit your head, did you?"

"No problem," Jeff said, moving his arm around in a slow circle. "I'm going to be fine." He kept moving his arm to stretch it out, to give himself more time to get his breath back. "In fact," he said, "I think I'm about ready for the next point."

"Good. I hope you know you're going to lose that one, too. You're just in over your head. I'm out of your league, Jeff. That's all there is to it. You're just no good."

"We'll see," he said, laughing. "We'll see," then after losing the next point, he won back his serve and made two straight aces.

"That, my friend," Herb said, "won't happen again," and soon both of them were back in rhythm and rallying, the process of the game—at least for awhile—good in itself. But a kill was coming up. Both of them even mentioned the fact as they rallied. More important than that, Jeff knew, was the fact—and he tried to push the thought away but failed—he was free from the horror of what he and his wife were sliding slimily into because of their daughter, her crazed obsession with trash, and though she denied that, though she said she and Buster were not even what they probably called *an item for pitysake*, Jeff did not believe her, not after Eileen said she had almost caught them once, or thought she had. Jeff didn't believe anything his daughter said anymore, then feeling both absurd and sick in his stomach for even thinking in this crazed way—ridiculously mixing up all kinds of things—he told himself right before it happened that he was going to flub his next shot and lose the point, and he did, his head lost in a swirl of red clay river mud, so much so he was not even alert enough to fully comprehend at first that Herb was both serious and right when he said—sounding as if he were speaking from a tunnel a great distance away—"Game, match, point."

The gesture a reflex—he was still lost in fog—he reached out to shake Herb's hand and said, "You got the wrong sport. You're talking tennis."

"Oh I know," Herb said. "I just wanted you to start thinking that when it gets warmer, I'll be beating you at that, too."

"You hope."

"You were tough," Herb said, no playfulness at all in his voice. "I don't know when I've gotten so winded."

That, too, sounded as if it were coming from far off, and for a moment Jeff did not know if Herb were simply chattering again or telling the truth.

"How's the shoulder?" Herb asked, laying his palm against Jeff's back.

"I think all right," Jeff answered, feeling as if he were coming back to his senses, and for a hitch of a moment—a second of startlement—Jeff thought again that Herb was saving his life, but that made no sense, no sense at all. Herb had only made him forget the horror for a moment, and that was all, and recognizing how mistaken his passing notion was, Jeff was troubled again to think he might have even sunk so low as to need help, any kind of help, and it bothered him, too, to think that just two days before, his friend the Capitalist had somehow gotten the notion that something was wrong. Someone knowing that about him, or even suspecting such, made him feel diminished, helpless, running the risk of being in someone else's control. He could not allow that. He could not allow that at all, and if he had to steel himself so he would not show—have no chance to show—even a bit of the mess that troubled him, that threatened to undo what he and Eileen had built, then he would do what he had to do even if that meant hiding the trouble from himself. But that would not be necessary, he told himself, his confidence back. Tonight he would go home and wallow around with Eileen, and all the trouble that tortured them would disappear just as it had for awhile with Herb today on the handball court. Tonight the good place would be the bed, and there, after he and Eileen had been touching each other through all their length, they would go unconscious, their grief something that had simply passed on beyond them, but thinking that, he saw a huge splash of blood exploding over him and washing all over his naked wife. Shuddering, he winced.

"You okay?" Herb asked.

"Sure," Jeff said. "Why?"

"You were shivering. You're not catching something, are you?"

"No," he said firmly, and forcing out a laugh, he told Herb, "I'm just having trouble believing you beat me."

"And no doubt about it, fellow," Herb said, clapping his friend's back, "I'll do it again, too."

CHAPTER 23

He told her they had to tell her parents. Looking at him directly, her eyes now hazel-colored ice, she said, "Why?"

"Because," he hesitantly told her—the subject itself seemed to frighten him—"if they find out on their own, there'll be hell to pay."

"Sweetheart," she told him calmly as she placed a hand on his thigh, "there's going to be hell to pay no matter *how* they find out."

They were sitting on the edge of the bed in his room in the boarding house. She had come here directly from school. It was usually the most regularly convenient time they had together, now that he worked the night shift. Usually no one was around except Buster's mother, and she was often in another part of the house or in and out on errands; but even when she was around, she was no problem. She did not try to insinuate herself in their presence. Ru-Marie, in fact, thought the woman had done everything she could to make her happy, to make her feel welcome in this place that was hers. She did not, however, push the romance, and never had, nor did she try to thwart it. Ru-Marie had the feeling that the woman had known about Buster and her for a long time. She just was not quite sure how thorough Annie Lopreis's knowledge was.

Ru-Marie had even asked Buster if he thought his mother might have an idea that they had gone off to Grandfield, the little Oklahoma town across the border the symbol for secret marriage among the young. He told her he didn't know. "The subject's never really come up," he said. "I doubt she'd be shocked."

"That's what I figured. It's just different with my folks. Sometimes I think there's going to be a blowup between us—I mean a real blowup—either with Mother and me or Dad and me or the three of us all pitted together in full-fledged war. I don't think anything would surprise me with them. I've even started wondering what level of violence there might be beneath that calm they're pretty damn good at presenting. I guess I wonder more about how much of their own layers they really even know about—or if there are even layers. But then there are other times," she told him, "when I think what they really want most is to forget it all, forget everything about you and me, to do *any*thing except acknowledge the possibility we've even come close to doing what we've done."

"You don't think their knowing about Grandfield would help take care of the problem—at least part of the problem?"

"Good heavens, *no!*" she said. "That would make everything worse. Then everything would be official and hard to undo. That would be much worse than thinking they can convince a couple idiot kids to get realistic and give each other and stupidity up."

"Okay," he said, backing down, his voice weak and his head hanging as if he were hesitant even to look at her, then seizing control of himself, he took a deep breath, took her hands in his and told her, "It's just—" but he hesitated, a wildly frightened look coming into his eyes, then that faded, too, and lifting his hands off hers, he limply turned his palms up, a gesture that seemed to confess helplessness. The look on his face turned blank, as if whatever thought he had had vanished.

"It's just *what?*" she asked.

"We *have* to," he said, but that idea, too, seemed to have vanished. Then trying to recover, he told her, "We can't—we just can't keep what we did a secret," he said as if he were pleading with her, "not even if we want to."

"Why not?" she asked insouciantly. "I don't think we have any other choice."

"But what kind of life can we have?"

"Pretty much," she told him, "the same one we have right now. We didn't, after all, get used to something else then have to change. Listen, sweetheart, I think I can hang in with what we have to do for as long as it takes. I just don't see the problem with that. We don't have to tell anyone anything."

"But what if you get pregnant?"

"I think we have that pretty well under control. Let's just not worry about what's not a problem."

He looked at her in disbelief.

"What's wrong?" she asked, smiling at him, her right hand moving up higher on his thigh.

He kissed the fingertips of his left hand then gently pressed them onto her breast.

She told him, "I like it when you do that."

But something other than touch and affection was driving his attention. "Do you mean," he finally got out, "you could go on like we are—indefinitely?"

"Sure," she said. "No problem. In the first place—as I've already said—we don't have much choice. Hell, Buster, if I'd been an ancient Greek, I'd have probably already died several years back during childbirth. Those idiots married their girls off at fourteen for heavensakes—except for the Spartans and they waited till the girls were eighteen. That's probably the only smart thing the Spartans ever did."

"Where'd you learn that?"

"Where else? I haven't gone to the library since I was a kid for nothing. You know what I am?"

"No, what?"

"Nubile. You know what that means?"

"No."

"It means marriageable. I'm biologically *ready*. That's what it means. And I'm not responsible if my parents aren't ready. Besides, what we have done is none of their business."

"Yeah, but—there's a bunch of stuff you've become aware of—in them—and that's a problem."

"Oh," she said, hugging him to her, her voice light and rapid and clear, "I don't see much of a problem at all—not for now. Of course, we might get into a big one with fireworks later, but I'm in favor of putting that off for awhile," she said, scooting back farther on the bed and away from him. "Just moving to get my balance back," she quickly explained. "I'm in no way trying to get away."

"I know that," he told her, moving close to her again.

"Then smile," she said. "We're not talking about anything sad. So what's there to fear?" Her eyes shining, she playfully asked, "Who else would have me? After all, love, you and your amazing body have just ruined me all to pieces—and again and again, too," she said, smiling. "So listen, love, it's just you and me. I, after all, am what the prissy idiots here call damaged goods—and thinking about that sometimes makes me want to sing out, really sing out. In fact," she said, both her hands on his thighs, "if your mother weren't due back right away, I'd ask you to damage me again, right now," and immediately they were in each other's arms, their kisses wild and happy, and now they were lying down, the lengths of their bodies pressing together.

"Maybe," he muttered, "she'll be late."

"Not a chance," she said, massaging his groin.

"So what do we do?"

"I'd suggest," she said, "we do what I've heard the Cajuns say," and going into what she passed off as a Louisiana accent, she said, "*Pass me you tongue, sha—I'm hot for you, bébé.*" Laughing, he rolled over on top of her and when he kissed her, she bit his tongue lightly. "Next time," she said, "I might bite it all the way off and keep it for a toy." Her eyes were shining at him as she asked if there might be anything else he would like for her to remove so she could take it home with her and get happy anytime she wanted to.

"Yes," he said, "me."

"And that will surely happen," she told him. "Maybe even sooner than we think."

He told her he liked the sound of that then dipped down and, cupping them in turn with his palms, he kissed one breast then the other. Her own palm now between his legs, she pressed upward as she slowly slid her hand around and around and back and forth over the cloth of his trousers. His palm was moving between her legs, too, his hand up inside her skirt. As he pressed his fingertips upward, they both looked directly at each other. For a time there was an expressionless quality in their gazes, then the look, from both of them, turned severe, turned grave. Catching her breath, she bit her bottom lip but kept her eyes directly on his eyes. He began then to unbutton her blouse, the sides of his fingers trailing slowly and softly along her smooth bare skin. She laid her hand over his to stop him from unbuttoning her blouse any more.

"We have to stop," she said. "I want you, but we have to stop. Your mother will be here soon."

"I know," he said, then added, "and the teacher who lives here will be back, too."

"If we made love now," she told him, "I'd likely scream till the whole city heard me."

"I'd like that," he said, smiling at her, a look of calm settling into his features. "That might be the best wedding announcement yet."

"Just think what a fit—no, I don't even want to say it."

"Go on," he told her."

"I was thinking they'd likely be so upset they'd both have a hemorrhage."

"That might not be a bad idea," he said. "I don't wish them much harm, but if they hemorrhaged bad enough, that might in itself solve our problem."

"It might," she said perkily, her mood now light. As they began moving to get up, though neither one hurried through the process, she beamed at him and kissed his face and neck when he told her he had just been thinking that if she were naked now, she would be pretty enough for him to take to church, and her smile turned again into laughter.

Soon they were up off the bed and brushing wrinkles out of their clothes and combing their hair back in place with their fingers. He told her he thought she looked just fine, and pinching him through his shirt near the navel, she told him he looked pretty presentable himself. "At least good enough not to kick you out of bed," she added.

They kissed each other lightly, but suddenly she frowned, as if something she had not expected had just passed through her.

"What is it?" he asked.

"Nothing. Just something I've been wondering about. Who knows why?"

"What is it?" he asked, frowning, too.

"It's something you mentioned. I guess at the time I was too shy to ask more about it. We were talking about something else, and the matter, the incident, the idea just seemed to pop up and then vanish."

"What?"

"You might've used a different word," she said, sounding more playful than offended, though there was a look of concern in her face.

"What do you mean?"

"It's a question I have, and it's probably not even my business."

"Hey," he said, palming her shoulders. "If it has to do with me, it has to do with you. So what is it?"

"Okay," she told him, "but if you don't want to say anything about it, that's fine."

"Sounds like an easy deal to me."

"Okay," she said, "and I know this happened years ago, and it's probably even beside the point."

"Go on."

"Why did your mother shoot your father?"

"She didn't," he said, a little laugh hiccuping in his voice. He did not look at all disturbed by the question. She was right. The incident had happened long ago, some ten years back, and he had not been around when it happened and had not seen his father since then, he explained, adding that he had not seen him often before the shooting either.

"What do you mean she didn't shoot him?" she asked.

"I'm telling the truth. She didn't shoot him. She shot *at* him."

"And missed?"

"Apparently," he told her. "I wasn't there when it happened."

"Did she mean to miss?"

"I don't know. It could've been either way. She and I never talk about it—and never really did back then either. I just happened to hear about it when I was a kid and asked her about it—I was just a kid, I didn't have any idea at all what it meant to shoot someone, it seemed all like a game or a movie. We just never, for some reason, discussed it. So I don't have any idea why she did it—other than the fact," he said, grinning, "he must've done something to get on her wrong side," and the hugeness of his smile allowed her to laugh.

"You don't take after her, do you?" she playfully asked.

"Not yet," he said dryly. "But then you haven't done anything that's really wrong either."

"Not yet," she said, mimicking him, and her arms going around his waist and his across her back and over her shoulder, they kissed before going through the doorway and into the living room. Soon she would have to go and she laughed again when he said, "Who knows? The time to meet the public might come sooner than we think."

CHAPTER 24

When Ru-Marie came down for breakfast, her mother was sitting alone at the table. No place was set for her father. That was not unusual because he often had breakfast downtown. Still folded, the morning newspaper was on the table beside Ru-Marie's place.

"A little late this morning, aren't you?" her mother asked coldly.

"I do believe I am. But thanks for getting the paper."

"Any particular reason for the sleep-in this morning?" her mother asked, accusation in her voice.

"I stayed up later than I'd planned," she said. "Doing drawings."

"Any particular subject?"

"Yes, as a matter of fact. I'm trying to get the hang of marble heads, and they're giving me fits."

"Any other subject?"

"Look," she said sharply. "Something bothering you this morning?"

"I saw your light on last night—saw it shining under the door," her mother said stiffly.

"Of course, you did. I don't, after all, tend to draw in the dark."

"Any other subjects you were trying to get a likeness of?"

"Not really. I did, though, do some scratch drawings to loosen up."

"What were those about?"

"Heads."

"Whose head?"

"What do you mean *whose head*? Whoever's head came out on the paper."

"Anyone we might know?"

"Mother—good lord! What the hell are you getting at?"

"I don't like you to use profanity."

"So damnit! In the holy name of the great lower place I won't. What're you driving at?"

"I just want to know what you're concerned about."

"Nothing, except trying to make a piece of paper look like marble. Nothing! Till awhile ago. But I am now. I'm getting real concerned. You're sounding idiotic."

"We just want the best for you."

"You're not making any sense at all. What do you think my sketchbook is—some kind of sordid diary done in code?"

"I didn't say anything like that at all."

"Seems to me you came pretty close. Sounds to me like that's what you were driving at."

"Maybe so. I'm just wondering if I might've been right."

"Listen, Mother, I don't have any idea what you're getting at—or trying to get at—other than trying to make me skip breakfast."

"You mean so you can get away from the house faster?"

"Yes!" she said. "You just nailed me. I've joined a harem. I'm just not very good yet on the initiation rites, so I need to get to our meeting early. The big crew of us plan to elect officers before school starts. But we won't know till this afternoon if his high great lordship the sultan approves. If he doesn't, it's back to the drawing board. But that might not be so bad. If I lose the first time, I might pull out a win the second time through."

"Listen here, young lady, you don't give me sass like that."

"And you don't talk to me like a crazy woman either."

"Don't you say that again—*ever!*"

"I think," Ru-Marie said, starting to get up, "maybe I need to go back to my room."

"That's part," her mother said curtly, "that's part of what I had in mind."

"Mother—if something particular is driving you nuts, just tell me. I frankly don't understand a thing you're saying."

"It's about your room last night."

"Yes? What about it?"

"Were you really there? That's what I'm worried about. Where were you really?"

"I was there in my room. I was there all night. You could've opened the door."

"And what would I have seen?"

"What do you think? Me with a pencil and sketchbook in hand."

"On the bed?"

"Good heavens, no! I was in my chair. You know I don't draw in bed."

"You used to," Eileen said with a tone that suggested she was about to catch her prey.

"I know and I quit. I didn't like the stiff back I got."

"You weren't really in your room, were you?"

"As far as I know, I was—all night. Of course, it's possible I had a bad spell of sleepwalking, but you know, for the life of me, I don't have any idea in the world where I went. I just hope it was some place pleasing—some place mighty different from what this pit is becoming."

Eileen reached out her hand to stop her daughter's talk—or was it to slap her—but Ru-Marie pushed her mother's hand aside and told her the next time she had one of these exotic episodes, she prayed to God she'd remember the great time she had.

"That's disgusting."

"You know," Ru-Marie said, pushing back from the table, "I don't know whether it was or not. But maybe it was.

You probably know better than I do. I just don't remember. I do know, though," she said, rising, "I've been at this table long enough."

She picked up the newspaper.

"Where do you think you're going?" her mother asked.

"Upstairs to my room. I think, if I hurry, I might be able to get through the paper before I have to go." She looked down at her mother coolly, as if she were daring her to say another word. Her mother met her gaze but was trembling, gritting her teeth to keep herself under some semblance of control. Her gaze still focused coldly on her mother, Ru-Marie asked, "Would you like for me to leave the paper when I go? Or should I just drop it in the trash on my way to meet my sisters from the harem?"

Her mother refused to look away. Scowling, she took a deep breath, her chest quickly rising, and her voice now as cold and as well-controlled as her daughter's, she said, "I don't think I like what you've become. And your father doesn't like what you've become either. In fact, neither one of us—"

"So *what* have I become?"

"I'm not going to say it. I'm not going to say anything anymore. But it's going to stop. Believe you me, it's going to stop."

At first Ru-Marie did not respond. She could pop off all day, but already she knew that was getting her nowhere. What she still did not understand, or even begin to understand, was what her mother was accusing her of. She *had* stayed up late last night, and she *had* done a lot of sketches, though only a few seemed to have even come close to working out, but there was nothing unusual in that. She could copy most things well, but last night she had been working primarily on effects—getting her pencil marks to capture the look of the sculpted textures of marble in different sprays of light, and different glooms of shadow. But she had no intention of reviewing that.

What drove her attention was her mother's crazed notion that she had left the house last night, but to do that she would have had to walk down the stairway and her parents—apparently going mad now with suspicion—would have heard her, just as they would have heard her unlocking the door, any of the doors she might have opened. So, she realized, there had really only been two ways she could have left last night without their knowing. Somehow her mother knew it, too. She could have climbed down from the sunporch on the ladder, although to do that she would have had to have had someone bring the ladder to her from behind the garage, and the only person she knew who was generous enough of spirit to have done that for her had been working the night shift at the refinery—*one* of the refineries, she corrected herself, the city had several. So with that option gone, there had only been one way out: to leap off the sunporch, but that also presented a problem. She had no affection for the kind of pain her landing in the yard might have brought her.

Thinking about all those missed options, she began smiling, rather liking all the extravagant absurdities she had not thought of until just now when her mother had ushered her into consciousness. Thinking again how amusing those wonderfully extravagant absurdities were, she turned her attention back to her mother who had a look on her face the people in the area called *bulldog blank*. Its appearance was stolid, rather leathery, but at the same time the eyes did not seem to have registered either grief or anger.

Looking directly at her mother, Ru-Marie said softly, "*What's* going to stop?"

"You—you know what I'm talking about."

"No, Mother, I don't," though that was not quite the truth. "In fact, to tell you the truth, I don't think I've understood much of anything you've said since I came down."

Her look turning bitter, but also gripped by a need to try to disguise that fact, her mother—putting on a sham of calm—said she guessed she had gotten so upset that she had been in no condition to talk, to have a real conversation this morning, there were things Ru-Marie did not understand, and maybe even could not understand.

"And if that's the case," Eileen added, "I'm sorry. I didn't mean to accuse you of anything. In fact, I'm sure there's no reason for accusation of any kind." They both, of course, knew that was a lie. "There are some things that have gotten out of hand. It seems—for some reason—I'm not quite sure why—I'm not in the right frame to talk. Maybe later. Maybe later we can talk. I think we both need to. Let's just forget that need for now—the way we had planned. Why don't we just sit back down—sit back down—back down right now—and have breakfast. And you can read the paper while I fix you something."

After Ru-Marie said nothing in reply—she was deliberately letting the ragged silence hang—her mother asked her if she might like an egg—and possibly bacon with the egg.

"No," Ru-Marie said flatly. Then her tone turning arch, she said, "That's not the kind of thing I prefer."

"Then what would you like?"

Maintaining her icy sense of control, she said, "I suppose more than anything else right now—I suppose I would like to know—I'm curious to know—what the hell gives you the gall to ask a stupid question like that? How—after all the weird accusations you've made—could you even ask what I might want for breakfast?"

"It's just—I—"

"No," Ru-Marie said, holding out her hand to hush her mother. "Let's not say anything more—not this morning. I think it's time for me to leave."

"*Leave?* What do you mean *leave?*"

"What do you think I mean? I do have obligations, you know. Do you want the state of Texas to declare me truant?"

"All right," Eileen said, determination and her own kind of iciness back in her voice, "if you're going to be like that."

"Like what?"

"I don't know how you came by it, though I do have my suspicions. There's developed in you—somehow—something that's mean."

"I do believe," she said peremptorily, unwilling to let her guard down, "that kind of malady is inherited—and only rarely, I've heard, contracted."

For awhile the two looked at each other stonily. Neither one would give in to the other, and this time Ru-Marie would not even try to break the tension—or had she deliberately enhanced the tension?—with a caustic remark.

Finally Eileen said, "I think we've both said enough."

"At least for awhile," Ru-Marie added.

A scowl disfiguring her reddening face, Eileen seethed. "Sometimes you—the way you talk—and *act*—you make me want to hit you, just slap the fire out of you."

A faint smile coming to her lips, Ru-Marie left the room, careful, as she did so, to affect an air of calmness in her walk. She reached the stairs and began to go up them, well aware that her mother was also refusing to break the ragged silence.

CHAPTER 25

Late the next afternoon when she got home, she found that her father had gone to Austin on city business. So once more, till they parted after supper, she and her mother would be pitted together, just the two of them.

She was determined to be correct, at least outwardly. She would not bring up the difficulties of the morning, the idiotic harshness that, with them, developed over small things. She also warned herself about becoming too glib in her lyricism. She needed to keep her smart mouth buttoned. She upbraided herself as well for drifting toward pretentiousness, at least a guise of it, an icy façade she found easy to keep in place. In an odd way—it felt odd to her—her own attitude toward herself threatened to unbalance her, threatened to push her toward a far drift outside herself. She had been hard on herself before. She knew she was not trying to change anything deep within herself. She was not even trying to change her own surfaces, except in those moments when sham was in order. She also knew that her inclination toward self-criticism had gotten more intense during the last year. That especially showed in the way she viewed her own drawings and paintings. She was not becoming harsh in her manner, but she was feeling freer than she had been in her willingness to scrawl a large X over a drawing. Learning to do that seemed to help her. Learning to do that seemed even to be improving her technique; and she began to understand what was happening in this: she was learning that her own impulse toward loyalty needed to be toward an effectively finished object, not to any project just because it came from her own hand. Her own hand, in itself, meant nothing; she was learning that it meant nothing, and that was intensifying her sense of freedom.

Still, she was hesitant to throw the scratched-out sheets away. She did not tear them from her sketchbook. She discovered that she liked having the rejected sheets around, the ones she had intentionally ruined by defacing them. Sometimes, too, she got new ideas from browsing through those pages.

It was time to put her pencil and pad aside. She had only been holding the pencil over the sketch pad anyway. There were almost no marks on the paper, but that did not bother her. There was nothing disconcerting to her about accomplishing nothing. She was not, however, looking forward to dinner. Maybe during the time of preparation, she and her mother could at least feign an air of cordiality. Maybe even the busy-work of preparing the meal would enable them to be civil to each other. What she was not sure of, however, was the degree of closeness she wanted with her mother. The two of them seemed to be driven in different directions. Thinking that, she laughed at herself. She knew she was only stalling for time. All she was doing was postponing the confrontation, the war that seemed inevitable. She hoped the explosion would not occur tonight.

Her mother was already in the kitchen.

"It's going to be awhile," Eileen informed her, "before supper's ready." She had just removed some carrots from the vegetable bin and emptied them onto the drainboard.

"I know. No worry. So why don't I pare them? I'll prepare the broccoli, too."

"That'll be fine," Eileen allowed, stepping away. "And a bit later—that is," she said, stiffening, "if you're in no big hurry to go wherever you go—I'll reheat the chicken from last night."

"Sounds fine to me, I'm in no rush," Ru-Marie said, determined not to respond to her mother's comment about her habit—*I'm sure she considers it habit, certainly not smart choice*—of going out at night to unknown places. Her mother's attitude seemed especially odd. Ru-Marie did not go out at night a lot. So now it was clear—her mother wanted to provoke her. But why? And what did she want to provoke her to do? Or to say?

Ru-Marie rinsed her hands beneath the faucet—amused by the thought she might be washing away the stain of sin—then set about paring the carrots then slicing them thinly.

"You do plan to go out tonight, don't you?" Eileen asked.

"No, not really. I hadn't thought I would. Why?"

Standing by the large ice box, Eileen said, "You—usually you do. I imagined tonight would be pretty much the way they all are—the nights, you going out so much."

"No," she said, affecting a matter-of-fact air, "I hadn't thought I would." Her mother, she knew, really was trying to stir up a fight. But why? Nothing would be settled by their arguing, but there was another possibility. Perhaps her mother did not really want to fight at all. Perhaps the woman—Ru-Marie smiled and told herself she liked the sense of distance the phrase evoked: *the woman*. Yes, she thought, that did press her back, *the woman*, put a distance between them; the phrase itself did that. Or maybe something else was going on, the influence of some impulse the woman was not even fully aware of was pushing her. She did know part of what was agitating her mother—no mystery in that. But what else? If there were anything else, it had gotten tangled in her concerns about—and this amused her, too, but she was determined not to show it—Ru-Marie's sordid, out-of-control, mindless and reputation-wrecking, nasty and unspeakably naked and oozing stains from her unspeakably

163

stupid and demeaning love life. It was hard not to grin at this, but Ru-Marie knew she was disciplined enough to keep the big smile to herself.

"Why not?" her mother said.

"Why not what?"

"Why aren't you going out? You usually do."

"I'm just not—no big reason about it. I've been planning on working on some drawings."

"What are these going to be about?" Eileen asked, her lips pursing bitterly.

Still busy with the paring knife, Ru-Marie realized even more how easy it would be to get into another fight with her mother, how hard it was going to be to avoid being sucked into belligerence. Maybe her mother really did want to fight. She knew she didn't, and she was sure, too, the reason had nothing to do with fear of her mother or fright about the consequences of the battle. She simply had no faith in anything being accomplished by another damn blowup. She had heard, read, that it was good to let the poisons out—whatever those poisons were—and calm would come. But fighting had never—as far as she could tell—let anything out except destructive confession; it never seemed to resolve anything either—at least her own fights with her mother hadn't. Fighting had only upset her and tangled her up even more than she had been knotted up to begin with.

Maybe she was wrong. She wondered if perhaps she should take the easy way, give in to the conflict her mother obviously wanted to bring about. Maybe she—or the two of them, what difference would there be?—ought to respond with more than words. Maybe instead of just yelling at each other they should hit and slap and bite and club each other, maybe get out some butcher knives and bloody each other up a bit, too. Buster had told her that guys often became friends when they fought—except with knives or guns—*Those change things, not much chance for society there.* Buster also told her that he didn't know if guys *really* became friends when they fought because, he admitted, he hadn't seen many fights, at least big ones. Then dancing with his own lack of clarity, he told her, *They might not really become good friends—oh hell*, he had said, *I don't have any idea at all if they do or don't, whether fighting's good or not. It's probably not. It's probably just not bad unless someone really gets clobbered then has to get a bunch of new teeth or go shopping for a new face. Why?* Breaking into laughter, he had asked her, *Are you suggesting you and I ought to get it on? Pull out all the stops and go nuts and bludgeon each other?*

She knew that the memory was only a distraction from what she knew was increasingly likely and increasingly appalling.

"I said," Eileen said, "I asked what these new drawings are going to be about. Something wrong with your hearing? You're not going deaf, are you?"

"I'm sorry. I just got distracted."

"Seems to me that's happening a lot lately. I asked what these new drawings are going to be about. You're not going back to something like those disgusting portraits you did last summer, are you? The ones you did of those two perverted, too-smart-for-their-britches murderers, are you?"

"You mean Nathan Leopold and Richard Loeb?"

"Yeah, those two that killed one of their cousins—the ones that atheist labor troublemaker lawyer got off—saved them from the electric chair or whatever they use up there in Chicago. You're not going to start drawing people like that again, are you?"

Trying to calm her mother down, she said, "You really thought those sketches were disgusting?"

"No, not the sketches—the people you drew. Why in the world would anyone want to do a likeness of people like that?"

"I was curious what I'd see."

"What do you mean what you'd see? You'd already seen them. You had a bunch of newspaper pictures right there before you."

"I know, but a lot of times when I draw something I see something I've missed before."

"That just sounds crazy."

"Maybe so. Could you hand me the colander?"

"You're not trying to avoid telling me what these new drawings are about, are you?" she asked, as she bent down to open a lower cabinet door."

"No. I just need to get the broccoli ready."

"If you had ever paid any attention, you might've washed the broccoli first."

"Okay. I'll try that next time."

"Here," Eileen said, handing her the colander. "Now once again—what're these new drawings about?"

"I don't know."

"What do you mean you don't know?"

"I haven't done them yet."

"I know that. I didn't ask when you're going to start them. I asked what they were going to be about."

"And I simply don't know. They—the images—come to me as much as I go to them. I usually discover them with my pencil. It's a process of discovery."

"I don't believe it."

"That's fine with me. I'm not going to try to convince you. In fact, I don't see what connection there is with you in the first place. So why would I try to convince you?"

"You're trying to hide something, aren't you?"

"Not that I know of. It's just that sketching is different from copying. At least it is for me. And even when I'm copying, a fair amount of the time I don't know beforehand what it is I'm going to copy. I might even discover I'm curious to draw this colander."

"Why would you want to draw a colander?"

Laughing through her frustration, Ru-Marie told her mother she probably didn't want to draw it anymore. She had just been entertaining the possibility. "But the impulse is gone."

"Then why did you bring it up? Look, don't go trying to hide things from me."

"I'm not trying to hide anything."

"Sounds to me you are."

"Well, damnit, I'm not."

"Hush! I don't want you to use that kind of language. Is that the way that boy and his trashy mother talk? I imagine it is, considering their backgrounds. There's just no reason to let yourself be influenced by that kind of people."

"I know," Ru-Marie said, "but it's tough not to. They're so exotic—especially to European aristocracy like ourselves."

"Don't you dare make fun of your family."

"I'm not. I'm just in awe of our gloriousness—and grateful as hell to be lucky—"

"I told you! I don't like—"

"—enough to be a small part—"

"—that kind of common talk."

"—of classy folks like yourself."

Eileen looked furiously at her daughter.

Turning even more blasé in her manner, Ru-Marie asked if there was a sauce pan nearby she might use.

"What for?"

"To sauté the carrots. Let's try having them that way tonight—unless you'd like to try them raw. Might be crunchier than you want, though."

"Don't you get snide with me. How much time are you—"

"Don't say another word," Ru-Marie told her mother. "You've been trying to get in a fight with me ever since I came downstairs. All you've been doing—no!" she said, raising her arm and pushing her open palm toward her mother's face. "Don't say another thing—not till I finish. I mean it." Her mother started to speak but Ru-Marie hushed her again. "I've about had enough of your nasty, suspicious, stupid, holier-than-thou attitude. What do you think you're going to accomplish getting me into a fight? I've been doing everything I can to avoid a fight—because I didn't think another fight between us would do anything more than make us both miserable. So hush, damnit, just keep your own damn trashy mouth shut! I'm tired of all your carping! You hear me? I'm tired of it. And that's all I have to say, so if you want to talk, go ahead and talk, but if you're just going to keep running off at the mouth, I'm not going to listen."

"Oh yes, you are."

Keeping her voice low, Ru-Marie said, "I doubt it. I learned to go deaf to you a long time ago. I'm just sorry I didn't do it sooner. And I'll tell you one more thing."

"What's that?"

"You can have *all* the carrots—broccoli, too—and anything else you can find, because I'm not hungry—not after all you've said."

"*You* shut up! *You're* the one I've been worried about. *You're* the one I've been trying to keep from ruining your life. It's all been about *you*—not me! I don't care about me—I've just been trying to watch out for you."

"Then stop it—you're making a mess of both of us."

"That's not what I wanted," Eileen said, trying to calm down. "That's not what I wanted at all."

"Well, it's damn sure what you got."

"Then maybe," Eileen said, taking a deep breath, then taking another. She was winded and having a hard time breathing. She put her palm to her chest, as if to press more breath into her lungs. Her face was reddening. "Maybe," she gasped, then inhaled again and slowly let the breath out, "maybe we both went out of control. I'm sorry if I did. I didn't mean to. Maybe we both ought to hush—and try to start over."

"With what?"

Eileen reached over to touch her daughter's cheeks, but Ru-Marie recoiled from her.

"Don't," Eileen said. "Don't back away—please."

"I don't want to be touched—not now and not by you."

"Please."

"Please what?"

"Okay," Eileen said, dropping her arms to her side. "I'll leave you alone if that's what you want. And I'm sorry if I sounded as if I were accusing you of anything. I wasn't. That's not what I intended. I just wanted to know about your drawings. And believe me, I wasn't trying to pry. I just don't understand things the way you do—not about drawing and painting. Everyone knows you have a gift. Your father and I both know that. We just don't understand it—I certainly don't—especially when you start talking about things like drawings coming to you rather than you just doing them. I don't understand that. The world's not the same as it was when I was growing up. And especially you—you're different from me, different from what I used to be. I'm—please—just try to understand—I'm not trying to chase you away. So please—if I said anything to hurt you, I'm sorry. I didn't mean to. Believe me. I didn't mean to do that at all."

"Well, you did."

"And I'm sorry. I said I was sorry—and I meant it."

Ru-Marie did not believe her. Fast talk came easily to her mother. She could run off at the mouth—full of accusation or pleading for forgiveness or just chattering—but it was all just talk. Still, it was not the chatter she minded. She did not mind chatter at all. In fact—and she was not embarrassed by this either—chatter was often as good as serious talk, at least it was to her. But her mother was asking her now to trust her in ways Ru-Marie couldn't. Not anymore.

She could, of course—and she knew it—drift easily back into a guise of softness with her mother. They could both settle down for awhile and admit their faults. They had done that before. One could apologize and the other one would graciously accept the apology, but the peace would not last. The spirit of viciousness and suspicion would always come back, only now the return was worse than it had been. Maybe, Ru-Marie thought, she had been naive to think, when she came downstairs awhile ago, that there would at least be a sham of peace between them, but that had not worked out. Still, she did not want to get into another argument. The rising and falling of their two voices did not make any kind of music she wanted to hear. She also knew she was incapable of just walking away, going back to her room. Not knowing what to do—how to leave or how to stay—made her feel dumb, abysmally full of limits. She also knew she was incapable of going through the motions of both of them vowing again to calm down. The choices, she saw, were fewer and fewer. She had thought about slinging the sauce pan—and before that the full colander—against the wall or across the room, but that kind of tantrum was alien to her as well. Some notions were not even temptations.

Something had to be done. Something had to be said. She and her mother both were taking slow, deep breaths, each one obviously trying not to let the other one know the level of tension in her, then Ru-Marie gave up trying to disguise hers. They would look at each other, a mere glance, then one or both of them would turn away to some idle distraction, then they would face each other again, but only for a time, a short time, the silence between them awkward.

Finally Eileen said, "Okay—I'll break the ice." Ru-Marie let her go on. "I'm interested in you, in everything about you—whether I understand it or not. And I'll admit, too, that I didn't go down to the library all the time when I was growing up either. We didn't even have a library—except a pitiful, small one at school, but the books there didn't draw me to them the way they've done you. I don't know why. They just didn't. Maybe I learned things in other ways. Or maybe I didn't learn things at all. And if that's the case, I don't know why that's so either. And who knows? Maybe I don't even know how to learn things now."

Her mother's gestures toward obsequiousness bothered her. She was sure her mother meant what she was saying—in spirit and word both—but she did not trust her. She was not going to sink into the thrall of her mother's gestures toward softness, the treachery of passing humility. She had done that before. She was not going to do it again. She was not going to fall into what would likely be another trap, though she knew, too, whereas her mother did not—or was not, not now—thinking of luring anyone anywhere, and certainly not into a trap, any kind of trap.

"Can we," Eileen said haltingly, "can we—maybe—both apologize?"

Realizing that she did not understand a lot of the reactions and feelings and notions of options that were passing through her, Ru-Marie stiffened.

"What's wrong?" Eileen asked, but Ru-Marie recoiled again. "Please. Tell me. I've apologized. I did. What's wrong?"

"It's the drawing," Ru-Marie said, not knowing where the drift of her reply was heading.

"What is it? What's the problem?"

"I'm having some trouble."

"Trouble? What do you mean?" Eileen nervously asked. "What kind?"

"With my figure drawing. It's harder than you'd think."

"Oh I know," Eileen said. "I'm sure it is. I couldn't even draw a straight line."

"There aren't any straight lines in bodies," Ru-Marie said coolly.

"Yes, yes, you're right. But you'll find a way. We always do—all of us."

"I don't know," Ru-Marie said, discovering a spirit of iciness beginning to seize her. "I've been doing the drawings—and I'm having problems with them. It's harder than you'd think. It's just harder than hell—at least for me," she admitted, then sighing, she went on and said, "it's just hard to get a good model for a penis."

She heard her mother gasp. She saw her gasp, but she felt as if the sound and image both were taking place in a distant room.

CHAPTER 26

Her mother seemed now to be perpetually on edge. Every time Ru-Marie was with her, Eileen would go rigid. She would grind her teeth and make quick slapping motions with her right hand, as if she were trying to pat down something on her leg, on the table, on the arm of a chair, whatever was there before her—the slapping spasm fast and short. She would repeat it again and again; and when she looked at Ru-Marie, her eyes would flash a look of bitterness. Sometimes Ru-Marie was even surprised that the woman did not suddenly flail her arms and scream, but so far she hadn't; and her father would not be back from Austin for two more days. Maybe it's good he's not here, Ru-Marie thought, unable to think of him as a moderating force on her mother. He was as bitter as her mother was, at least in terms of any concern that included Buster, or even a ghostly remnant of him.

Her mother had also started bringing up again the incident of last fall when she had discovered Buster and her daughter on the bed on the sunporch. For awhile she had seemed ready to believe Ru-Marie's explanation that things were not what they seemed to be, that Buster was wearing a swimming suit, not, for heavensakes, underwear. Ru-Marie had been convincing in acting both shocked and indignant at her mother's accusations. She had even issued a warning to her mother. She had told the woman, "You'd better watch out. If you think I'm as low and cheap as you're making it sound like I am, you'd better not be surprised if my disgust at what you're suggesting turns out to be an inspiration to give you *real* reasons to think I'm even *worse* than you're suggesting I am. And frankly, lady, it's going to be a pleasure to embarrass the hell out of you. And don't forget this: you're stuck here, I'm not. So get off my back. I'm not letting anyone talk to me the way you are—nobody, neither you nor Dad nor anyone else. So hush! Just hush!"

Although she had meant everything she had said, she also knew that she had been bluffing; and for awhile her ploy had worked. Her mother had backed away. Her mother had even explained that in wanting only the best for her daughter she might have gotten carried away. And if she had, she told Ru-Marie—she had lost her breath again and was having to breathe deeply to keep dizziness away—she had not meant to be accusatory and disrespectful because that's not what she felt. "Please," she said, "please. If I've truly crossed over a line, I apologize. I do, I apologize."

Hearing her mother go on at the mouth, as she called it, Ru-Marie thought the woman was disgusting, but she softened her attitude when, for awhile, her mother started seeming benevolent. The woman quit prying, and it soon became clear that she had not said anything to her husband about finding Buster and Ru-Marie on the sunporch late one night months ago. Jeff had also been to Austin on business that time. The silence on the subject was not going to last. Ru-Marie was sure of that, but at this point she did not know what she should do to prepare for the aftermath of her mother releasing the old news. That, she had become convinced, was bound to happen. The only thing that had ever seemed to work was for her to stay as unguarded as possible, and she did have some options, ones that only included herself. Buster could not come to her at night on the upstairs sunporch. His working schedule prevented that. Even if he did find a way to skip work one night, the weather was too cold for anyone to go out on the upstairs porch for any length of time; and if Ru-Marie tried, her parents would find the stunt so crazed they would go into another fit and she would be even more under their watch than she had been. For now, there was nothing to do but endure the strain of the wretched limits she had to live with. Her drawing, however, was flourishing. Of course, if her mother ever found what Ru-Marie called her memory sketches, the woman would likely, she thought, have a hemorrhage and die. *Ah yes*, she mused, enjoying a respite from the tension in the room, *what a pleasure there is in the power of art. Who knows? Maybe I could pick off Mother and Dad both, and with just a few sketches.*

"There's something," she heard her mother say, "I've been meaning to ask you."

"Yes?" she answered distantly.

"About that night last fall."

The battle had begun, again.

"There were several nights last fall," Ru-Marie said.

"You know what I mean. The night I caught you and that guy together."

"I don't believe *caught*'s the right word, and you do know, don't you, he does have a name."

"I'm sure he does. I just prefer not to say it—or even hear it."

"Then I prefer not to have any conversation about it—about him or me or anyone or anything else."

"You can think what you want, but we're going to talk about it, young lady."

"Don't use that kind of talk with me. It's not impressive. All it does is make you sound old."

Holding back her rage, her mother was digging her thumbnails into the sides of her index fingers.

"I mean it," Eileen said. "We're having a talk, and we're having it right now, too."

"Go on," Ru-Marie told her coolly.

"I want to know how far things have gone with you and him."

"He's a very good friend—and as great a pleasure to be around as anyone I know."

"Are you telling me that's all?"

"What do you mean *that's all*? How much better could it get, his being a good friend and great to be around? That sounds pretty good to me. Is there something else you'd want?"

"Now look," Eileen said, pointing at her daughter, "don't go trying to slick me out of what I'm trying to get at. I want to know—and I want to know exactly—whatever the truth is—what's the nature of your relationship with him?"

"I thought you and Dad had already decided that. Just look at it my way. One of you threatens him with a tire tool and the other one won't quit bitching and babbling about him. So what's there to say? How can I improve on what you both obviously already know?"

"I'm serious," Eileen said, straightening her posture. "I'm as serious as can be. I want information, and I want *good* information—the truth—no skirting around after phantoms. In fact, let's just forget the past. Let's forget it altogether—whether I caught you two in the middle of something or whether—in some crazed way—you—both of you—were innocent, and believe you me, I'd like nothing better than to be able to believe that. But let's just try to forget that because all it does is torture me because I can't understand how you've become whatever it is you've become, and I don't even know what it is. Let's just forget all that—and even somehow start over. But please! Tell me. I want to know—I *need* to know—for my own sake as well as yours. What's going on with you and him?"

Apparently not much, she thought, *I'm in school all day and he's at the refinery all night*, but she didn't say that. She was not sure at all how to answer her mother's question. She did know there was likely no advantage in trying to find a sure line of attack or a clever line of defense either. She had no faith in certainty, not with her parents, not now, not with what her mother was demanding, and not with what her father had already done, what he had cruelly threatened to do.

"Did you hear me?" Eileen insisted. "You don't go silent on me. I want an answer. What's going on with you and him?"

"Okay," she said, apparently ready to give in, but that, too, was a sham she raised to separate herself from her mother. "Okay," she repeated, stalling for time, "but I think you ought to open up, too. It's simply unfair to put all the blame on me. You're the one who's really beating around the bush. You might not be silent, but you're certainly not saying what you mean."

"I think," Eileen said, bristling, "you'd better explain that. I'm being as direct as I can be. I asked you a question, and I asked it clearly, and I asked it politely, and I think it's time I got an answer."

"I'm not sure whether it is or not," Ru-Marie told her. "You're not asking if we go out together—even though it's clear you'd certainly never approve of that if that's what we did. You're not even asking if we're sweethearts—or whatever your term for the malady might be—though that one sounds a bit sappy to my taste. I wonder if you even know what it is you want to ask. And I'm really not sure if you really want an answer to what I assume you think you're thinking."

"You're the one, young lady, who's confused, and you're trying to make the rest of us confused with you."

"What do you mean *the rest of us*? There's no one else here."

"You know what I mean, and don't pretend you don't."

"What's really wrong? Are you just scared I'm going to waste the rest of my life on a poor boy and won't even give myself a chance with an oil well?"

"I've never said anything like that at all."

"You've sure thought it, though."

"So what if I have? I want you to have a good life—an even better one than you've had with us. And I think it's also time you started getting realistic. In fact, you don't have as much time as you think to make your decisions. Not much time at all. So you need to start settling down and get realistic."

"Realistic? I don't even know what you're talking about."

"I'm talking about catching you with a trashy young man."

"I thought we were going to try to forget that."

"How could I? How could any mother—and thank goodness you ought to be grateful I've never told your father about that night."

"Good God, Mother! You just fill me with a wealth of confidence. Have you ever thought what it might feel like for me to have you—my own mother—shoot a gun at a good friend who wasn't even close to doing anything he wasn't supposed to be doing?" *Like making love with his wife*, she thought. "Talk about truth! Do you call shooting at your kid's friend classy? I damn sure don't. You and Dad might think you've arrived somewhere special—the whole damn country's gone idiotic over athletes—or former athletes like Dad. If you want to be classy, you might start acting classy—tire tools and guns don't cut it. To tell you the truth, from what you're saying and from what you and Dad have already done, you *both* seem pretty goddamn trashy to me. Did you ever hear of the Prince of Wales taking a damn tire tool with him when he went to see someone he might not like? I doubt it. So quit putting on airs."

"I'm not!" Eileen shouted. "And neither is your father. We've earned—we've both earned what we've achieved. We've earned every bit of it."

"No, you haven't. You didn't earn anything. Dad just got a smile from the Capitalist, and who knows why? But without that nod you wouldn't belong to any country club and Dad wouldn't ever have come close to being mayor—or even thinking about the possibility. Hell! You two wouldn't have even become Presbyterians. What did you have to do to get that distinction? Kiss up to local royalty?—such as it is."

"I've told you before," Eileen said, taking a deep breath to steady herself, a number of deliberate breaths, "and I'm telling you again—you've become one of the nastiest ingrates I've ever run across. And for some strange reason, you even think you're smart. And all I can do about that is wonder, young lady, where in the world did you come up with such a ridiculous notion? Believe you me, everything about you lately sounds like stupidity. You don't even have enough sense to be ashamed."

"Ashamed of what?"

"You know what I'm talking about."

"I'm afraid I don't," Ru-Marie told her.

"Oh yes, you do. I'm talking about you and—it's Buster, that's his name, isn't it? It's Buster! There! I said it. Are you satisfied now?"

"What about him?"

"Just who in the world do you think you are?"

"You might look around," Ru-Marie told her. "You'll probably find a lot of things about this place you've never noticed."

"Like what?"

"Let's just don't go into that. Let's don't go into that at all. There's probably a lot around here you don't know anything about."

"So what makes you think you do?"

"Let's just not go there either. I've noticed you almost never read the paper—and I doubt that those women you go around with—let's call them what they are—*wives*—as if that's something wonderful. I doubt any of those women have any idea what the city they're living in is really like. It's not nearly the grand place you think it is. But you and your crew just never look around."

"I've told you before—and I'm warning you—don't try to slick me. There's something you're hiding. You're the one full of nasty accusations, not me. There's something you're hiding. You're sneaky. And I want to know what it is." Her voice rising, she said, "I want to know it *now*, too! You hear me?" she screamed. "I want to know it *now!*"

But Ru-Marie kept her voice soft. She was not going to be tricked into a shouting match. Yelling, like fighting, she thought, would solve nothing. At the same time she knew she would not be able now to slide away from the confrontation her mother was insisting on. Walking away would solve nothing. Her mother would follow her. If she retreated to her room, her mother would open the door. And when she was gone—to school, to anywhere—her mother—in the state she was in now—would likely invade her room, pore through all of her things, including her sketch books—especially her sketch books—and at some point she would undoubtedly find the *memory sketches* and be horrified—the faces immediately recognizable—and the war would then enter another phase. Nothing could stop it, no matter how ridiculous the central concerns of the conflict were.

"I said," Eileen repeated, "I want an answer *now*."

"I think," Ru-Marie said, her throat constricting but her gaze coldly locked on her mother's scowling face, "I think what you're trying to draw out of me is simply one thing—and only one thing. The only thing you really want to know is whether we're fucking."

Eileen glared at her as if she had been knocked into shock by a blow that had come so suddenly and powerfully that no pain had registered, only the quaking sensation of a jolt. Her lips trembling, her hands turned into fists at her side, she stared at her daughter. Neither one was making a gesture toward speech. Neither one even seemed inclined toward making a statement or asking a question.

The one lamp that was on in the room cast a delicate glow against the increasing darkness of the late afternoon. Evening was already here, twilight disappearing into a moonless, starless night, the overcast so thick all day. The only thing that Ru-Marie had now was a thought, a memory that seemed altogether beside the point: her suggestion, made months ago, that the world here would seem a lot brighter if people painted their houses white, inside and out. Her parents had said that was ridiculous, and maybe they had been right, Ru-Marie allowed herself to think. She knew, too, that she had no great commitment to the idea herself. All she had been doing was having what she had thought was easy conversation, but their opposition to the passing suggestion had turned them defensive, then caustic; and that seemed odd. Ru-Marie had allowed herself another thought, this one a question she did not give voice: *Are we going to stand here till one of us has to go to the bathroom? Or is that, too, too much of an intimate concern to be fit for conversation?*

Maybe an involuntary smirk changed the alignment of her lips, maybe even a tic in one of her eyelids or cheeks appeared, though she had not registered any sensation of such, but something—and perhaps it made no difference what the stimulus had been—broke her mother's silence. Ru-Marie heard the woman now saying, "I'd prefer to think I never heard you say what you just said. That low level of language has *never* been used in this house—*never*! I can't even imagine what would possess you to talk like that. To call your speech common would be to exaggerate its worth. What have you sunk to? I don't even want to imagine. I think, to tell you the truth, I've found even more than I even dared expect to discover. If that's the kind of language you're using now, I can't even imagine how low you must've sunk."

"Shut up, Mother. You're the one who's pretending."

"No, I'm not pretending at all. I'm just shocked."

"I don't believe that either. But in case you really are, would you prefer I use a more Latinate term?"

"I don't want to hear you use *any* kind of term. I've heard more than enough from you."

Her cool demeanor another protective sham, Ru-Marie said it probably made more sense to quit trying to talk since the day was getting late and the sounds of animalistic growlings in their guts were indicating it might be past time for them to begin preparing supper.

Her mother not responding, Ru-Marie asked, "Or would you rather ask if—being the lowbred animal I obviously am—if I've run off and gotten myself turned into an old married woman."

"Have you?" was all her mother asked.

"What do you think?" Ru-Marie asked with contempt.

"I certainly hope not."

"So there. We're both happy now."

"Good," her mother said. "At least that's a relief." She was breathing deliberately again. "And as far as that other goes, what I think you said, I think I prefer to think that you took a notion—for some misguided reason, some awful drop into what I can only call bad taste—you took a notion to shock me—to get back at me because you had gone so out of control. And if you thought you were being funny—making some kind of awful joke—I want you to know you weren't doing anything of the kind because it wasn't even close to funny—and I don't ever want to hear such awful talk again. The least you could do is apologize. That's the least you could do—the very least. Then maybe we can go on from there."

Hearing her mother now, Ru-Marie was the one surprised. She had never even considered, never even hoped, that her bluntness would defuse the explosive character of their talk, but apparently it had.

Careful not to sound condescending, she told her mother she was sorry she had upset her. Her mother said she accepted the apology. Feeling she had accidentally bought time, Ru-Marie had to admit that she had no idea how long this guise of calm would last. Surely there was little depth to it, but for a time at least the electrifying quality of the air about them was gone. For a time it was gone, though Ru-Marie still could not fathom how the horror of one word had shocked her mother away from what she had thought she wanted to know but some powerful part of her could not stand to hear. Ru-Marie also had no idea that two days later, when her father got back from his trip to Austin, her mother would tell him about the terrible conversation she and Ru-Marie had had, and she would also tell him about what she had come upon last fall on the sunporch one night; and he would not back down the way her mother had; and she had no idea how little time it would take for her mother to loudly drive her father on in his own drive toward murder.

CHAPTER 27

Her father, she would learn, arrived back in town by mid-afternoon, well before the time Ru-Marie got home. She had gone to Ima Jean's but had called her mother to tell her where she was. Half an hour later, Eileen called her back, obviously to check on her, though the excuse she used for the call was to ask when she might expect Ru-Marie home. Her father had gotten back from Austin, she told her, so she thought they would all three eat together. She needed to plan the time of the meal, she said.

Ru-Marie found the ruse aggravating, her mother so transparent. They almost always ate at the same time, and there was nothing unusual about the three of them having the evening meal together.

But playing along with the ruse, she told her mother she was flexible. She even asked when her mother would like for her to get home. "What time would be most convenient?" she asked, a knot crimping her gut. Although nothing had been said, she knew the easy calm that she and her mother had experienced for the last day and a half was over. No one had said anything unpleasant, and neither one had raised her voice; but the fact that her mother had called to check on her told her—though she did not know how or when it would arrive—trouble was coming. Sounding as polite and as matter-of-fact as her daughter just had, Eileen said that sometime around six would be good—"if that's convenient."

"Sure. I'll be home by then—maybe earlier," she added, as if a gesture of cooperativeness would keep things calm, at least awhile longer.

But that did not happen.

Darkness was settling in when she left Ima Jean's. The blustery cold wind of mid-afternoon had died down. The dampness in the air, however, made the chill cut deep. She was walking as fast as she could to try to warm herself, but little relief came. Then, as if surrendering to the misery, she slowed her pace to a more relaxed gait. She gripped the collar of her jacket to her throat, but nothing could stop the shivering that after awhile told her it was good no one was with her. She would not have been able to talk, her teeth were chattering so much. Her momentary sense of amusement at her own inability to speak disappeared. She found herself thinking that, though it would still be several hours before Buster had to catch the streetcar to go to work, she was glad she had not been with him when her mother had called. She did not want him implicated in the noise between her mother and herself, though she knew, of course, he really was the center of the trouble. She wanted to protect him, but she was not yet sure how to do that. She wished some kind of magical mist would surround him and make him invisible to her parents, but there was nothing even close to convincing about such a notion.

In every way, comfort seemed unattainable. She still tried to convince herself that the deep coldness in the air was what was making her miserable. It wasn't and she knew that. The notion was only a feeble diversion. She did not know what to do. The only hope she could conjure now was to wish for a loud explosion, a powerful eruption, maybe even by tomorrow, she feared, and she knew she was contradicting herself. But maybe an explosion would distract her from the bone-rattling shivers that a sense of desperation was bringing to her; and as she kept walking, finishing now another block, she began to think that she had not even been coherent with Ima Jean. They had actually said little to each other during the afternoon, Ima Jean willing, with no trouble at all, to let Ru-Marie idle away the time by drawing—scribbling, Ru-Marie described it to herself—while she went back over the lessons she had already mastered.

A little laugh quickly blossoming from her, Ima Jean had confessed to her friend that she ought not be bothered by her own distraction: "I can't ever spend too much time on Latin. Just keep drawing. And maybe tomorrow I'll be able to recite my lines for the day with a bit of quality. I thought what I did yesterday sounded clunky."

"Don't worry," Ru-Marie said, glancing up from her tablet. "I'm sure Vergil will forgive you."

"I'm sure he will, too," Ima Jean said. "The problem, though, is the fact that I doubt I will."

"You weren't so bad—just not especially shiny. What I was mostly thinking about was what we'd read on Monday."

"I knew that. I knew exactly what you were thinking. I couldn't help thinking it myself."

"You mean about Dido and Aeneas in the cave?"

"Of course," Ima Jean said. "I was thinking exactly what you were thinking—how the night in the cave was like our own—*your and Buster's*—trip to Grandfield."

"Yes," Ru-Marie said, brightening. "In fact, I almost broke out laughing, though I'd read the passage carefully the night before but didn't think anything of it other than I liked it. Then in class, everything suddenly came together and I didn't dare even glance at you, I was so scared I'd crack up laughing about Aeneas, after that fine night in the cave with Dido, going out the next morning and building that cairn then putting his dagger on it to celebrate the home-made marriage night, and knowing that what he was doing was something as goofy as Buster might do—and did do."

"What was that?"

"I'm going to keep that part private, at least for now. Maybe I'll tell you when we're old."

As she turned another corner—lamps in the houses lighted now—the wind seemed to be blowing harder than it had been. It was coming at her directly as she headed, chin tucked, northward, her home just a block and a half away now.

When she started up the stairs to the wood-plank front porch, her legs felt heavy. Dread weighing her down, she wished she were back at Ima Jean's, or even at Buster's, anywhere but here; and though part of her found the comfort both slight and absurd, she felt there was at least a gesture of protection in the fact that she and Buster were actually married. Undoing that fact would be difficult, and there was solace in that. Maybe her parents, too, would hope the scandal of the tie would go away somehow, and maybe their hope for that would lessen their anger as they all, finally settling down, began to accept what had happened.

She almost cried out when, through the window, she saw her father. He was sitting in his armchair. He was facing the front of the house, the chair even angled toward the front door. It had always been positioned that way—she knew that—but now the placement seemed threatening. He had no magazine, no book, no newspaper in his hand or lap to while away the time before supper was ready. He looked as if he were coldly ready for his daughter to come back into the house. There were things, she assumed, he was thinking, things that needed to be said; there were also things, she assumed, he was thinking that needed to be done.

Stepping up to the door, she hesitated before taking the cut-glass knob in her hand. There was some relief, she felt, in knowing that, placed where she was now, she could not see her father. She gripped her books more tightly to her chest and, as she opened the screen door, took the cold glass knob in hand, she warned herself to quit making assumptions about what was getting ready to happen. Her mother had given her a test by calling to check on her, and she had passed that test. She had passed it effortlessly. There was no reason for anyone to be suspicious or to feel hostile. No reason at all. Then, as she turned the knob and opened the door and came into the house, the thrill of a needlelike pain came to her face as she blew out a breath and gushed, "It's cold out there!" She closed the door quickly behind her. "It's as cold as can be," she added, looking directly now at her father.

His gaze fixed on her, he remained impassive, stonily impenetrable.

He told her to put her things up in her room then come back down.

Stopping, she looked directly at him. Surprising herself, she found herself thinking she had no intention of letting him bully her. He never had before and he was not going to start now. Immediately, instead of worrying about the belligerent tone in his voice, she found herself thinking that in the lampglow he was sitting in, his light blue eyes looked as if they had been bleached or maybe scorched by a thousand days in the sun.

Out of the corner of her eye, she saw her mother coming from the kitchen. She stopped in the doorway.

"Need any help?" Ru-Marie asked her.

"I told you," her father said. "Put your books and such in your room then come back down."

"You don't," Ru-Marie snapped, "think there's any possibility of trying to sound half-friendly, do you?"

"Don't," her mother warned her, "don't start in with your smart mouth."

"What's eating you? Both of you? I told you when I'd be home, and here I am on time. So what's going on? Do you two want a pre-supper fight for some reason? You might at least tell me what's going on."

"I think," her father said, rising, "you're the one who ought to tell us."

"I don't even know what you're talking about," Ru-Marie told him as she briskly walked away from him and started toward the stairway.

"Where do you think you're going?" he asked.

"To put my books and *such*, as you say, *up*—but, of course," she said, having turned all the way around now, "if you've changed your mind, I'll come back down. Which," she said slowly, "would you prefer?"

"Go on," he said, motioning her to go on up the stairs. "What I have to say can wait a bit longer."

As she started toward her room again, she heard her mother saying, "I think we all ought to wait. If we get started in on her, we might never have supper. Believe me, I know."

"Sure," he said, agreeing.

Ru-Marie thought she heard a tone of relief in his voice but considered it more likely that she was simply hearing what she wanted to hear. At this point, and she knew this clearly, she did not trust anyone, including herself.

During the evening meal, the family's mood never turned clearly harsh, but it never became friendly either. Careful to ask what her father had likely accomplished on his trip, she listened while he told her about several paving projects that he and the others testifying with him had been able to link with state highway programs.

"That should help," she said.

"I think it will," he agreed. "And what's been happening with you?"

"Not much beyond staying here most nights."

"What do you mean *most nights*?"

"Sorry," she said, "I mean evenings. Studying and drawing."

"What're you drawing now?"

"Nothing sustained. I'm basically trying out some ideas—techniques as much as ideas. I guess I'm also, as often as anything else, trying to find some ideas that seem worth pursuing."

"So you're not doing much copy work?"

"Not recently. I guess, more than anything, I'm trying out some new things."

"What kind of *new* things?"

"Let's just put it this way," she said. "There are a number of things I just haven't mastered."

"Okay," he said, sounding finished with the subject. "I suppose you know whatever it is you're doing."

"That's the trouble," she said, laughing, "I don't—not yet—I just trust I will in time."

"Well," Eileen said, entering the conversation, "I'm glad it's you and not me. I can't even draw a straight line."

"Neither could God," Ru-Marie said, and the table went silent.

Finally her father asked what she was aiming at.

"I'm not aiming at anything. Just look around outside. You almost never see a straight line."

"That's better," Eileen said. "I thought for a moment there you were trying to be blasphemous again."

"What do you mean *again*?" Jeff asked. "Something I missed while I was gone?"

"I'd like to know, too," Ru-Marie told her mother. "What did you have in mind?"

"Just forget it," Eileen said. "I don't think I really knew what I meant."

By the end of the meal Ru-Marie was ready to dismiss the tension at the table as a normal level of familial awkwardness, the ragged effects of people being so close to each other that they mindlessly bruised each other. Beginning to relax even—perhaps there would be no explosion, one did not appear to be developing—she envisioned going up to her room and reading till it was time for bed. She even considered bringing a book downstairs. That might help ease the tension even more. She thought the ploy would at least be worth a try, and whether it worked to her advantage or not, her spending the evening in the living room would at least prevent her parents from drifting back into another conversation about her bad judgment, about how wretched she was in not dismissing *him*. The strangest element in their obsession was the fact that, as far as they knew, or could know, she was almost never *with* him. He never came by to pick her up or drop her off from some event they had gone to. She did not talk to him on the phone when either one of her parents was around, so why did they keep insisting he was such an important part of her life?

She had no idea what was driving them. She would, though, spend the evening with them—unless they insisted on retiring to their own room. She doubted they were planning to leave the house.

Helping with the dishes, she heard her father say, "You're not going to answer me?"

"What do you mean?" she asked, turning around and wiping her hands dry on a dish towel.

"I asked you what your plans were for tonight."

"I'm sorry. I didn't hear you. I must've been daydreaming."

"You ought not do that," he said, and something told her not to laugh, "not if it's going to interfere with your manners."

"Okay," she said, careful not to challenge him tonight.

"So what are you going to do?"

"I had in mind getting a book and coming downstairs with it."

"What book is it?"

"I don't know. I haven't decided. I've got several going."

"Sounds to me you're just drifting," he told her. "I understand you've been doing a lot of that lately."

"What do you mean?" she asked.

"Idling away your time. Drawing with no apparent purpose at all. Not even hearing me when I ask a simple question. What else are you drifting around about? Sounds to me as if you need a better sense of focus. You drift around much more you're likely to end up in bad trouble."

"Look, Dad, I don't even know what you're talking about."

"I'm talking, damnit," he said, "about that boy. I'm talking about that night last fall."

"What night?"

"When your mother caught you in bed with that boy—out on the sunporch."

Bristling, she looked straight at him and said, "I wasn't in bed with him."

"That's not what your mother says."

"Good lord, Dad, all we were doing was visiting."

Narrowing his eyes in anger, he said, "I didn't know anything about that"—he was now coming toward her—"not till this afternoon when I got back. And what I want to know is," he said, stepping close to her, "what do you think you're trying to get away with? I don't think that night with him upstairs was an isolated event. And if you're going to be that brazen here at home, what do you expect me to think you're doing when there's no one around and you two are out no telling where? What do you expect me to think? I want to know how far this goddamn relationship has gone. I also know the kind of language you've been using. It's pretty clear to me that guy's ruined you."

She put the dish towel down on the drainboard then carefully, and slowly, laid another dish into the water with the table utensils she had not yet cleaned. She picked the dishtowel back up and laid it over the hook on the wall of the cabinet. She was biting her upper lip. Fidgeting, she was doing everything she could to keep from breaking into sobs. But tears began streaming down her cheeks. She tried wiping them dry with the back of her hand, but they kept sliding down her cheeks.

"You're hurting me, Dad," she heard herself say. "You're hurting me a lot."

But he would not give in or back down or soften his tone. As awful as she felt, she could see that clearly, though it jolted her, as much as if he had hit her, when she heard him say, "What I want to know is when the sonofabitch seduced you. And I want to know that, goddamnit, *now*, because the sonofabitch is not going to get away with it—no matter how far back it was."

The moment she opened her mouth to speak to him, she knew she did not dare continue. If she tried to speak now, she knew she would break down and cry. She felt she had already begun. Again she wiped tears away with the back of her hand. She was trembling, as if a terrible chill had blown in and engulfed her then entered her. Feeling off balance, she looked toward her mother, someone to help her, to give her back her balance, but what she saw was a woman who looked as bitterly stiff and cold-eyed as her husband was. They had undoubtedly been talking intensely since her father had come home. Ru-Marie felt helpless. She did not even know—she had no way of knowing—why they were attacking her. Nothing had happened to trigger their horror. Blinking, she glanced again at her mother, but no look of tenderness softened her face. No gesture of help. Then she turned to her father who was battering the silence again.

"I said," he told her, "I want to know," and with effort he was working to keep his speech measured, "*when* he seduced you."

This time she did not even try to wipe the tears away. Instead she looked him directly in the eye and surprising herself that she did not break down, that she somehow was able to speak, however briefly, she told him, "He didn't seduce me. No one has ever seduced me."

All he said back was "I don't believe you."

"I don't even know," she told him, "what seduction means."

"Sure you do," her father said contemptuously. "It's what he's done to you."

"You mean want to love me?"

There was suddenly a look of disgust on his face. "I don't want to hear you," he said, "use language like that again."

"You mean *love*?"

"I said *hush*!" he yelled at her. "Don't try to make a mockery."

"Of what?" she asked.

"When did it happen?"

"You don't understand," she said.

"Of course, he understands," she heard her mother say in a tone that suggested something foul had gotten into her mouth. "We *all* understand—*you're* the only one who doesn't understand. You've ruined yourself and you're trying to ruin us."

Her father held up his hand to stop her. Eileen's face flushed as she turned away from her husband and glared at her daughter. Ru-Marie was crying softly, weeping, but she would not let herself break down, not in front of these two, her parents, and though she was shaking as she fought to stay in control of herself—there was no one else to talk to—she would not let herself break down before these two people who seemed so alien to her. Then, in a moment, when she heard her father shouting at her, she flinched and closed her eyes.

"I said I want a damn answer, and I want that answer *now! Now!*"

Feeling battered, she looked at him, pleading for relief with her eyes but saying nothing. Her palms open, she reached out toward him, but he kept his hands to himself, as if there were nothing here, not even the ghost of a notion, for him to reach out and touch her or even want to touch her, the filth of her was so overwhelming.

"You—" she began.

"Don't even say it," she heard her mother telling her, but she was not going to back down, not now.

"You don't," Ru-Marie said, glancing at both of them. "You don't understand at all." She coughed. "Not at all," she told them fiercely, but still kept having to fight the fit of coughing. Then, after managing to hold herself in silent stillness, she was able to tell them, "We're married."

CHAPTER 28

Her face flushing, her mother screamed, pressing her palms across her mouth, the noises she was making: incoherent hitches of sound. At a loss for breath, she gasped, and at that same moment she threw her hands back across her face, against her throat, the spasms of movement crying out that she was trying to swallow, but she could not swallow. The sound that emerged then was at once a cough and a cry. Aghast at the horror of ruin, she gagged and began muttering, "You didn't, how could you—*why?*" she cried. "Why? Omigod! Now you're—why did you let him make you do that? You didn't have to, you didn't have to run away. Why did you let him force you to?"

For awhile no answer came. Ru-Marie was more concerned now about her father, an oddly unreachable man. Like her, he had so far mouthed no response. The look on his face seemed at first to her unreadable, as it often did, and though he did not change expression in any way that she could see, she suddenly understood that he was not really as impassive as he seemed to be. The man was furious. She knew that, yet, for however long a time, he had also been apparently paralyzed by what he had just heard.

The two of them, father and daughter, were facing each other. Neither one was going to give in to the other. It was not that they looked defiant, for no look of rage controlled their features, not yet. Their eyes were serpentinely cold; and later Ru-Marie would say that she would not have been surprised if her father had hit her, though he had never raised a hand against her before.

When he finally did speak, he told her that, though he already knew what she was going to say, she ought to answer her mother, which Ru-Marie did, though, for her own protection, she kept her eyes fixed on her father as she said, "Mother, he didn't, and he never has, tried to force me into anything."

"I just don't," her mother managed to say, "I don't understand. What ever possessed you? You've ruined yourself."

"No, I haven't," Ru-Marie said, "and the situation is not very complicated either," she added, still looking at her father. "We just want to be together. And now we can."

"No, you can't," her mother told her. "They don't allow girls like you—married girls—in school. You'll have to quit if the story gets out. You're ruined. That's all there is to it—you're ruined."

"Not in my eyes."

Then slowly, and his look still cold and controlled, her father shook his head and told her, "No. You're wrong there. You can't be together. Not now you can't. We'll arrange to have the marriage annulled."

"No," she told him, "that's not what I want."

"I'm sorry, young lady," her father said, summoning an illusion of frightening authority, "there's more involved in this than what you want."

"No, there's not," she insisted.

"You listen to your father," her mother told her, "and be glad that he's keeping himself in control. You don't even know how close I'm coming to wanting to hit you. How could it *not* have occurred to you what you've done—and not just to yourself, but to us as well?"

"That boy," her father said, "and I won't say his name, not in this house—he should never have quit school."

"Why not? He wanted to be able to support me. I am, after all, his wife."

"I doubt he'll be working much longer at the refinery," he told her.

"What're you going to do? Try to get him fired? Go ahead. I'm frankly not sure that you—or your damn position in town—is as important as you think that you—and *it*—are."

"Everything," her father said, doubling and unclenching his fists nervously, "will be easier, much easier," he said, "if we get this mistake annulled. That way that boy won't have to get hurt. And I have no doubt he'll see things my way. People like him always do."

That was such an odd thing, she thought, for him to say. Who was he trying to fool? Himself? He didn't even know the one he called *the boy*. Why was he trying to sound as if he had had a world of experience he had never had at all? Was he really simply desperate and flailing at fantasies?

Hard of demeanor herself, Ru-Marie kept her eyes on her father without saying anything to him. She had in fact, she realized with a curious yet untrustworthy sense of relief, nothing to say to him, and nothing to say to her mother either. There was nothing any of them had to say to each other, not anymore. There was also no reason for her to stay here with them, not anymore. She would stay here in the house for the night then decide tomorrow where to go. Her attention was not on her parents but on the narrow planks of varnished oak on the floor in the kitchen, a throw rug by the sink to catch any water that spilled on the floor. At one time, she mused, tolerating the absurdity of the notion, she might have suggested that they consider covering the floor of the kitchen with tile.

She knew that it made no difference what she preferred, at least in this dark place which soon, no matter what ended up happening, would no longer be her place. In several ways it had quit being her place sometime back. She could not, however, name the time when that had begun to happen.

Finally pulling herself away from herself, she looked up, and glancing at each of her parents in turn, she told them she thought it would be better if she went upstairs. She was afraid, she said, that if she stayed down here much longer, things would likely turn unpleasant, much more than they are, she added, and for the sake of all three of them she told them she preferred that not happen. But in spite of her gesture toward formality, they seemed to pay no attention to her, to what she had just said.

Her father cleared his throat then announced, "I'll talk"—he cleared it again then added, "to him, to the boy, tomorrow."

"I'd rather you didn't," she told him.

"Well, I am. There are things in this situation—and I think you ought to grow up and face what they are. But, believe me, there are lots of things more important than what you might think you want—lots of things."

"Oh indeed," her mother gushed, "indeed there are," and hearing that, Ru-Marie wondered which wealthy dame in town her mother was trying to sound like.

She tried to keep quiet but was helpless in her desire to sustain the protective ambiguity of silence. Turning her attention now to her mother, she said, "No, that's not true. There's only one thing that's important, and that's the fact that I'm married—happily married, I'll add—and ready to do anything—and I mean *any*thing, to stay that way. And if you can't accept that—for whatever reason you're trying to latch yourselves onto—then both of you can go—" but she stopped herself, then turning away from them walked briskly toward the stairs.

They called out after her, both of them did, and they cursed her when she did not turn back around to reply to them. Mustering all the strength she could summon, she was determined to look thoroughly self-contained and able in her sham of arrogance to pay them no mind.

The next afternoon Buster told her he would have given anything to come by and see her last night, and laughed as she reached over to squeeze his arm. They were sitting on the top step of the back porch at his mother's boarding house. She told him what a good thing it was that he hadn't come over.

"Why?" he asked.

She told him what had happened. Ru-Marie knowing they were fooling themselves, they both agreed there might be some relief coming from the fact that her parents now knew about the marriage. His own mother had known for awhile, he said, and there had never been any problem with the news.

Ru-Marie kept having the sensation that Buster was distracted. She asked him what the trouble was, and after a time of stumbling around in the confusion of his phrases, he told her that her father had called him here this morning, just after he had gotten home from work.

"Omigod," she said, "he actually did that. You didn't agree to see him, did you?"

"No, I put him off. I said I couldn't get loose today. I was trying to sound friendly and told him maybe later, some other day soon. Thank heavens," he wanly laughed, "I resisted an urge to ask, if he really didn't mind, would he leave his tire tool locked up in the trunk of his car?"

Ru-Marie slid her arm across his back and, with her fingertips, massaged him gently. She leaned over and kissed him on the cheek. Then he asked her what she thought was going to happen.

Her gaze drifting to the spare and strawlike grass in the backyard, she told him—her voice scarcely audible—that she had no idea, none at all. "Just don't," she said, "agree to see him. Please."

"I don't how long I'll be able to put him off."

"Keep trying," she told him, laying her palm on his

thigh. "Keep trying for a thousand years."

"You really think it's that bad?"

"Probably worse," she said. "Maybe more than anything, I think I'm surprised to learn how poorly I know them."

"But maybe they feel the same way," he asked, sounding desperate for hope.

"Maybe so," she said, glancing past the property line to the wheel ruts in the unpaved alley. "But I'm not a threat, not to them—and neither are you, love. This is one time—and the only time—I'm sorry there's no mean wilderness in you."

"At least I can run twice as fast as he can." When he flippantly added then that he and her father had never really raced, not formally, she broke into a great smile and kissed him. "But I know that I can," he told her. "I just hope some night on my way to work, the streetcar's not late. We might both get bothered, me out there with nothing but the light from the street lamp for company if he drove by and shot me." Narrowing his eyes to exaggerate his mockery of his own fear, he said that something like that would likely be worse than having to get an annulment. "He doesn't have a gun, does he?"

Closing her eyes, she said she didn't know. "But Mother does. She keeps it in her nightstand."

"Oh," Buster said, sounding as if he were dismissing the information, "a lot of women keep guns by the bed. Mother even has one. That's nothing to worry about. No telling how many women in town keep a gun." Then cocking his head toward her, he said, "You don't have one, do you?"

"No. You know I don't."

"Just being careful. Husbands," he said, "need to know what equipment their wives have. You can't be too careful."

Squeezing his thigh, she said, "I think you know pretty well what kind of equipment I have."

"Oh, I do," he said, "and everything about you makes me sing."

"Good. That makes me sing, too. And it's a shame," she added, tilting her head back behind her toward the house, "there are so many people inside."

"Don't worry," he told her. "We won't have to deal with them forever." Then he kissed her ear and told her that her hair tickled him, then looking toward the alley himself—twilight was settling—he told her she probably needed to start thinking about getting on home.

Noting that he had not pulled his pocket watch from his trousers, she asked him how he knew. He told her the cloud cover wasn't as thick as it looked, and he could see there ahead in the west where the sun's glare was "just partly off the horizon."

She asked him when he had learned to do that—read time by the sun—and he told her, "Years ago—a few years ago," then getting up off the steps, he held out his hand for her to take, and as they squeezed their hands together, he asked her if she were going by Ima Jean's on her way home.

"I don't think so," she said. "I think it's time I learned to live without her cover."

"Just don't get too far away," he told her. "She's too good a friend to make her have to miss you."

Throwing both of her arms around him and kissing him quickly, she said, "Don't you ever just think about yourself—instead of bothering first about others?"

As he wrapped his arms around her, he laughed and said, "Probably. Is that bad?"

"No, sweetheart, not at all."

"You know, there are some things—likely lots of things—that just don't ever occur to me—not the way they do to you. How could I harp on myself when you and Ima Jean—every time you're together—show you know so much more than I ever will?"

Shaking her head in amazed delight, she smiled directly at him. She thought she detected at least a hint of a blush on his face. Then squeezing him to her, the lengths of their bodies pressing together, as if the clothes separating them were nothing but illusion, nothing but a thin and pointless sham, she told him, as she pulled away and put her arm through his, "If you will, I want you to escort me through the house on my way out. I think that now that the news is known, this place is even more mine than it was."

CHAPTER 29

Leaving the house, she told Buster she would call him tomorrow and, beaming at her, he told her that she always did, and the sound of her voice really did make him want to sing. Yes, she told him, she felt the same way, and waving goodbye, she walked on toward the street. She was hoping that he had not registered the terrible worry that was waving through her. She was frightened, and though she had done this before, sometimes for simply sentimental reasons, she was going to take the longer route home so she could pass by the corner where each night he caught the streetcar that took him to the stop near the refinery. She liked to stand where he had stood and where he would stand again.

Almost all the day's light was gone, yet even that gave her a notion of comfort. She would be traveling through darkness soon, just as Buster did each night on his way to work. Before long she would be at 17th and Bluff, and though she considered it silly, the name of the intersection had a lilt to it because that's where he had been for so many nights, and where he would be again later tonight when likely she would be in bed.

When she got to what she had to call the fine place, the corner where her husband would wait for the streetcar, she lingered in the chilly light wind and was glad that this evening the wind was not gusting and the dampness in the air had dried enough so the needling air was not, the way it often did, going through her flesh and into her bones. She buttoned her collar around her throat. Several blocks back she had taken her gloves out of her coat's side pocket and put them on.

The walk tonight was diverting. For a time it even dissipated the fear that had waved through her, the fear she knew would return. The many uncertainties—in her and in Buster and in her parents—ensured it would. She discovered herself taking a deep breath then realized she had almost gasped, and a wave of fear returned just as intensely as it had awhile ago at the doorway of the boarding house. In some ways it shocked her to think that her father had actually called Buster to talk about annulling the marriage, but even she knew the source of her shock: the vain hope that her father would leave the matter alone. She knew, too, he would try again, that he would never abandon his drive to undo what she and her husband had done. The illusion of his own prominence guaranteed that, and so did the odd vulnerability of a cadre of her father's prominent supporters. It was as if, in every dimension of their lives, they conducted themselves within a system of elders.

Barely two generations back, this place had been a frontier, a postless, borderless expanse of wilderness. Neither forest nor desert, the place had characteristics of both. It was a world of rolling plains, and its weathers were rough. There were stories, too, that said long before the white settlers came, the Indians never set their camps here. There was a reason for that, and it, too, was curious: God, the old lore said, had abandoned this place. That had happened farther back than anyone could remember. The early settlers had not known that. Hearty and often wild-eyed themselves, they had tried to tame the area, and in some ways they had made good progress in that, but the changes coming to the place were so great that threats of incoherence, the dissembling pressures of chaos made it necessary, so many seemed to think, to keep present the comforts that images of order brought. And though a girl and a boy running off across the Red River a few miles to get married was no rare thing—it happened all the time and would continue to happen for years—it became a major concern, her parents thought, and maybe some others, too, if the girl were the mayor's daughter and the boy lived fatherless and in poverty in a boarding house that might well fail because the income was so meager and repairs so common and expensive that it seemed clear to those who reflected on it—and she knew her parents considered themselves as members of that tribe—that it was likely that soon everyone would see there had been no progress at all, that the girl—and socially her parents with her—had fallen back into the hopeless and useless mess of a slough pit; and that, as people like her parents said, would just not do. Legal or not, measures would have to be taken, and with several kinds of wilderness still present in these people—the tribe her parents had gotten attached to—violence was no alien matter. Aggravations like mesquite had to be cut, bulldozed, and burned so farmers could plow and then harrow their fields. That happened all the time, and even mesquites, like certain people as well, were ambiguous things. Even the scientists disagreed on whether mesquites were shrubbery or trees. What was certain was the fact that they needed to be cleared away. If they weren't, the land would go back to a useless and poor wild state; and that would not do.

Finding herself weeping at what was beginning to seem like a hopeless plight for Buster and her, Ru-Marie walked away from the meagerly lighted corner where her husband would later be. She could not stay here forever and dream, and she knew that and could even accept that it was time to go back into the darkness, to walk her way through the paths of this portion of the city's labyrinth of streets toward what, whether she liked the fact or not, was home. She passed by house after house whose windows made the lights inside them visible, and these places she passed seemed so calm, but she knew that, too, was in some cases—who knew how many?—an illusion. Still weeping—though at the same time feeling oddly distant from grief—she sniffed. It was not the cold air that was making her eyes water and her nose run. She knew she needed to get better control of herself. This was no time to break down, not with what was getting ready to happen, however it happened. She knew why she had started weeping. There was no mystery in that. There was simply the presence of the awful fact that she had no faith now—hope had fled—in the possibility of what her Latin teacher last fall had called the triumph of holy persuasion. The Romans had gotten the idea, the teacher said, from the Greeks; and when she had heard the teacher say that, she had been thinking about Buster and herself, the two of them already married; and, as if the concept of holy persuasion itself was a reason for hope, she had been thrilled by the new bit of knowledge she had gained, but at the same time she had been overwhelmed by it. There was so much to learn.

She did not know what would happen, not exactly, not even vaguely. The imagery of possibilities passing by her and through her all seemed undependable, so many of them ridiculous in their melodrama, that she even began to feel a wave of relief coming to her, but that frightened her, too, because there was no chance at all she could talk—*persuade*—her parents into leaving well enough alone. There might have been a chance if her father had not called Buster this morning. But he had, and unless Buster fell apart—and there was no reason to think he would—gestures toward discussion would solve little. It bothered her even more to think her father might forgo discussion altogether. There would be no chance for what her teacher had called holy persuasion to be triumphant; there might not even be a chance that anyone might try it. If only she could walk all night, she thought, and all the next day, too, and the night after that, with her only companion a breeze, maybe then whatever it was that was going to happen would never occur. That's such a sweet thought, she told herself, mocking herself. She was glad she had found a chance to berate herself, because now she was no longer weeping, she was angry, though she had to admit, too, there was something frightening in her quick shifts of mood. She had to find some way to be more contained. She wanted to be able to intimidate her parents and their world into distance, but she did not know how.

She was now at her own house, and though she did not expect anything pleasant from the evening, she was glad she would soon be out of the cold.

When she opened the door and walked in, she found both of her parents in the living room. They were not sitting together on the sofa, but in separate padded chairs. Sounding impatient, her father asked her if she had been at Ima Jean's all this time, and Ru-Marie said no. Then her mother asked if she had even been to Ima Jean's at all, and she told her mother no.

"You've been with *him*," her mother said curtly.

"Yes, I have."

"Where?" her mother asked.

"At his place," she said.

"After all we went through last night," her mother said indignantly, "do you think that's smart?"

Ru-Marie said she really did not understand what her mother was saying, or trying to say, and her mother puffed up in anger but did not try to rephrase her question.

"I had a talk with him," her father said. "I'll be having another—probably tomorrow. In just three weeks we can get all this taken care of." He stopped speaking—the silence vivid in its suddenness, but Ru-Marie did not reply. "Do you understand that?" her father asked gruffly.

"No," she said, "not really," and turned her gaze toward the floor.

"In just three weeks," her father said, "we can have all this over, and I think he's going to be—that boy—agreeable. Three weeks and it's done," he said, snapping his fingers to emphasize how quick and easy the process was. She could not tell, however, if he were trying to intimidate her or convince himself that he really knew what he was talking about.

Determined to breathe evenly, she stayed silent, then raising her gaze to meet her father's, she said, "You mean three weeks for the process to work its way through court?"

"Yes," her mother said, "that's exactly what he means."

But again Ru-Marie said nothing.

"You don't have any response?" her father asked.

"Not really," she said, a sense of distance in her voice. "I imagine most legal procedures have time-frames associated with them. I don't see any reason why annulments should be any different."

"That's not what he's asking," her mother told her.

"Asking?"

"It's *clear*," her father said, ignoring her biting question and sounding so self-assured that she wondered if he had even rehearsed his part, "it's *very* clear that an annulment will be the most painless way to get rid of this trouble—the best way for everyone."

"You don't have any reaction?" her mother asked impatiently.

"Why should I? You've both come upon a plan, and it doesn't seem to me as if I'm a part of it—other than a name on an odd piece of paper."

"What do you mean *odd*?" her mother asked, and Ru-Marie saw her father sneering, though she had no idea who or what the object of his contempt was. There were several possibilities, including a bleakness of mood whose source even he likely did not know, but that notion, too, she knew, was an idle gesture of self-protection on her part.

Bracing herself, Ru-Marie said, "Please. Let's stop this talk. If we keep on, we're just going to make each other more miserable than we already are. So why don't we forget the matter for awhile and have supper—though I'll confess I'm really not hungry. Maybe it would even be better if we all went our own ways tonight—or if I did. So please. Let's all just hush. I'm tired, very tired."

Both of her parents were glaring at her, but she was determined not to confront them. She knew she had made a mistake. She should have gone to Ima Jean's tonight and stayed there. Maybe she could even still do that. The two here with her, her antagonists she considered them, would fuss and accuse her of insulting them by lying about where she was really going when they knew for sure where she was going. Hearing all the loops in their rhetoric made her dizzy. She had to spend tonight at Ima Jean's, but not to have any long talk with her friend. There was nothing they needed to discuss. She simply needed a friendlier place than she had now to lay down her head and drift into the nothingness of sleep. Even if dreams interrupted unconsciousness, they would not be threatening. They would be distractions. After all, she had never been bothered by nightmares and had only had a few of them; but in spite of that she knew she would never be able to drift off here.

CHAPTER 30

Without identifying himself, Jeff Coleman told Buster on the phone that he needed to see him, needed to talk to him—family matter. "I'll pick you up in my car."

The moment he heard the voice, no question who it was, he backed away from the scratched mahogany-stained stand, placed in a narrow hallway just off the kitchen and near the stairway. No one was here with him; and Mr. Coleman, he hoped, was in some distant place.

"You still there?" Jeff Coleman asked impatiently.

"Yes, sir," Buster said, overcome by fright.

"I said I need to talk to you."

"I understand that."

"I'll pick you up right now—soon as I can drive over."

"I'm afraid," Buster said, "I can't. I need to go to work. I'm on a different shift now."

"What time're you due there?"

Buster's shift at the refinery had not changed. He knew, too, that he and Mr. Coleman would eventually need to talk—just not now. Nowhere near ready for the conversation, Buster was going to put off the meeting as long as he could. He knew, too, that no matter when they talked, no good would come from it. But whenever they met, it was not going to be in Jeff Coleman's car. Again and again he had imagined what the meeting would be like, and he could never conjure up an image of the two of them talking. No image or sound of discussion ever materialized within him, and he did not dare dwell on another time Mr. Coleman had gone someplace to see him, at the party that Ru-Marie had left early. Mr. Coleman had been carrying a tire tool behind his back. He might as well have held it out before him and presented it as the weapon it really was because there was no way to hide such a thing.

After awhile the image began seeming ludicrous, cartoonlike even, as if some unlikely creature had had a weapon thrust into his grip and was embarrassed and aggravated, too, by the presence of the thing in his hand, as if he could never find a comfortable grip for it. Buster knew that he was only trying to protect himself with such notions. He admitted, too, that he was the one who was ridiculous. What was even more disturbing was the fact that he did not really know Mr. Coleman. He had no way to predict the man's actions. He did not even have a way to predict—or even come close to understanding—the textures of the man's moods. Even Ru-Marie had said she had often thought her father seemed to wear a mask, but she had modified her own impression. She had told him that she had likely been wrong—the swirl she and Buster were in was dizzying her more and more. Her father was not likely hiding anything, she had told him, then added there was often no way, she felt, for her or maybe anyone else to register what was going on behind the blank, harshly vacant guise of her father's face. She had begun to notice, she had told him, that a number of men were like her father.

"I think it would be terrible," she had said, "to live with someone like that."

"But you do," Buster told her.

"That's not the way I meant it. I meant to be married to someone like that."

But that image, that fleeting distraction, had passed. Buster realized now that he was unable to drop the receiver. He felt as if his hand had spasmed around the thing that was now locked coldly in his hand. He could still hear the man asking him, more and more impatiently, when he could be free, and why couldn't he simply come by now and "drive you to work myself?" That would, Mr. Coleman added, "save you the price of streetcar fare."

The chatter kept on—that's what Buster wanted to think it was, just chatter, though he knew it was deadlier than that. The man's voice had a ruthless yet ghostlike quality to it, then Buster began rising from the fog where awhile ago he had gotten lost. The world was still blurry, but clarity—maybe that was also an illusion—was coming, and now he knew for certain that, whenever he and Coleman talked, the conversation could not occur in Coleman's car. Buster knew he would be impossibly vulnerable there. The Coleman car was a Franklin. There would be no way to jump from it if the situation turned threatening, and it would. Most other cars were open, but not the big Franklin.

Having drifted away again from the presence of the man he was supposedly talking to, Buster heard himself say, "I'm sorry, Mr. Coleman. I just can't meet you today." The sharpness of his own tone—he had overheard it more than willed it, he would later tell Ru-Marie, felt good. He was not at the beck and call of this man, so to clarify his position he added, "There's nothing I can do. I have my own obligations. The time's just not right for us to talk about whatever it is you think we need to talk about. The time's not right."

But Buster was thrown off-balance again when Mr. Coleman didn't sound as if he were affected by what Buster had just told him.

"Son, I said we need to talk. I doubt you want to be around me any more than I want to be around you. But there's an obligation we need to deal with. I'll come by and get you. We can take care of the trouble, maybe even to both our points of satisfaction."

"No, Mr. Coleman, I'm not going anywhere with you in your car. I have my own concerns and they're staying that way. I also need to hang up. There are others here in line to use the phone," he lied. "So you and me getting together today just ain't gonna happen."

"I believe I can accept that," Jeff Coleman told him. "You name the time, and you name the place."

"Let me think about it," Buster said, feeling he was now in control again. He liked the sensation. It softened the dread he had about the meeting he knew really did have to take place.

"Time's important," Coleman said, but Buster had no idea what that meant. He also had no impulse to continue the conversation.

"You name where we meet."

"I'll meet you downtown," Buster overheard himself saying.

"When?"

"I'm not sure yet, but soon," Buster said.

"Where?"

"I said downtown," Buster told him, knowing the sidewalks would be busy with people. That in itself would protect him, at least as long as he stayed in full view of the people milling and hustling around them.

"Where downtown?"

"In front of a bank," Buster said, as if his own vagueness would stall the fact of the meeting itself.

"Goddamn, son. We got three banks downtown. You think you're up to making a choice? Or do I have to do that, too?"

"The City National," Buster said. "There at the corner."

"When?"

"I'll let you know," Buster said hurriedly. "I'll pass the message through Ru-Marie."

"I'd rather get the message directly."

His Honor, Buster called him, as if the small gesture of mockery might relieve his fear, called the next day and said he had not gotten any message about their meeting. "How about today?"

"Because, damnit, I don't want to meet you today. I'll meet you tomorrow morning."

"When?"

"Ten o'clock—or maybe nine-thirty."

"Which one, son? I'm a busy man."

"I'm sure you are," Buster said, trying on a snappy air of confidence, "but I have obligations myself. I'll be downtown sometime between nine-thirty and ten. That's the best I can do, and if that's not good enough, then we probably don't need to talk at all."

Buster then heard the click of Coleman's phone being slapped back on its cradle.

When they met the next morning in front of the bank, neither one offered to shake the other's hand.

"Let's walk," Coleman said. "The matter at hand's not meant for the rest of the world. You do know, don't you, you've put me in an awkward situation."

Buster didn't answer, and after a moment Coleman said it was going to be necessary to get the marriage annulled. "Under the circumstances, there's just no kind of life you two could have. I can't even imagine what got into you two."

"It's pretty simple," Buster said. "We love each other."

"Oh for heavensakes," Coleman said, "idiots like you don't even know that silliness like that comes and goes. I used to play baseball with some guys who'd fall in love every time we had an out-of-town game. At least they were smart enough not to try to turn their damn rut into something idiotic like marriage."

"I don't see what you're saying has to do with Ru-Marie and me."

"Let me just put it this way: everybody'd be better off if this thing got annulled. I'd be more than glad, too, to pay the filing fee myself. We're also not but three blocks now from where we have to go."

"What you don't understand," Buster cried, his voice going high, "is that I don't think I want an annulment—or divorce or separation or anything even close to anything like that. Look, I'm doing what I can to make things right."

"Oh hell, son, you're not set to provide anything except trash to be around."

"I damn sure am! Look—I dropped out of school in December and went to work full-time at the refinery. I'm making good money and more's on the way when promotions come along. I'm getting things set so she and I can have a good life together—a good life, damnit, a good life."

At first Coleman said nothing in response. The silence began to bother the young man who started to say again what his plans were, how good his prospects were, that he was glad to work the nightshift, that he had always known how to work, that he had faith in his own abilities—he wasn't any slouch and the people at the refinery knew that, and Ru-Marie knew it, and he loved working hard—then suddenly feeling off-balance, he realized he wasn't keeping quiet, he wasn't just thinking these things, he was actually saying these things out loud, and the string of his chatter was undermining his gesture toward strength, toward control of this awful situation. He even had the sensation of Ru-Marie fading away from him, her face as expressionless, as threateningly blank as her father's, and that scared him. Any sense of domination he had felt with this man had been as illusory as it was brief.

"You need to understand," Coleman said icily as he grabbed his hat's brim to keep a wind gust from blowing it away, "there likely won't be any promotions. You might also be careful about counting on the job—any job—being permanent. I want you to consider these things. I'm telling them to you because of the great respect I have for my daughter, my family, the position we represent now in the community. You've put me in an awful damn awkward situation. Listen. There won't be any promotions—*ever*!"

"You're threatening me, aren't you?"

"No, young man. I'm not threatening you at all. I'm just telling you the facts of life. I'm letting you know that you haven't done anything yet to earn anybody's respect, and as a consequence of that there's no one around here who has any obligation to you. That's not a threat. It's just a series of facts. I'm telling you, there's not much I know for you to count on. And I'd be remiss if I didn't suggest you consider employers as being among the most undependable matters in your life. Damn undependable."

For a moment the two looked at each other with neither movement nor expression between them.

"Hello, Mayor," a man said, passing by.

"Fine day to you, too," Coleman said. Then turning his attention back to Buster, he told the young man he should not have dropped out of school, that the only hope he had was getting a diploma. "There are a lot of young men," Coleman said, "who'd be glad to have your job. And more are coming into town every day. I've told you already, but I'll tell you again: I'd be glad to pay the filing fee. The annulment is the best way for both of us. In fact, it's the only way. So let's be sensible. Let's go take care of it now. It's the only option there is, and I'd appreciate it greatly if you'd go with me."

"I don't know," Buster said. "Maybe I should. I just don't want to let go of, or *lose*," then he quickly turned away, his eyes glazing with tears.

"If you do love her," Coleman said, "you'll give her this chance, just as you'll be giving yourself a chance. The way things have moved, there's no other choice."

Swallowing then coughing through the downtake of air, Buster made an unintelligible sound, then nodding weakly, started walking faster, not to get away from his father-in-law, a term that made no sense to him, neither now nor before, their being such distance between them.

Coleman was striding beside him. The man had no trouble keeping pace with the boy. Neither one looked at the other. They were simply hurrying in the same direction, and the courthouse was in view.

Speaking softly but with no tone of compassion in his voice, Coleman said, "What we're doing—it's right. Right for you, right for us all—for anyone here who counts."

Buster did not reply. He would later tell Ru-Marie that he simply couldn't speak, he was trying as hard as he could not to collapse into sobs. He would tell her then it wasn't just the horror of losing her that upset him—he couldn't even imagine losing her, he felt so close to her—it was the raw fact that told him he had no way that he knew of yet to handle, to counter what her father was driving him to do. He did not even know, he admitted, if he truly thought her father had the power he was implying he had—the power that would get him fired, make him unemployable anywhere near here. Weeping in shame, he told Ru-Marie that he felt helpless because he didn't know really what he was up against. "So I ran," he said, "I turned around and ran, back to where we'd been, then turning at the corner onto Eighth and, hollering back, *No! No!* I ran as fast as I could up the steep hill and I kept running down streets and through alleys so no one could find me. I ran faster than I ever had before," he said as she put her arms around him and hugged him to her breast.

What he did not tell her that day was what he heard her father say when he broke away from him, the man's voice coming calmly through a fog: "That's it. You're dead." He did not hear the warning as a yell but as a statement delivered coolly, and that frightened him more than anything else.

CHAPTER 31

The house itself seemed frantic, though on the surface no one seemed in a rush. The air itself, however, seemed charged; but after a time Ru-Marie found an advantage in the chaotic mood. She had not understood much of what her parents were saying to each other, but at the same time she had not tried to listen to them. At this point she wanted nothing to do with them and was glad for their inattention to her. They were finally leaving her alone. She even began to sense that in some so far unknown way something had shifted so she could now go where she wanted—to her room or out of the house—without being badgered by the two who now seemed not only in conference with each other but in conference with the telephone, too. One of them would make a call, the muffled conversation short, then before long the phone would ring, and again one of them—there seemed to be no pattern here—would be back on the phone for another short conversation.

It was already past six and no one was saying or doing anything about supper. Ru-Marie was not famished herself, but she did want something, so almost in passing she said she would go ahead and fix herself something light—and if they wanted her to throw together something for them as well she would be glad to. She had added that last, in effect, as a test. Had they even been aware of her presence here? And they had, each one of them, in oddly casual gestures of politeness, waving off her offer, and thanking her for it, but they would be in later: no need for her to bother about them at all. All three were being polite. The drift of their flurries of conversation on the phone, however, did not seem pleasant. She had not registered anything especially tortured in their speech or in their features or their gestures, yet everything about the situation seemed swept up in an attitude of frenzy, the strangely non-familial façade a mask for something that later she would likely come to know. At the same time, even though the turns of their bodies and voices did not indicate they were hiding anything from her, she could not understand why she had not even heard any phrases that, rightly or not, suggested some specific point of concern. Maybe she—and she let this idea, as she had others, pass through her then vanish—was occupied by her own portion of the world much more actively than she thought. Yet, even if that had been true, she thought she would have felt some terrible struggle between choices or desires or movable points of awareness, but she didn't.

Instead, what registered most keenly—and she had just become aware of this—was a dinning in her ears: tiny, ceaseless waves of a slightly scratchy sound, too low in its register to be called ringing, too high in its register to be called drumming; but it seemed to be keeping her from hearing much of anything else. The tinnitus continuing, she found herself staring at a sepia-tinted print of a narrow Venetian canal flowing ripplelessly between two stone buildings. A gondola, apparently moored, though neither rope nor docking post was visible, floated unmanned in the twilight-darkened water. Ahead was an arching stone bridge that appeared to join the two buildings, but no people were visible in the scene.

She had seen the image countless times, but had never been especially interested in it till now. She had responded to it as a decorative cliché, a nod toward the foreign, she had said to herself, to *exotic up* a place whose people were likely going nowhere, or certainly nowhere far away. A time or two she had admitted that she was being harsh—perhaps even pretentious in her judgment—but she also knew there was nothing major at stake, and if one idea canceled out another, as one passing judgment invalidated another passing judgment, that was fine with her. At this point, at least to her, matters of judgment seemed curiously beside the point. The peopleless quality of the image before her—she was standing halfway up the stairway now—did not seem haunting or threatening or even a revelation of emptiness inclined to aggravate the viewer. Amused, too, that in her distraction she had forgotten to get anything to eat—she would do that later—she kept looking at the image and thinking that maybe some day she would go to that place, Buster likely with her of course.

Then a wave of coldness swept through her, and she found herself close to shivering, though the room itself had not seemed cold before. Besides, the breath of chill was gone now, but her chest felt tight. The image from Venice was still before her. Maybe it was the bridge that kept drawing her back to the scene, but why? What was the story? The façade of the building on one side of the canal looked essentially like the one on the other side—no shore here—and both foundations were covered by water, then quickly she understood what matter in the scene was affecting her so intensely: the brazen absence of tension that, while preventing the eruptions of laughter or grief or anger or horror or despair or victory or defeat or endless perplexity, included all of those. She had never seen the piece, this lithograph, in this way before, and it did not concern her that she might or might not see it this way again. What she was coming to understand, though—if only for a moment or two longer—was a body of water with neither beginning nor ending, and in it was a boat—this one a gondola, but that seemed idle enough, too. Everything here was still. Nothing was moving, no image of a current was present; and no one but she was present to mark its absence.

Turning away to go back to her room for awhile, she thought she would go out, ostensibly to see her friend Ima Jean, though that was not her plan at all. She began to think again about what awhile ago she had referred to as the brazen stillness of the print; and whether the maker of it had ever considered this or not—and likely the creature hadn't, she assumed—the piece she had found herself gazing at was perhaps much more threatening than it, for a long time till now, had seemed. An image of explosion would, in the aftermath, define who or what the antagonists had been. That's why the print was threatening. One had no idea who or what or if anything was behind the expressionless walls, or beneath the rippleless waters.

A few minutes later she came back downstairs and told her parents she was heading over to Ima Jean's. Still aflurry with phone and odd glances at each other, they waved her on in an almost friendly way, as if they had never been bothered by whom she might really be going to see. She had never seen them this way before.

When she got to where Buster lived—she knew he would be leaving for work before long and they would have no real chance for privacy while they were together this evening—she knocked on the door, as she always did, though Buster had said that was not necessary if the front door were unlocked.

Mrs. Lopreis let her in, giving her a big hug and kiss on the forehead, the way she always did when she saw her. Months ago, the woman had told her she had always loved children—had had four of her own, and all of them living here and there, as she put it, then added that she had always loved, too, her children's good friends. Her openness seemed so different to Ru-Marie from her own parents' closed-in attitude. Her own parents seemed to find it necessary for her friends—more likely her friends's parents—to pass some test in order for them to be worthy of their own or their daughter's attention, as if everyone needed to get the approval of what amounted to some sham of a council of elders.

"How've you been, sweetheart?" Mrs. Lopreis asked her; and feeling the uninhibited richness of the hug she was getting, there was nothing that Ru-Marie was able to say but:

"Fine, just fine."

"Well," Mrs. Lopreis said, "Buster will be thrilled to see you. This'll be a great surprise for him. He didn't think you'd get to come by. So run right along. You know where he is, and I'll be taking care of the kitchen." Ru-Marie knew that the woman was telling her not to worry at all about being disturbed.

As she was getting ready to tap on his door, the door swung open, Buster excitedly saying he had just now heard her voice. She threw her arms around him there in the doorway. Still embracing, they moved on into his room. With her heel she pushed the door back against its jamb.

They kissed then pulled back to look at each other and embraced again, Buster finally getting enough control back to ask how things were at home.

"That's the oddest thing. They were half-huddled together there in the living room and seemed scarcely aware that I'd come in, and it stayed that way, even when I left to come here. They didn't even grill me—just waved me on almost. I don't know what to make of it. They've never been this way."

His look turned serious.

"What's wrong?" she asked, pulling back.

He kept shaking his head. "That doesn't make sense," he told her.

"Oh, I know that," she said, "but, lord, I was glad for a

bit of relief."

"Something's wrong," he said.

"What do you mean?"

"I saw your father this morning—downtown."

"Oh no," she said, covering her mouth.

"He called me again and offered to pick me up, but I made up some excuse that I'd have to meet him downtown, near the City National Bank. I wasn't going to get in a car with him. I wasn't going to get anywhere with him that was closed in."

"What happened?"

"More of the same—annulment talk. He's not going to give up on that. I know it. He'll never give up."

"He didn't threaten you, did he?"

Buster was having trouble getting his breath back.

"He didn't, did he?" she asked again.

Finally he was able to tell her, "I don't know. I really don't."

"What do you mean?"

"I don't think this has ever happened to me before."

"What?"

"Thinking I heard someone say something then at the same time thinking I hadn't heard them at all—I'd just heard some odd part of myself saying what it was that I'd heard though I knew I hadn't said anything out loud. That's all I knew, and all I know now."

"I don't understand," she said. "What was it?".

"That I'm dead—some voice saying *you're dead*."

Crying out, she threw her arms desperately around him. "No no no," she said, "he didn't say that, he couldn't have, it's just the fear. He didn't say that at all."

He squeezed her now as hard as she was squeezing him, then letting her go and backing away half an arm's length, he said, his voice shaking, "I don't know what to do, but I haven't told Mother, and I'm not. I don't want to drag her into this—she'd just worry. Who knows?" he went on. "Maybe nothing's going to happen."

"It won't," she told him. "I know that. We're going to be just fine."

"You will," he said. "No question about that."

"Listen, sweetheart," she told him, taking his hands in hers, "if he calls again, just don't agree to see him. *Please.* Just don't agree to see him—no matter where. And you don't need any excuse either. Just say you can't and leave it at that. There's no way to reason with him in the first place—or Mother either. And you know that—so don't try. You don't owe him or them a thing, and if they can't like you or accept you, that's tough—for them it's tough. Just let them miss out on what they could have had."

Moving his hands out of hers, he put his arms around her and pulled her to him. "I love you," he told her.

"Oh, sweet one," she said, "I love you—so much. And everything's going to be okay. I know it will."

"I hope so," he said.

"Just remember," she told him, forcing herself to look ready to tease him. "Most people are pigs—and probably more often than we'd like." She was finding it hard to sound light-hearted. "So remember: there are two good reasons we should never try to teach a pig to sing. And I'm talking about my parents."

"How you mean?"

"It's a waste of our time," she said, "and it irritates the pig."

Looking at her, he finally began smiling, then told her, "I'll remember."

"You'd better. You don't owe either one of them a thing. And if some time in the next year or two I turn up pregnant, they'll go nuts—and I'll love it. We're going to be okay," and she kissed him and told him again, "We're going to be okay. Besides," she added, "this is Valentine's Day."

"Omigod," he said, "I forgot that."

"No problem," she told him. "I'll let you make up for it next year."

Before long they both agreed it was time for her to go to Ima Jean's. Her parents would likely check on her there. She'd call her friend so in case her parents called before she got there, Ima Jean could cover for her.

Ima Jean told her that her parents had not called. Everything, she saw now, was going to be fine. Her cover was in place, and there were numerous reasons she could not come to the phone if they called, and some of those reasons involved the body in such a way that if Ima Jean were clever—and it was likely it was impossible for Ima Jean to be anything other than clever, especially if Ru-Marie's father called—she would hint at something, like a problem with the time of the month, and if that happened, Ru-Marie knew that her father would try to get away from the phone as fast as he could, and Ima Jean, feigning innocence, would likely play with him awhile longer, to make him more nervous than he already was, to keep him on the phone for a wonderfully miserable time longer. It amused her, too, to realize that things would not be much different with her mother. Some things, after all, it didn't do to talk about outside the home, or even there if you didn't have to.

Thinking all these things and loving the delight of Buster, she did not mind the chilly walk at all. She was wrapped up as well as she needed to be, and the knitted scarf looped around her throat was soft and warm. The night seemed ripe for pleasure, a perfect time for snuggling in bed. She smiled as she thought how easily Buster made her laugh and sing inside.

CHAPTER 32

The streetcar was due to arrive at Buster's stop, 17th and Bluff, at ten-fifteen. Jeff Coleman knew that and the other city schedules as well. He and his wife, however, were not going to wait there. The streetcar stop was likely going to be their last stop tonight, and they might not even have to go there. They were looking for their daughter. For everyone's sake, they would later say, they were hoping she would be on the street and by herself, and they could simply pick her up and all go home. In court that prompted some laughter. Their finding her mattered more, they would say, than where she had been or what she might have been doing.

Earlier in the evening they had stopped at Eileen's sister's house. When asked why, Jeff testified that they needed to pick up a gun—"in case there was trouble." That also prompted snickers. Then he said, as if defending himself against troublesome opinions in the audience, that he had been concerned about the safety of his wife and daughter. If he had to, he said, he wanted to be able to protect them, and that required preparation. He added that he thought that's what anyone would do—or like to do: be present in the time of his family's need.

The pistol they had picked up from Eileen's sister was a .45, the same model as the one Eileen kept in her nightstand. The District Attorney asked Jeff why he needed two guns. Jeff said he wasn't sure the other one was in good working order. It, he said, had not been fired in a long, long time—maybe never, though maybe once or so.

"So to be safe," the prosecutor said, "you got another one just like the one you didn't trust. Is that right?"

"Yes, sir."

"Was the gun you got—the one you said you borrowed—was it in good working order?"

"I think it was. It seems to have been."

"You mean it worked when you fired it?"

"Yes, sir. It did."

But none of this discussion had happened yet. They were not yet in a courtroom. They were enclosed in their automobile, the big Franklin that Buster had refused to get into. He had been afraid he would get trapped in there. But the Colemans were not concerned about a complaint like that. They were glad their car was able to keep out the cold night air. They had a lot of driving to do. They had already passed by the places where Ima Jean and Buster lived. They had driven the various routes, and across the routes, their daughter might be taking on her way home, or from one friend's place to the other. Neither one of them wanted to say the young man's name or even to identify in any way a degree of kinship with him. They referred to him—if they had to refer to him at all—as *the young man*. What he had done to their daughter showed he was no mere boy. They did not like to talk about him, and within several weeks they would both affirm that. Refusing to use his name, they insisted, was no crime—no crime at all. Developing the theme, Eileen explained on the stand that in some odd way the term *son-in-law* sounded worse than *our daughter's husband*—which he wasn't, "He wasn't really," she explained. "They had been planning to have the marriage annulled." Consequently, she said, she and her husband wanted nothing to do with him or his mother or anyone else of their kind—*ever*.

The city, though its grid of streets was simple enough in most areas, seemed like a labyrinth that night. There were so many places their daughter might be. They even drove down alleys, but failed to find her—no matter how intricate and careful and deliberate their search was. They got angrier and angrier, so much so that, though there was little conversation going on between them, it became impossible to distinguish the frustration they felt at not finding their daughter from the anger at what she had let herself get involved with.

Now and then on the long drive they would glance at each other, but in those glances was a blankness of look that registered little: no look of assurance, no look that projected a cry for help, no look of affection, no look of accusation, no look that showed anything definite other than a set of the jaws in both that appeared so rigid it countered both the inclination and the ability to speak. Ru-Marie had seen that look numerous times. She had even wondered—several times as she was blithely passing into or out of daydreaming—if that look of rigidity they seemed to find so easy to slip into might be the reason they got so wrought up when they asked her what her drawings were going to focus on and she would—maddeningly from their apparent points of view—tell them calmly that she had no idea at all, that whatever they were going to focus on she was going to have to discover. She just did not know the answer, she told them; and when she said that kind of thing they might even huff away from her or swell up red in the face and try to turn their attention to something else, but usually they could not even distract themselves with that, not for awhile, not until their frustration with their daughter's odd notions passed beyond their attention spans. "They were often blessedly short," Ru-Marie, years later, would say with a smile as she remembered moments that, she said, were not really severe from her own perspective and nowhere as devastating as what would come to happen that night her parents drove for more than two hours, and only one of them would be able—or allowed—to drive back home.

The only conversation they were having now involved sudden questions and pointless observations about what they were passing by and about how bad their luck seemed to be.

"Do you think we ought to just go back and wait?"

Both of them would say things like that, but each time the other would snap back, "No! We've already waited and you can see what happened. We should have stopped all this a long time ago!"

During these outbursts, raw as they sometimes were, neither one directly accused the other of being lax or naive. They didn't praise themselves either. As sizable as it was, their car seemed to be closing in on them, as if in time it would crush them. Jeff kept pulling at his collar, as if he were trying to free himself from something that was determined to choke him, and Eileen was also pulling at her clothes, as if they, too, had begun to wrap around her tightly, even threateningly. They both testified about that, both of them saying that might have been part of the reason that what happened actually occurred. Each time they spoke that way, the young District Attorney would look disgusted, as if both of them—he didn't care what their position in town was—were sorry violations of everything decent and just and responsible.

"Omigod!" Eileen cried out.

"What?" Jeff asked, sounding alarmed.

"This is where he'll be! He'll be here soon."

"That's right," Jeff said, sounding distant. "The streetcar stop," which was where they now were, and the time was after ten.

"Get away!" she said. "Drive away! He might see us! I can't stand being around that filth."

Shifting, Jeff started to speed away, but Eileen cried out, "Stop! Stop!" and he did. "Look!" she said, gazing into the darkness behind the streetlight glow at the intersection. "There's someone coming."

"*Him?*"

"I can't tell. Just don't drive away."

Jeff was trying to read the shadowlike figure himself. Then he reached down to the floorboard, moved his fingers around till he found the gun and pulled it up into his lap. His wife opened her big purse and reached inside it as she continued staring into the dimness.

"I don't think it is," Jeff said. "He's too tall."

"You can't tell," Eileen told him. "He's the only one around. We can't tell—not yet."

The features of the man were now becoming discernible. He was walking toward them but not angling his gait in a direct line to their car. He had turned his head toward them, as if to try to see why these people had stopped their car here.

"It's not him," Eileen said, sounding relieved.

"I know," Jeff told her. "I just wish it was," he said, giving a slight wave to the man to tell him there was no problem here, then muttering to him, though there was no way the man could have heard, "I thought you were someone else."

"He's early," Eileen said.

"Who?" Jeff asked.

"That man—coming to the stop."

"Yeah," Jeff agreed, as he shifted to drive away. "I just wish he'd been someone else."

Then a shout crying "Wait!" came from the darkness. Jeff braked to a stop.

"Who's that?" Eileen asked.

"I don't know," Jeff said, straining back to see who had called out. Had the cry been for them?

As he backed up, Eileen told him, "Be careful. Can you see who it is?"

"Not yet," Jeff said. He had now backed up to the intersection, parking just outside the curb. "There are two of them," he told her.

"Be careful. Just be careful," she warned him.

Almost immediately, as the two moved across the street toward the lamp post, it became clear that the figures were a young man and a woman. The woman, they soon saw, was considerably older than the young man who was running toward their car.

"Mr. Coleman!" he called out. "Mrs. Coleman! It's Buster!" his voice full of guileless energy, and now he was at the front passenger's side of the car. Eileen was rolling down the window. "I saw your car," Buster said. "I had to say hi."

In a slow growl, Jeff asked, "Where's our daughter?"

"Oh, I haven't seen her for a long time, sir. She's likely at Ima Jean's—maybe even at home by now. She probably is."

"She wasn't when we left."

"I don't know when that was, but she should be there. I imagine she is."

Only one side of this conversation was friendly, and the brightness on that side was fading. The openness of the young man now sounded as if it were being replaced by fear, as if the inclination toward friendliness had been revealed as nothing more than an unfortunate impulse he should have held back.

Nervously Buster said he didn't know where Ru-Marie was—that all he knew was that he had been surprised—and glad, too—to see their car here at the streetcar stop when it was time for him to be here, and he had assumed, he told them, that there might have been something they wanted to tell him. He was certainly open to talking to them. "This is my mother with me," he said quickly, but she was standing back, and his chatter stopped.

He glanced down, away from Jeff Coleman's hat-shadowed face. He glanced at Mrs. Coleman, as if for support, but her gaze was straight ahead and had been for awhile, and for good reason, too, she would later make clear: she had nothing to say to this young man who was much more treacherous than a lot of people knew. But she knew. She knew very well the unspeakable thing he had done to her daughter, had gotten her daughter to do, how he had manipulated her—*and worse*, she would add, the look on her face an unwelcome admission that somehow filth had settled on her tongue. This was what she would testify to, but not in her husband's trial—in her own.

"I saw you," Buster said weakly, pulling back a bit from the side of the car. He sounded certain now—there was no question left—he had misread the situation and made a terrible mistake, though he still could not hush. He was determined to turn the situation friendly; and whether they liked it this time or not, the three of them were connected in the most important way possible. He was married to their daughter, "and I thought since I saw you in the car here you wanted us all to talk—just to say hi if nothing else. Just to say hi."

His mother looked horrified and helpless. Her hands kept fluttering to cover her face. The other person at the streetcar stop, everyone but Buster would learn, worked at a refinery, too, but not at the one where Buster worked. The man was a nightwatchman; and as such, according to the laws of the city and the county, he was, because of his position, a deputy sheriff and policeman, too. He was watching all this warily.

Bolstering himself with what had just passed through him, Buster told Jeff and Eileen, as chipperly as possible, though his voice was shaky, that he had thought—because they had driven here—that they had wanted to see him and just by chance his mother was here with him and he wanted to introduce her to them. They would certainly want to know her, and he was sorry that Ru-Marie wasn't here, too, with all the rest of them, but that was okay, he told them, that was no problem, because he only had a few moments longer before he had to catch the streetcar to go to work and they wouldn't have had a chance to visit anyway, not tonight. Sounding lost, he said he thought that was why they had come here—to tell him something, or maybe just to visit.

They said nothing. Then Jeff opened his car door. He walked around in front of the car, the engine still running, the headlights still on. Seeing him outside now, Buster looked as if he were trying to smile, the nightwatchman at the intersection later said. Mr. Coleman was coming around the front of the car, Buster's right hand was out now, as if he were ready to shake hands with the man who, after all, was his father-in-law. Jeff stopped then took another step toward him. The brim of his fedora obscured the look in his eyes, then quickly stepping back, Buster gasped and retreated still another step.

"No!" he said, his thin voice high, "no, sir, *please!*" Then, as if all his energy had disappeared, he said, "You're going to shoot me." The statement itself sounded as if it had come from a ghost that had drifted away from wonder. A cry then broke from the young man. "No, Mr. Coleman," he said, "*no!*" but the older man, Ru-Marie's father, still saying nothing, pushed the pistol forward, the barrel a long, thick needle against the boy's belly. Then a fiery explosion shattered the night.

Screaming, the boy's mother ran toward her son who was now on his back, the blast of the .45 having knocked him, like a block of cement, backwards. His mother kept screaming, "Don't go, don't go, love," she wailed, "don't go."

Looking upward, but at nothing in particular, Buster said simply, even quietly, distantly and weakly, and with a voice that sounded touched by surprise, "You just killed me."

"No no no!" his mother cried, and scrambling down to her son in the scraggly strawlike grass, what little of it there was on the clay, she brought her son's head onto her lap and frantically stroked his forehead, as if that might push the unspeakable away, then she began trying to comb his hair back with her fingers and smoothing it down with her palms because, she would later volunteer in the trial, it had gotten mussed in all the confusion. During her frenzy another source of noise delivered the racket of heartless chaos. Jeff Coleman was standing motionless at the boy's feet, the barrel of his big pistol angled downward now, pointed at the young man, and Eileen was screaming. She was yelling at her husband to get back in the car, but not to try to escape. She was yelling that the kid might not really be dead. She said, in fact, that he might be pretending. She was stretched out the window as far as she could and yelling that she still couldn't get a good look at him. "You might've missed!" she shouted. "It's so dark I can't see—he's pretending! Get back in the car! You have to back up—shine your lights at him! Get in! Now!" and he did. He put the car in reverse, backed up quickly a-ways, then a bit farther back, then forward now at an angle that let the big headlights spill their light across the motionless boy.

Something liquid purled from the young man's lips. Jeff burst from the car, the engine still running, the headlights still shining, the pistol still in his hand. As if shoving against something no one else could see, he stepped in front of the car then across the curb so he was close to the boy, Eileen again yelling, "Is he dead? Is he dead? We have to kill him!" and two more shots followed, or possibly three.

"I think," the nightwatchman would testify, "it was three. It might've been two, but I think it was three."

When the final shots were fired, everyone there flinched at the loud, stunning crashes the explosions made, and Buster, or his remains, quaked, too. His mother was screaming, wailing uncontrollably and rocking back and forth over her son, his head in her lap. She had scrambled to get his head back in her lap after those last shots, and screaming even louder than she had before, she looked up and, her eyes wild with grief, she screamed at Jeff Coleman. At the top of her voice—louder than her voice had ever come close to going—she screamed at him, "Goddamn you! Goddamn you to hell! He was just a *boy!*" Sobbing and shivering, and unable to even try to stop sobbing—so little strength in her voice—she began muttering, phrases coming from her that sounded like *damn you damn you damn you he was just a boy*, and as she cried, her hands going over her son's face and blood-soaked body, she was saying, "He needs some cover, some warmth," she moaned, and the nightwatchman stepped forward.

But Eileen started yelling again. She was yelling that her husband had to get back in the car, they had to get away, they had done what they had to do, they had done what they had come here to do, and amid the cry of orders she was giving her husband, the nightwatchman told her, "Shut up, lady. Neither one of you is going anywhere."

The nightwatchman then turned to Jeff Coleman and said, "I'll have to take your gun," and looking adrift, Jeff handed it to him. Eileen started barking again for her husband to "Hurry! Get back in the car!" but before she had said much more, the nightwatchman told her, "Damn you, lady, I said *hush*! Goddamnit, hush!" and she did.

Identifying himself, the nightwatchman told Jeff Coleman, "My name is Frank Bracken. I'm a nightwatchman at the Red River Refinery. That means I have deputy's rights, and you're under arrest."

"I understand," Jeff said.

"I don't have any handcuffs, but I don't think we need them."

"You don't. I'll go where we need to."

Then squinting, Frank Bracken said, "I know now who you are. You're the mayor, aren't you?"

"Yes, sir," Jeff said. "I am."

By now several people, having heard the shots, had come out of their homes, some in nightclothes and robes. Frank Bracken told the small gathering crowd that everything was under control. He asked if one of them would go back inside and call the police. "Tell them we need an ambulance, too—though I'm not sure," he added, "we do." Then he told Jeff Coleman, "You'll have to be taken in."

"I understand," Jeff said. "What about my wife?"

"I'm not sure about that."

"What do you mean?" Jeff asked.

"Mrs. Coleman?" Frank Bracken said, but when she did not answer, he said again louder, "Mrs. Coleman? I have another question."

Jeff told her to go on and tell the man what he wanted to know."

"Yes, sir?" she asked.

"Do you have a gun, too?"

"What do you mean?" she asked.

"I asked if you have a gun."

"Why?"

"Because," the deputy said, "I'm not sure all those last shots came from one gun. I'll have to ask the policeman to search the car when he gets here."

Her voice cold and firm, she asked the man if he were telling her she was under arrest, too. "No," he said, "but there needs to be a search."

"Well, I don't know why," she said, refusing to back down.

"Listen, lady, I don't want to argue with you, but there are, frankly, a lot of things a lot of us don't understand, and you might not be the least of them either. There's only one thing I care about now. A boy's been shot, and I'm not the only one who saw it. So if you don't mind, I hope you'll put a lid on your mouth till the policemen come."

"Do I have to stay here?" she asked.

"Yes, ma'm, you do."

The streetcar came but the nightwatchman told the driver to go on: "I'll get another ride."

Shortly after that, an ambulance and a police car drove up. After a quick examination of Buster's body, the two medics laid a blanket over him, then the two policemen came up, pulled the blanket back, looked at the corpse, down past the groin where the blood stopped then put the blanket back over him. As they did that, one of the medics helped the boy's mother to her feet. She asked if she could ride with them. Saying that, she started sobbing again, but this time she tried to stop herself, but she couldn't. She did, though, finally manage to get out that when they took her boy to the hospital, she didn't want him to have to be alone, not after what all had happened to him. Choking, she said, "He can't be alone. Don't make him. Please, not after what he's been through."

"Sure," one of the medics told her, "we'll let you ride with us."

By now the deputy had explained to the two policemen what he had seen happen and what he had done: taking the gun away and putting the man under arrest. He mentioned, too, the advisability of searching the woman in the car. "She might have a gun, too."

Nodding, one of the policemen then turned to Jeff Coleman and said, "I'm sorry, Mr. Mayor, but we'll have to take you in."

"I understand. You don't have to use handcuffs, do you?"

"No, sir—not in light of who you are—and your willingness to go with us. And when we get down to the station, if you need to, you can use the telephone."

"I appreciate that."

Before long Jeff Coleman was at the police station. He was booked, charged with murder, and the District Attorney set bail at $20,000. The mayor was then given a phone to use. He called his friend the Capitalist; and though the hour was late, long before the night was over he was out on bail. Although one of the policemen had found a .45 in Eileen's purse, he let her drive herself back home. She told him she kept the pistol for protection. She said her husband, "as you must know, is often gone away on business." He said he'd let her keep the pistol, and she told him she appreciated that. He said, "We might be talking with you later—routine obligations—but I don't think any charges are going to be filed now." She thanked him again and said he was truly a comfort.

The Capitalist and two of his friends, including his brother-in-law who was the Colemans' neighbor, picked Jeff up and drove him home. None of the men asked him how he was doing. The Capitalist said they'd be getting some business in motion in the morning. They dropped him off in front of his house. He thanked them for the ride, and the Capitalist nodded, saying, "There's no reason for us to go inside with you."

With his wife now, he found that their daughter was not here. Sounding aggravated, Eileen told him she had no idea where the girl was. "She wasn't here when I got home. I don't know where she is."

CHAPTER 33

The information Ima Jean had just given her on the phone shocked her. Buster had been shot at the streetcar stop. Without saying anything at all to her friend, Ru-Marie laid the phone back in its cradle, grabbed her coat and ran from the house, almost losing her balance on the front porch steps, but she caught herself and was running again, going back to the same intersection, 17th and Bluff, where she had lingered earlier tonight.

She had not even told Ima Jean goodbye. She hadn't said anything to her, and she had no idea how Ima Jean had found out what had happened. Later she would learn that Ima Jean's father had called her. He had heard the news at the hospital. He'd been walking past the emergency room when he heard the report.

Running block after block, she kept stumbling but kept catching herself, too, as she asked herself, *How did Ima Jean know? How?*

To get to the intersection faster, she began cutting through yards. Still running, she began to feel odd. The night air seemed strangely calm. No wind was about. There was nothing in the air to mark the urgency of what she had just been told had happened.

Near the intersection now, she saw a police car driving off, and her parents' car was following it. There must have been some mistake. She stopped to watch the two cars, then her parents' car made a turn, and she knew she had been wrong. The back car was not following the front car. The back car turned into a different street from the one the front car was following. She did not know what that meant.

The only vehicle still around was the ambulance, but that was pulling away, too. She cried out for it to stop, but the ambulance drove on, picking up speed. As she watched it, her legs threatened to collapse beneath her. A block away now, the ambulance didn't seem to be going fast at all; and no siren screamed at the night.

As if they were oddly independent of her, her arms began flailing, and her mouth flew wide open, but no cry broke from it, only the rhythmic whispering of her breath. She was panting. Then addressing herself to no one, she asked, "What happened? They aren't in a rush. Why not?"

Two people, coming to her, put their hands on her shoulders and back. Thinking they were trying to restrain her, she jerked away, to free herself from the viselike grip the man and the woman had tried to clamp on her, though all she really did was shiver. She had not even jerked against them. She had only thought she had.

Her voice soft and lost, she asked, "What happened? Was that my husband? Why weren't they in a hurry? That's my husband who's with them. He's hurt, I heard. My father must've hurt him."

"You're the Coleman daughter, aren't you?" the man said.

"Yes," she answered, her glance floating toward the little crowd gathered beneath the streetlight. "That's my husband they're taking away. Someone shot him," she said, crumpling, but the two people grabbed her as her knees barely touched the ground. With little inflection in her voice, she kept giving these people information. "Someone told me someone shot him. My father shot him. Someone told me that. That's what he did. My father shot him. I think he thought he had to. My friend is the one who told me, but she didn't tell me that. He didn't kill him, did he? Maybe that's why they're not going fast. The wound must not've been bad."

"Oh, you dear," the woman said, hugging her, the embrace feeling like a massive wave of protection going around her, and again the woman said, "You sweet, sweet dear," as she stroked Ru-Marie's head, her hair, as if Ru-Marie were her child, a little girl who needed to be soothed asleep.

"Who are you?" Ru-Marie asked, but all the woman said was:

"Don't worry, don't you worry at all. We're all of us here to take care of you," and hearing that, Ru-Marie settled again against the woman's bosom, the woman keeping her arms fast around her.

After awhile she did not try to move, or even turn her head when she said this, when she asked, her little voice high, "Sir? Sir?" and the man who had, just awhile before, come to her and touched her shoulder and back to brace her, to keep her from falling, told her:

"I'm here. I'm still here. We both are."

"Sir?" she asked. "Sir? Is he hurt? How bad?" But when the man did not answer her, she said, "He's not in much pain, is he?"

"No, ma'm," the nightwatchman said, "not likely much pain at all."

"Was anyone with him?"

"Yes, ma'm," he told her. "The boy's mother. And I was here, too. He wasn't alone at all."

"Did she go with him? Did she go with those people who aren't even hurrying?"

"Yes, ma'm. She went with them. They let her go with them."

"Thank you," Ru-Marie told him as she pulled away from the cradling arms of the woman. Still in a daze she said to them both, as if they needed to know this bit of information that was all she had to offer them: "He shouldn't have to die. He shouldn't have had to die. He didn't do anything to make him need to die. He loved me. Have you ever loved anyone? I have. I loved him."

Then she started walking away, the man and woman both reaching out to stop her, but neither one of them touched her. Instead they seemed to be holding their arms out, not to restrain her, but to offer her support if she turned and came back.

For a moment she gazed at the crowd, at least her eyes were pointing in their direction, then she turned back around and faced the two who had come to help her. Heaving to pull in a breath, she touched her upper chest and drew in another breath then mumbled, "I think I feel faint," and again they rushed to her, but she tried to gesture them away. "It's okay," she said, "I've been dizzy before. There—over there—a lot of people here. Why? Did they come for my husband? Or just for the noise?"

Then taking deep breaths to steady herself, she said she needed to go. She said there was somewhere especially she needed to go. Both the man and the woman said they would be glad—even honored, one added, the man—to accompany her wherever it was she needed to go, but Ru-Marie told him, told them both, that was not necessary. The place where she needed to go was not far away. "It's a good place," she told them. "I wish I could say I've been there a thousand times before, but I haven't. A thousand means forever, you know. But I haven't been there close to that number. But you don't need to worry," she said, walking toward the crowd, not to meet them, but simply because they were in the path she needed to take. "Don't worry," she said, and without looking back, she told them, "I know the way."

Sunday was a blur, as it had been since Ru-Marie had walked to Buster's mother's boarding house on Saturday night. Boarders there had taken care of her as best they could. One of the women staying there suggested that Ru-Marie take her room, that she would arrange to stay with one of the other boarders, but shaking her head at her, Ru-Marie began sobbing, and another boarder, hearing them, rushed to the linen closet and changed the sheets on Buster's bed. She also removed Buster's clothing that was hanging on a hook on the wall beside the chifforobe. Then she went to Ru-Marie and, with the other boarder helping her, said she had gotten her room ready, then added that "all of us here—for longer than you've known—we've thought of the room as yours—for a long time it's been yours."

"You mean Buster's room?" she asked.

"Yes, honey," the woman said, hugging Ru-Marie to her, "and now it's your room."

"Did you know we were married?"

"Oh yes. We've known that a long time."

"I'm staying here tonight," Ru-Marie told her. "I'm staying here for more than tonight."

"We know. This is your place. All of us know that. Just think of us all as your sisters and aunts. And you've got a couple uncles, too," the woman said, laughing.

"Thank you," she said, as they led her into the room. Crying out, she broke away from them and, sobbing, threw herself on the bed, her arms and legs wildly awry, as if she were trying, with everything she had—limbs and voice—to find, to touch somehow a remnant of Buster. The surges in her mind and body could not accept that he was no longer here. Suddenly curling up into herself, she began shivering—she was sobbing again, then her moans became intermittent and weak and her gasps for breath slight. Shortly afterwards—it seemed just a few moments though she might have been dreaming and it was much longer—she had no idea how much time had passed—she heard voices in the house. Someone had come in, then Ru-Marie heard one of the women telling someone, "She's here. We fixed the bed for her, she's here," and Ru-Marie then, though not at first, began to understand that they were talking about her, and the woman they were talking to was Annie Lopreis. Coming further out of the blur, she heard a cry as the door to the room opened. She twisted onto her back and rose up, and another cry pealed, and she and the woman, Buster's mother, were in each other's arms on the bed.

"He's not here," Annie said.

"I know that," Ru-Marie told her. "This is my place now," and Annie hugged her even more tightly then told her:

"Yes. This is your place for as long as you want."

The phone was ringing again, and each time it did one of the boarders answered it. Often they said, "She's not available now. ... Yes, that's true, but I'm sure you understand." Then another time the one who answered quit being friendly, began sounding wary, coldly distant even, but also sounding as if she were keeping her anger in check, she said, "That will not be possible. She's already told me: she's taking no calls. ... That's true. ... Yes, but we'd prefer you not to call her here. She'll call you tomorrow—that is, if she chooses to. I'm sure, sometime, she'll get back in touch. ... No, I've told you before—and please, if you have any decency at all, don't call again. She'll return your call if she wants. ... No, you'll just have to wait."

Hearing a portion of what had just been said, she wondered if that was one of her parents, most likely her mother, and feeling Annie shifting, she realized her mother-in-law was struggling to get up. As if it might help her, she stretched herself out of her inward-turned curl, and the two women rose.

Standing, though unsteadily, Annie reached across the bed and cupped her palm against the back of Ru-Marie's head. "Don't get up," she said. "This is your place, love. I need to go now to my room. I'll see you in the morning."

Ru-Marie reached back with her left hand and squeezed the woman's wrist, but she did not turn around. She kept sitting on the edge of the bed and looking straight ahead. She was looking at the window, at its mullioned panes, but because it was dark there was nothing out there in the yard, the back yard, that she could see, but that was okay. There was nothing out there she needed to see. Then after awhile she realized the phone was not ringing anymore. Yes, she found herself telling herself, it's time for us all to be back in bed—long past time, she muttered, surprised at how sleepy she felt. Long past time, she muttered again, time for the thousand tongues to hush.

Then somehow Monday came. The flood of people coming to the boarding house on Sunday had kept both Ru-Marie and Annie in their rooms. One of the boarders even made a sign to put on the front screen door saying the two women appreciate *your love and concern* but were unable to receive visitors. Before long the boarders agreed to leave the front door open because so many had assumed they were among the exceptions to the note. These included friends of both. The boarders had taken turns staying near the front of the house so they could personally instruct the concerned that Annie—or Ru-Marie—had had to retire. That at least kept the racket of doorknocking and bellringing down.

The funeral was to be Monday afternoon, at 2:30 p.m. at the First Methodist Church downtown. But even that morning hundreds came by the J.T. Rhodes & Son funeral parlor, so many that the body and casket had to be removed to the boardinghouse till it was time for the funeral. The funeral parlor had had to do that. There were other funerals and visitations the company had to take care of, so many that if they did not remove the Lopreis remains from the premises the other families and friends would not be able to get into the funeral parlor. School was also let out at the high school and junior college for those students who wanted to go to the memorial service; and many did.

Hundreds came. Every pew was packed, every available folding chair at the church was occupied, and well before the service began there was not even standing room available. The church doors, front and side both, were propped open so the crowd packed in the narthex and on the two landings and steps outside might have a chance to hear at least part of the service. They would certainly be able to hear the hymns and sing along with the congregation that they had come to be a part of.

Ru-Marie and Annie sat together, and with them was one of Annie's sons, as well as one of the male boarders, and others Ru-Marie did not know. Annie was unable to walk without help; but weak as she was, Ru-Marie was able to get around on her own. Remnants of rage were keeping her upright. The vicious absurdity of what her father—both parents—had done made her sick to her stomach. The day before, she had thrown up and gone into dry heaves so many times she had stayed for long periods in one of the bathrooms. Stretched out on the field of tiny hexagonal white tiles, she was glad they were cold. Only the chilly feel of the hard, unyielding floor kept the nausea at bay.

Now she was hot again, the air in the church uncomfortably close and warm because of the crush of people; but after several deep breaths to give herself the illusion that she had more space than she actually did, she knew she would be as fine as she needed to be. She was not worried anymore about the nausea. Sudden waves of grief were a different matter, but sometime the day before she had quit trying to fight that, too. When a surge of uncontrollable sadness came, she would accept it, though she would never pretend to embrace it as some of the well-meaning ones had suggested she try to do.

Her loss was bitter, and if one more person—she had said this out loud, and sharply, too—tried to tell her that everything happens for a reason and that, though we don't know why, Buster had been called home in God's good time—she would scream at the top of her voice. "God," she had snapped, yesterday and this morning, too, when someone tried to comfort her, "God had nothing to do with this! No one, damnit, called anyone home! So don't try to sweeten the horror. God didn't kill him—or call him home either. My parents killed him. They shot him to death, so damnit, quit bringing God into this!" Well enough then to consider such idle support as nothing but aggravating bother, she had run back to her room, but not in tears, in anger for what had been done. In their own ways, both of her parents had pulled triggers.

That notion, too, disappeared. The minister was beginning the service. In fact, he had begun it some time ago, but her attention had come and gone so often that at times she did not know if she were hearing him speak or remembering something someone had said to her or she had thought. At some point in the service—she would never know exactly what part—she heard the minister, his big voice booming, though not yelling, forcefully telling the people gathered here, "young and old alike—your ages mean nothing—so none of you—none of you should say God caused this—or even accepts it in some mysterious way, for God had nothing to do with this. This boy," he said, his voice rising again, "was murdered. Murdered," he repeated, "not taken away—murdered. And yes! God gave this boy life, but one of us—not God!—one of us took that life away from him. And the Lord had nothing to do with the crime—and it is a crime, but the Lord is still with us—and mighty is his presence in our grief. God is also present with us in joy, and I hope—though I know memory causes terrible pain now—I hope that this young man's mother and his wife—and loyal friends gathered here with us—will remember forever, as long as they take breath, that God was with them in their joy just as God is with them now in their grief." And the congregation answered with a loud *Amen!*

There was more that he said, though his message was not long, but the small part she did remember she cherished, though she knew she had nothing like the measured balance that the minister seemed to have. At the same time, the thought passed through her that he was not requiring or even encouraging balance in her or in anyone else at this time, and she was thankful for that, though she would never hear him preach again. In just a few months he and his family would move, called to another church in another city, as the rhetoric said. She asked someone why: Had there been some kind of trouble? She was wondering, after finding that the minister was moving, if his funeral message for Buster had upset influential people.

"Oh no," she was told by Ima Jean's father, a long-time member of the church's Board of Stewards. "The congregation loves him and his wife, too."

"So why does he have to move?"

"Oh, sweetheart," he said, putting his arm around her and speaking in the gently fatherly tone she liked to hear him slip so easily into, "it's just the way we Methodists do things. We swap our preachers around pretty often—the bishops and presiding elders do. That's one way we're different from you Presbyterians. But I do think I agree with what I think you're thinking—it's sometimes a questionable practice."

The sky was clear at the burial service in the cemetery, a fertile stretch of bluff whose back border overlooked the

Kiowa River. The clay-red color of it looked to some—and they said this—as if a flood of blood had poured into it. She would remember little of that time. Her sense of drift set in again. There was a lot of handshaking and hugging and chatter—she did remember that—and she had been a part of it, but only flickering images, and none of them telling or moving registered in memory. But one thing struck her: overhearing someone saying that the District Attorney was asking—or was going to ask—the judge to revoke the $20,000 bond and set no bail—no bail at all—for the mayor. "The crime's too serious," the man said, though at that point she was not certain if the statement was quoting the District Attorney or only stating the speaker's opinion. "It's too serious a crime," she heard the man say, "to let the perpetrator walk free."

CHAPTER 34

When the funeral parlor's chauffeur drove Buster's mother and older brother home, Ru-Marie went with them. She had stayed at Annie's boardinghouse since Saturday night and had no plans to leave. She did not, however, feel that she had settled in there. Nothing about her was settled. The blur of the funeral and burial service continued, and with it frenzy. The same was true of Annie, and the wild throes of grief were even worse when they saw each other. Neither one could accept Buster's death. They were living in wreckage.

If they had perhaps lapsed into some semblance of wonder, they would have likely found a few moments of calm; but to those around them, that did not seem to happen. One woman would see the other, and both would go into new convulsions of grief. That happened so often in the closed quarters of the house that some of the boarders tried to keep the two women apart. Several of the boarders had already taken over the kitchen duties, and the others helped with the cleaning. Everyone knew that Annie was incapable of functioning coherently, and some said they were worried she might fall apart permanently. She kept collapsing into unconsciousness, but no sense of rest seemed to come from that. Instead, she seemed increasingly weary, dangerously fragile; and the same was true of Ru-Marie.

Ima Jean came by each afternoon and was graceful in the presence of her friend's frenzy which pitched back and forth between grief and rage. Ima Jean kept telling her, "Yes, yes, I understand. Don't worry about me. Just go ahead and say whatever you want—and if you feel like throwing curses at me, do that, too." Comments like that seemed to soothe Ru-Marie, at least for awhile, but never for long.

Time and again Ru-Marie threw herself on her bed, Buster's bed, and sobbed. She heaved and sometimes pounded the mattress and covers with her fists. When she did that, the sounds choking free from her throat sounded like coughs she was trying to swallow. Nothing rattling in her throat or escaping from her mouth came close to achieving a sense of language during those times, and when Ima Jean touched her, in gestures meant to give comfort, Ru-Marie would flail her arms and sometimes even flop herself over on her back, but when she did that, she would instantly throw herself, face and body, forward again.

"It's okay," Ima Jean would say, and once again she would reach out and touch her friend, her palm on her back or cheek or arm. Sometimes Ima Jean would stroke her friend's back, and Ru-Marie would let her, but her body would often go undulant again, and the awful sounds of choking came back into her throat. She sounded as if she were smothering herself, choking herself, determined to erase herself from any level of awareness. Everything was so painful, she moaned, then fell into incoherence again, a cry then a ragged gagging sound broke in her throat, and sometimes threw her back into moments of unconsciousness, a spasmless state that looked like sleep. Other times the sounds she was making seemed to shock her back into a sham of alertness, but that did not last either.

The look on her face—her gaze directly pointed toward her friend—was the look of one who was altogether lost, numb, then waves of pain seemed to move across her eyes and lips, and she would wince, wince again and again, as if something sharp had scraped a part of her raw. Then that, too, would disappear; and sounding as if she were speaking from some place distant from the one she was in, she would even turn lucid for a time. When she did speak, there was only one subject she spoke of, and she spoke about it again and again.

"Go ahead," Ima Jean told her. "Don't worry. Tell me again, you need to—tell me again. Go ahead and say it. Say whatever you need to."

"What hurts the most," she would say, her voice thin, then she would stop, and Ima Jean would tell her she knew she was talking about her parents, and Ru-Marie would nod and say, "Yes. They thought he was nothing but trash. He wasn't. He might have even—he wasn't just hauling stuff, the way they made it sound he was doing—just some common kid too stupid for words. That wasn't him—that wasn't Buster at all. He worked in the lab. He didn't haul stuff, and you know why he got that job in the lab. He was good in Chemistry. You knew that. He did better than both of us—at least in Chemistry. He wasn't just trash in a dead-end job. But they never would accept that. They were frightened of him, weren't they? But why? I wasn't frightened of him."

"Who knows what they had in mind?" Ima Jean sighed.

"Do you know why?" Ru-Marie asked. "I don't. He never frightened anyone I know. Did he ever bother you?"

"Of course, not. We both know that."

"But he's not coming back," Ru-Marie said. "He's not ever coming back. I know that."

"Yes," Ima Jean said, putting her arms around her friend. "Yes," and she started smiling as she said, "I'd love seeing him again just one more time—surprising us all, the way he did that day when he whipped himself around that tall ladder and climbed—hands only—down the back side of it—with the cat in his shirt."

"I was thinking the same thing—but quirky little things like that don't matter."

"Oh they might," Ima Jean told her. "It's possible that quirky little things like that mean more than we dare admit."

Still in each other's arms, the two would be silent, for awhile, until Ima Jean said she had to go home, but Ru-Marie should call her if she needed or wanted anything. "You might think, too, about coming back to school. Give me a call some morning. I'll drop by and we can walk the rest of the way together."

But her attention had drifted away again. She looked as if she were somehow floating, unattached to anything, including herself, then she began making a sound, as if she were humming, but in a moment the hum would sound as if she might even be getting ready to sing, though softly, but never with enough effort for the sounds to resemble even rudiments of muffled speech. The sound would become merely humming again. The look in Ru-Marie's eyes then would not suggest anything but a painless absence from self.

Later, Ima Jean would tell her, "I think at times, during that week, you were actually demented, and that bothered me. You don't know how much it bothered me. I even told Dad."

"I figured you did. You know he came by?"

"I know, and I'm glad, and what he told me, when he came in off his rounds, made me feel better."

"What *did* he say? When he was here, he didn't say much at all."

"He just took me in his arms," Ima Jean told her, "and held me, then not long after that, when I calmed down, he told me that, of course, you looked and acted as if you'd lost your mind. Then he added—the calmness of his manner even shocked me—he said, *For awhile she probably had lost her mind, but don't get alarmed about that*. He said that after what you had been through, losing your mind for awhile was not all bad. Then he laughed, for just a second, that little laugh of his, then he told me that sometimes losing your mind for awhile is one of nature's blessings, *one of nature's blessings*, he repeated then told me to keep on doing what I was: going to see you. *She's going to be just fine*, he told me. *No doubt about it. She's going to be fine.*"

CHAPTER 35

RM told me:

 I still had a long way to go. Then and even now when I drift back over that time I keep thinking I stayed there with Annie longer than I really did. That's what I *think*, but when I start counting the days, it wasn't long at all. Just Saturday night till Thursday when I went back home. I guess the only decent thing my parents did during that time was to leave me alone. As far as I know, they didn't even call—or if they did, the others in the place kept the news from me. But even if they had called, I don't think I'd have talked to them. At least I hope I wouldn't have. You just never know. There's often a gap between what you want to think you are and what you truly are. And I don't know if Ima Jean's father would have called knowing that fortunate or not, the way he said that period when I lost my mind—being in shock—was a blessing.

 I think I don't usually talk—or even think—about things in terms of blessings. Somehow that term, when I think back, is one I've never been drawn to, though—and I have no trouble confessing this—I always did like the way Dr. Wolfe, Ima Jean's father, talked. Ever since I first knew him, when Ima Jean and I were just girls, I always thought I could have listened to him all day, no matter what he talked about. Of course, and I'll admit this, too, there's some oddness in that notion, too, because I almost never heard him talk. He was gone so much. But his coming to see me, I'll always call that a blessing, though I'm really not sure that visit—hazy as it's always been—was really what jolted me back into some semblance of control—or, more likely, for a long time, what I'd call a sham of control.

On Thursday afternoon, as I said, I went back home. Some of the women staying in the boardinghouse told me they thought that would be best, and even then I thought they were likely right. Of course, if they had asked me to stay, I'd have probably done that, too. I was still too much in a fog to make any kind of decision on my own. But they told me that Annie and I weren't doing each other any good. They said we weren't doing anything but upsetting each other. I'd see her, they told me, or she'd see me, and we'd both fall apart, and it was clear, even from the first, that, crazed as I was, it was clear what was going on. There was only one thing on our minds, and we both knew what it was. She would break down and I would break down, and then again we'd both of us break down together.

So I went home, and thank heavens, no one made anything of it. I didn't say I was glad to be back, and they didn't say they were glad to have me back. We almost didn't even talk, about anything, for a good while, and believe you me, the silence was welcome. I don't think I saw it then, but I started realizing later how close to explosion the three of us had been. I still don't have any idea in the world how we avoided it, other than the fact that we were all three wrapped up so tightly in our own troubles that, thank goodness, we had little time for anyone else's concerns.

Then the trial came, Dad's trial, and several people urged me—Ima Jean among them, bringing word from her father—not to go to the trial, and I didn't. I went along with what they wanted. They knew what the testimony would be, and they doubted I could take it, and likely they were right—especially considering how I broke down and sobbed later on during Mother's trial when Mr. Bracken, the night-watchman, described Buster and my father and Buster's mother and my mother, Buster getting shot and blown apart again and again. I still wince when the image comes back.

I sat with my parents during Mother's trial, and I'm still not sure why I did. In fact, every time since then, when I've remembered being there with them, I feel like crossing myself and confessing how wretched I was. I really do. I even felt that way back then, and I'd never even been in a Catholic church. But I wanted to cross myself and confess. I think I felt that I was violating something by sitting with them, but by then I had—or at least I thought I had—some distance from them. That was another foolish notion. But I do know when a fundamental sense of distance from them occurred—not just when I became aware of it, but when it happened. It happened, in fact, twice. The first time occurred when I read the morning newspaper early on during Dad's trial and heard—actually read—what Mother said when the District Attorney asked her why Dad had shot Buster. I'll never forget her answer.

The DA asked her the question, and she told him, "He wasn't at himself."

"He *what?*" the DA asked.

She said, "I told you. He wasn't at himself."

I read the statement again, then again and again, and I cursed. You don't know how much I cursed, I was so disgusted. But in a wicked way, too, I was amused and found myself laughing. There for a second I thought I really had lost my mind. I felt guilty for laughing because I was still finding myself pitching into uncontrollable sobbing. Years later, though, I adjusted to that disconcerting fact about humor. It's no respecter of anyone's mood and seems altogether alien to anyone's sense of decorum. Constitutionally I knew that. We had never, Buster and I, as far as I can or could back then recall—ever talked about humor. How could we? We just laughed a lot and felt comfortable doing it.

We weren't, after all, much older than kids ourselves, but his way of easy laughter, I kept realizing, taught me a lot. I'll add, too, that most of what I've come to know has never seemed momentous—nothing I ever felt qualified me or even inclined me to offer insight to someone else. But at that moment when whatever buried part of me let me laugh—*made* me laugh at my mother's wretched mangling of the language—I didn't feel superior to her. What happened was the great distance there was between us became more apparent than it had before. I also knew—whether I liked it or not—that the sweet, tricky meanness of laughter let me know, too, that in laughing at her I was also laughing at myself. No doubt about it: I'd been proving again and again how inadequate I was.

No counselor's wisdom rescued me, though the blessed arms of Ima Jean's father, Dr. Wolfe—the memory of those strong arms around me in the boarding hose—probably held me together more than I knew. I somehow began to learn, too, that though falling apart was nothing to be proud of, I didn't need to drown in shame, and I did feel shame for being so weak when dear Annie Lopreis needed a kind of support I was in too sorry a state to give her. Sometimes—even these decades later—I cringe, I still cringe when I remember how useless I was. That's why learning to laugh—at myself or anyone else—seemed more a blessing than a lapse into heartless bad taste.

Not long after that moment in Dad's trial when Mother made a fool of herself—I read something else, and I'm still about half-surprised I didn't do something drastic—to a lot of people. Dad's lawyer—no question he was being paid by the elders—the Capitalist and his crew of elders—called a woman to the stand and began asking her questions about Annie's boardinghouse, things that she and the lawyer indicated *many* people *knew* went on there. To hear her talk, you'd have thought the place was a whorehouse more than a boardinghouse, and the only good thing about that sorry slut's testimony was the fact that the day after Dad's trial was over, the District Attorney charged her with perjury. The District Attorney had already ripped her apart on the stand during cross examination, though she stuck to all her lies. He wasn't finished with her, though. And when that young DA, barely twenty-five himself, announced he was charging her with perjury, he told the press that lying under oath was serious and he had no intention of giving anyone who committed perjury any slack. "No slack at all," he said.

The pleasure of revenge like that, however, was not even close to being as powerful as the desperate and pitiful condition of Buster's mother who had to be helped—not just from the stand but from the courtroom itself—again and again. She was falling apart and sobbing hysterically, "He killed my boy, he killed my boy." And I was sobbing, too, though all I was doing was staying at home and holding a newspaper. I still felt I was with her, both of us bawling our eyes out.

I think if I hadn't known what the trial was about I wouldn't have had any idea sometimes what some of the people were testifying about. If you were even only half-gullible, you might have gotten the notion my father was a knight in shining damn armor defending his helpless daughter—or at least whatever meager sliver of her virtue there was left, the rest of it having been cynically and unspeakably seduced away by this low-rent filthy man all hot to better his deservedly sorry station in life, and that Dad, my great protector, had gone crazy—but understandably and virtuously crazy—after coming back from his trip to Austin for the city he was the re-elected mayor of—and finding out that Buster and I had been married for seven months, and no telling what I'd been forced to wallow in. This wasn't murder, this was honor, and the motivating factor—according to him—was me trying to hide my hideous damn shame.

Then he turned right around and shifted his story by saying that Mother had gotten the pistol at her sister's house that night the shooting occurred, and she was waving it around in some kind of awful joke that was getting out of hand and he had to get the gun away from her or someone was going to get hurt, and he couldn't stand for anyone to get hurt, he had—after all—a position to uphold.

According to all the accounts I read, the young DA was withering, just not withering enough. Because of all the circus acts the defense put on the stand, the murder charge ended up turning into a verdict of guilty—but not for murder, for manslaughter, and the early possibility of execution became a three-year prison sentence, but not much more than half a year—not even that—was served. The idiot clairvoyant governor pardoned him, and I don't have any idea how much that cost, though it's pretty clear who paid it—the Capitalist and his elders.

I know it sounds awful for me to talk this way. I never have wanted anyone put to death, for any reason, then or now, but the sham of what went on in that trial made me sick. I even found out—but this was years later, too—and who knows if it really reveals anything, though it does seem right: the judge who took over the trial because of the change of venue had been run out, as they say, of North Carolina when he was nineteen. It seems some family there got bent out of joint when he shot their son in the back after an argument. That's when the judge, the kid who became judge, decided to pull up stakes and move. You almost get the idea that back then the whole culture—maybe it's just as true now—was, as my daughter once said about a bad song she and I were hearing on the radio: "Awful. They sound like they're just making it up as they go along."

And, lord, was she right, and in a lot more ways than she even had in mind.

CHAPTER 36

Her mother's trial began on Monday, May 25th, and a verdict was delivered on Friday afternoon that same week. The first witness for the prosecution was one of Ru-Marie's friends, a young woman who had also gone across the border and gotten married the summer before. Her name was Alma Carpenter.

The young woman's initial testimony was so short-lived she barely got to identify herself. When she took the stand, she was trembling, and her rapid breaths were shallow and short. She looked pale and desperate, frightened and wild in the eye. The young woman looked as if she were about to burst into tears. But why? Nothing sad had happened to her, except some friction with her parents, but Ru-Marie knew that had not lasted, maybe no more than a day or two, and that had been almost a year ago now when they found out she had run across the river to get married. Alma had even been able to live openly with her young husband Mark.

As far as Ru-Marie knew, the girl had not witnessed anything at all, at least nothing associated with Buster's death and the trial. So why was she on the stand, and why did she look so distraught? Just seventeen herself, the girl had no idea either that her marriage would not even last another two years and that she and her husband would each have married two more times, and once even to each other again before a decade had gone by.

Alma's cheeks looked sunken, and that was odd, too. She did not look emaciated; she looked as if she were sucking in her cheeks. What was going on? She didn't even look like herself, Ru-Marie thought.

Speaking for the prosecution, the County Attorney from Haskell, the small town where the trial had been set, approached her after she had been sworn in as a witness. For the record, he said, he asked her to give the court her name.

Suddenly looking desperate, she turned away from the crowd and faced him directly, but no look of recognition brought life to her eyes. Her lips were quivering, at first grotesquely, as if she were gumming something in her mouth. She was shaking all over. Looking stunned, she was whimpering, then suddenly pitched forward off her chair in a faint. Dropping his pad, the attorney lunged toward her and, breaking her fall, caught her, both of them tangled together on the floor. As the judge called for a doctor, the attorney pulled away from her, looking as if he had been touching something he shouldn't have had his hands on. Gathering himself back into a semblance of propriety, he took her head in his hands and eased her back down on the floor. He pulled the hem of her skirt down, though it had not hiked up in the fall. Then another man, a doctor, nudged him aside and began ministering to her. The doctor and attorney were both mumbling to her, but she did not seem to be responding. The doctor pulled a small packet from his coat pocket as the judge announced an hour-long recess. The doctor moved the packet he had ripped open to her nostrils. The girl flinched, and soon the bailiff and another man brought in a stretcher and carried the young woman out. Stirred and confused, the people began clearing the chamber.

Calling out to the bailiff that he would be right with him, the doctor stepped back to confer with the judge. After they had talked for awhile, the judge rapped his gavel and announced to those still crowding the doorway that the trial would resume at one-thirty in the afternoon.

It was about two o'clock before the trial actually got underway again. Alma Carpenter, the doctor told the judge, was indeed ready to testify. She had fainted, he said, because, in her nervousness, she had not eaten or slept for two days. She would need to testify from a cot. She was not yet strong enough to walk into court, or even to sit upright in a hard chair. The judge agreed that the cot was acceptable. The main problem, in terms of the trial, was not the young woman's health. The main problem was the absence of the defendant. Eileen Coleman had not returned from the recess. A flurry of alarm broke out in the packed chamber.

By herself at the defense table where she and her parents and her mother's attorney had sat this morning, Ru-Marie glanced around, then kept turning around to check the closed door, but her mother and father and her mother's attorney were nowhere in sight. She had not gone to lunch with them. She had told them she preferred to go to a café by herself. She kept twisting around, the look in her eyes increasingly severe. Their absence made no sense.

Soon the three entered the court room, the defense attorney offering his apologies to the judge, but the judge cut him off and told him sternly, "One-thirty, sir, means one-thirty. One more stunt like this and I'll hold you in contempt."

"Yes, your honor."

"Sit down."

The judge then told the attorney for the prosecution to proceed.

"Thank you."

What Alma Carpenter, there on her cot, testified to was family news that was almost a year old now. Although the content of it did not really surprise Ru-Marie, she would later tell Ima Jean that she had not heard the conversations

Alma said she had had with Ru-Marie's mother. She had not even heard about the conversations, other than a passing remark Alma had made about how much Ru-Marie's mother hated Buster.

"But why?" Ru-Marie had asked. "She doesn't even really know him. He's only been over here a few times."

"Well, believe me," Alma had said, "she doesn't like him at all."

"That's her problem," Ru-Marie had snapped, dismissing her mother's opinion as irrelevant—"and of no concern to me," she had added. She had not, however, asked Alma what exactly her mother had said. Why should she have? Her mother had always had airs, she thought, and Ru-Marie did not think it was her place to try to reform the thick-bodied, dull-eyed creature. Ru-Marie didn't intend to let anyone boss her around.

But a chill sliced through her during Alma's testimony. Still, Ru-Marie was not surprised or even especially interested when she heard Alma saying that Mrs. Coleman had said she wished that Buster would leave her daughter alone. Ru-Marie already knew that. *He's just trash*, Alma reported Eileen as saying. *Anyone can see that*. But Ru-Marie's mild drift into daydreaming stopped when she heard Alma say that Mrs. Coleman had also told her—she had been over at the house on a Saturday, she said, and Ru-Marie had gone down the street to get something from the store, she forgot what, she testified, seeming a lot livelier than she had this morning, but Mrs. Coleman had told her, she said, that if Buster didn't start staying away from her daughter that she was going to have her husband kill him—and he'll do it, believe you me, he'll do it, Mrs. Coleman had said.

The attorney asked her to repeat what she had just said, and she did.

"Did she say anything else?" the attorney asked.

"Yes, sir."

"And what was that?"

"That if her husband didn't shoot him she'd kill him herself."

"Did she actually say she would kill him?"

Looking more like a pasha on the cot than a witness, Alma said, "Yes, sir."

"Did you hear her say that just once?"

"No, sir, she said it a couple times."

"How many times?"

"At least twice, sir."

"No further questions, your honor."

Then Alma Carpenter started waving her hands at the attorney and opening and closing her mouth, as if she were frantic. There was something she had to say. "Please!" Alma cried. "Please!"

"Yes?" the attorney asked.

"Can I have a glass of water? I think I feel faint."

Frowning, the judge said he had a pitcher at the bench and a clean glass, too. The attorney reached to take the glass after the judge had poured it half full. He handed it to Alma. She took a sip then pressed the glass to her forehead, then her cheek, then against the top of her chest after that.

"Are you all right?" the judge asked.

"Yes, sir. I think so. Just a wave of weakness there. I think I'll be fine."

"Are you able to continue?" the judge asked.

"Yes, sir. I think I am." Then after sipping from the glass again, she said she was fine. Everything, she said, was fine and okay.

The judge told her to let him know if she needed more water. She thanked him. Then, as she readjusted herself on the cot, the judge called the attorney for the defense.

Approaching Alma's cot, the defense attorney reminded her that she was under oath.

"I know that," she said, sounding irritated. Amused, as if she were watching a curious scene in a play, Ru-Marie did not find Alma's tone surprising at all.

The attorney then asked her if she had quoted the defendant accurately.

"What do you mean? You already asked if I knew I was under oath. Of course, I said what I said accurately."

"Did the defendant actually say what you claimed she said?"

"I already told you."

"And I'm asking you, young lady, if you quoted her exactly—not approximately—exactly."

"You mean word for word?"

"That's exactly what I mean."

"Well, maybe not," Alma told him, "not exactly word for word. I mean I wasn't taking the conversation down in shorthand."

"Just answer the question, please."

No doubt about it, Ru-Marie thought. Alma was feeling much better. She had always been flighty, and sometimes moody, but when she seemed to feel truly fine, she often had a caustic lip. A time or two during her daydreams over the last couple years, Ru-Marie had begun to wonder if the only way to keep Alma stable would be for someone to keep her miserable. Otherwise, she'd likely be worthless as anyone's mate.

"Maybe not exactly word for word," she heard Alma say, "but I'm telling you—and this is the truth—I'm not reading a thing into what that woman told me. So how many times do I have to say it?"

"So you are admitting," the attorney said, "that you are *not* quoting her exactly. Is that correct?"

"Maybe, but just maybe," she said sassily, "if that's the way you want to put it. That's correct."

"Listen, young lady, all I care about here is accuracy—

not your ability to see into anyone's mind. Do you understand that?"

"Yes, sir," she said, "I do. But what I said was true. You think you're capable of understanding that as well?"

The attorney told the judge, "I'm through with the witness, your honor. No further questions."

Then the prosecuting attorney rose and said the state was resting its case. A gasp of surprise went through the packed chamber. The trial, however, was not over. The defense had its own witnesses to call. The first to be called to the stand was Mr. Bracken, the nightwatchman who had witnessed the shooting. He was asked to describe the killing, and he did, his testimony the same as it had been in Jeff Coleman's trial.

As he described the events at the streetcar stop that night, Ru-Marie began weeping. She closed her eyes, as if that would help the information go away. But it didn't, and when Mr. Bracken winced as he described Buster being shot—first when he was standing face to face with Mr. Coleman, then again when he was on his back and Mr. Coleman—"urged on loudly by Mrs. Coleman"—shot him several more times, Ru-Marie looked as if someone had struck her in the head with a club. She bolted upright, her mouth open in a soundless scream and her eyes looking wounded and wild. She was standing now, the look on her face suggesting she had just discovered that fact, and that confused her. She had no reason to be standing. She coughed, just once, then sat back down, a look of bewilderment overwhelming her. She began sobbing loudly—*bitterly*, the next day's *Kiowa Times* said.

Her father glanced at her, but her mother did not look at her. A look of irritation on her face, her mother kept her gaze lowered toward the floor. Then Ru-Marie, still shaking, her cheeks and eyes wet with tears, wrapped her arms around herself. She was shivering and still crying, and though she tried to stop herself by gritting her teeth and shaking her head violently, she could not stop herself from sobbing, and the tears did not stop either until a woman—Ru-Marie never learned her name—stood up and made her way to the aisle and walked resolutely to the railing. Reaching over it, she stroked the back of Ru-Marie's head, then after squeezing her shoulder, she said, "You just go ahead and cry all you want. You're the only one of us here that matters."

As the woman walked back to her seat, Ru-Marie felt a wave of calmness sweeping through her. She knew that, kind as the woman was, the woman was wrong. Buster's mother Annie was every bit as important as she was—and so, probably, she thought, in their own ways, was everyone here; and though she had no idea why, she was glad that she knew almost none of them.

Looking up now, she saw the judge looking down at her. She took a deep breath and wiped her cheeks dry. Her eyes still welled with tears. She took another deep breath then nodded at the judge to let him know that she was okay. Turning to the nightwatchman, the judge told the witness, "Proceed."

The nightwatchman testified that he had seen no indication that Mrs. Coleman had even tried to fire a shot. Under questioning, he also said he never saw her with a gun.

"So, are you saying," the defense attorney asked, "that you never saw Eileen Coleman with any kind of firearm?"

"Yes, sir."

"No more questions, your honor."

The prosecuting attorney said he had no questions either.

Eileen's sister was then brought to the stand and was asked what Mr. Coleman's demeanor had been like the night of the shooting.

"Upset," she said.

"Was he out of control?"

"Objection," the prosecuting attorney said. "The witness has no expertise in—"

"Sustained," the judge said.

The defense attorney asked her what she had heard Mr. Coleman say that night."

"He, as I said, was upset—terribly upset. He kept crying out, *What have they done to my daughter?* He kept crying that out over and over."

"What did he mean by *they*?" the attorney asked.

"I don't know."

"Would you say then, to use a layman's terms, that he was *beside himself*—so much so that you had questions about him being in control of himself?"

"Yes, sir. I didn't even think he ought to have been driving that night—not in the state he was in."

"What was your sister, the defendant, like that night?"

"Upset—very upset—as anyone in her circumstances would be."

"Did she seem to be aware of how distraught her husband was?"

"Yes, of course. Anyone would've been."

"What did your brother-in-law say—other than that something terrible had happened to his daughter?"

"What do you mean?" she asked.

"What else did he say?"

"You mean that he was going to get him?"

"Is that what he said?"

"Yes."

"And who did you understand *him* to mean?"

"The Lopreis guy—the one who kept bothering Ru-Marie."

"What did you understand *going to get him* meant?"

"To kill him."

"How do you know that's what he meant?"

"Because he said so. He used his name—that Buster

guy—he used his name a number of times."

"Was your sister present then?"

"Yes."

"Did she say she was leaving the house to kill Buster?"

"No. Of course, not. She didn't say anything of the kind."

"No further questions."

The prosecuting attorney then asked her if her sister had actually been present when Jeff Coleman had threatened to kill Mr. Lopreis.

"Of course, she was present. I already said that. They came to my house together. What're you getting at?"

"So your sister, the defendant, was present when your brother-in-law, Mr. Jeff Coleman—later convicted of killing Mr. Alvin Lopreis—a young man known as Buster—made threatening remarks about said son-in-law? Is that correct? Was she present when he said that?"

"Yes, sir. She was there the whole time."

"And in your judgment, was she close enough to have heard her husband's threatening speech?"

"I've already said that," she said impatiently. "We were all in the same room together."

"Did your sister seem upset?"

"Of course, she did."

"Why?"

"Because she hated that guy—that Buster who kept bothering her daughter."

"What do you mean *bothering her*?"

"Going over to her place when he wasn't welcome."

"Did you ever hear your niece Ruth Marie complain about him coming over?"

"Not in so many words."

"Did you ever hear her complain at all?"

"Maybe not, but I'm telling you that guy, Buster whoever, wasn't welcome there."

"Did you ever hear your sister say she wanted to kill him?"

"Maybe, but I think it was just a figure of speech."

"What exactly did she say?"

"Something like if Jeff doesn't have the stomach for something—I'm not exactly sure what the word was."

"Go on."

"That if Jeff didn't do something, she would—or wanted to—something like that."

"Did she ever say anything like that to you before that night?"

"Maybe—a time or two—but not much. She didn't even like to use the guy's name."

"But she did say that if her husband didn't kill Mr. Lopreis, she would. Is that correct?"

"Yes, but that doesn't mean she actually did it."

"No further questions," the prosecutor said, then the defense attorney said he had no more witnesses to call.

The judge said closing remarks would begin the next morning, at nine a.m. "Each side will be allotted three hours. This court is adjourned till tomorrow morning at nine," he said, rapping his gavel, and the sound of the gavel striking the wood block made Ru-Marie wince. It sounded the same way she imagined shots sounded.

Neither side used more than an hour of its allotted time. The young District Attorney from Kiowa spoke for the prosecution. He reminded the jury that no one had testified, or even suggested, that the defendant had had possession of a pistol that night or had fired any kind of weapon that night. What had been testified to under oath, he said, was that Mrs. Eileen Coleman, the defendant, had been present in front of at least one witness when her husband had threatened to kill young Mr. Lopreis, their daughter's husband. "Knowing what a terrible rage her husband was in," he said, "and having heard him threaten to kill the young man—which he did that same night, and in front of witnesses, too—you have heard in sworn testimony that the defendant—clearly aware of her husband's state of mind and having a belligerent attitude herself toward the young man—went with her husband to seek out this young man. And the defendant, well before that night, was quoted under oath as having said that she would get her husband to shoot the young man if the young man did not stay away from their daughter. She also said, in front of at least one witness—and more than one time—that if her husband would not kill the young man himself, *she* would kill him. No one," he said, "has disputed any of these facts.

"So what we have," he said, "is simply this: a defendant who herself had threatened to murder the young man who did get shot—at least three times in cold blood. And this same defendant, on the night the killing actually took place, went with her husband to find the young man. Then, mind you, right after her husband had said before witnesses that he would shoot the young man to death, and he did, she, the defendant, was with him. And as two other witnesses have testified under oath, the defendant encouraged her husband to make sure the young man was dead. She even yelled at her husband to back their car up, to shine the car's lights on the young man—lying helpless on his back before them—and her husband did exactly what she told him to do. He backed the car up then got out of the car again and shot the boy at least two more times.

"Gentlemen of the jury, under the law, as it is written and as precedents have affirmed, the defendant is guilty of murder by aiding and abetting a murder. One, according to the law, does not have to pull the trigger to be guilty of murder. If one," he said, "is even in willing company with the one who fires the weapon, and has even encouraged said offender to fire his weapon, as is indisputably the case with the defendant—one *must* return a verdict of guilty. That's the law," he told the jury. "Gentlemen," he said, finishing his statement, "there is neither confusion nor qualification here. There is only the defendant who, according to the laws of the state of Texas, must be judged guilty of murder. That's the law. She went to the murder site willingly, knowing her husband's state of mind and intentions. And she also, in front of witnesses, encouraged her husband—even ordered her husband—to make sure he had truly sent the young man to death. She *must* be judged guilty—of murder. That's the law." Then he took his seat.

The defense attorney tried mocking the prosecutor. He said, "All this young District Attorney wants is to stride back into the town where he lives, sporting victory in a prominent case. He has his ambition—I think almost everyone knows that—but this case is not about a young man's political ambitions—no matter how clever he might try to make you think he is." He went on to say that no one saw the defendant fire a weapon or even have a weapon in her possession, that what one must say about her was that she was passionate about the welfare of her daughter, as her husband was—the twice-elected mayor of his community, mind you—both of them loyal to their responsibilities to their family and community.

"They wanted," he said, "what was best for their daughter. How can you," he cried, "convict anyone of murder when that person did not commit murder? How can you? She had no weapon, and she used no weapon. She was with her husband, no matter what state of mind he was in. She was not just with him in times that were happy. She was with him for better or worse. This is no criminal," he told the jury. "This is a woman—a mother, a wife—who has shown a level of loyalty to child and mate that I, frankly, stand in awe of. Long before the events this trial is addressing took place, she showed herself to be one who inspires admiration because of her sense of loyalty to her family and her willingness to sacrifice her own comfort for the welfare of others. She—with her own great abilities and fineness of character—stepped aside to give others their chance. No scandal has ever touched the defendant, none at all, none at all. She pulled no trigger. She committed no crime. She is innocent—innocent before the law, and innocent before God."

In his instructions to the jury, the judge said that Mrs. Coleman's mere presence at the time and scene of the shooting would not be sufficient to convict her. "But," he added, "if the jury finds beyond a reasonable doubt that the defendant's husband, Mr. Jeff Coleman, maliciously killed Mr. Lopreis and that she, the defendant, was present and knew of the unlawful intent of her husband and aided him by acts or encouragements of words or gestures in commission of the offense, or if before the killing she agreed with her husband that he should do it, or so advised him and was actually present at the killing, whether she aided or not in the commission of said offense, if any, then the jury is instructed to find her guilty of murder and assess her punishment at death or by confinement in the state penitentiary for life—or any other term of years not less than five, as the jury may determine." Then he added, "Unless the jury believes her guilty under those circumstances, it must bring in a verdict of acquittal."

Those instructions were given at one-thirty. The jury then went into deliberation, and by four-thirty that same day they sent word to the judge that they had reached a verdict. The court was called back into session, and the verdict was read: The defendant was guilty, and the recommended punishment was ten years in the state penitentiary for women.

CHAPTER 37

RM told me:

She unfolded a thin sheaf of paper and, in a curiously formal way, began to read:

Jeff Coleman, my father, finally went to prison in June. He was locked up, however, for less than six months. In mid-October he was furloughed home for a month to recover from the flu. The week after he went back, Eileen Coleman, my mother, was due to go to prison herself; but that never happened. On Saturday, Nov. 20—the week before her husband, my father, was due back in prison and less than a week before Mrs. Coleman, my mother, was to go to prison, the governor of the state, a woman named Mrs. Miriam Ferguson, called a press conference, during which she issued a full pardon for my mother. "The main reason for such action," the governor said in a prepared statement, "is that after a careful investigation and consideration of the facts I have come to the conclusion that the defendant is not guilty of the charges against her and therefore ought never to have been convicted."

During the press conference, the governor also pardoned another person. The two cases were unrelated. That same day a spokesman for the state legislature said there would likely be an investigation into the issuing of the two pardons. Mrs. Ferguson's husband, governor a decade back, had been impeached himself for corruption. Then running for office herself, Mrs. Ferguson promised the voters that if she were elected they would be getting two governors for the price of one, and she was elected. Soon after that a joke began circulating across the state. In it, Mrs. Ferguson was in a crowded elevator that jostled as it came to a stop at a floor. Bumping against her, a young man said, "Oh pardon me," and bristling, she said:

"Listen, young man, you'll have to talk to my husband about that."

Numerous people from Kiowa—doctors and dentists, the two legislators from the area, and thirty women the newspaper called prominent had signed a petition asking for a pardon for Mrs. Coleman. There were others as well who had signed the petition: eleven members of the jury that had convicted her, the city's new mayor, the Sheriff-elect, and the chief of police.

Those are the facts, but no one at our house seemed thrilled about them. My parents and I sustained the distance that had grown between us. I do not think any of us had any desire to put our pasts away, to begin life anew, as they say, and try to love each other. I don't think we were bitter, but we were not interested in overtly forgiving each other's debts. That was not the way we thought. But who knows? Maybe we were still in a state of shock. I don't think so, though I will admit that's a subject I don't to this day have any curiosity about.

I know I have had my blessings, and I'm grateful for them, but the two I'll mention now—my second husband and the daughter we had together—have never seemed like gifts that came to me from some place or source distant from me. That may be why I turn rather shy—wary even—when people start talking about blessings. Talk like that has usually seemed odd to me, and I know the reason why. My husband Grover and our daughter were (my daughter still is) powerful and even lyrical parts of my life. I loved them both, though Grover has been gone for more than ten years now. But all that is another matter, and I know you respect that.

I have a few more things to tell you. The first is simply an observation I found myself making that long-ago winter when Dad came back from prison and all three of us seemed to accept that no one of us, for whatever reason, had any inclination to ask anyone for forgiveness. I'll go ahead and add this as well: I never saw any indication of a feeling of pride in any of us, but I also saw no sense of remorse. Somehow all three of us seemed inured to pride and guilt both. That, however, was not what I meant when I mentioned discovering myself making an observation.

I even tried to paint what I had observed. I tried to paint it again and again, but I never could come close to making the image work. The painting looked abstract, not because I had intended that but because, in zeroing in on the image that kept returning to me, I lost its context. When I translated the image into a painting, it became ineffectively abstract. To begin with, the image was nothing more than a patch of ground, a small patch of ground. I saw it—I noticed it time and again—in our yard and in so many other yards, too: straw-colored dry runners of grass that sprayed thinly across the hard, cracked earth, that unyielding hardpan. That's all the image was, but it stayed vividly with me, like an after-image burned into sight. Who knows? Maybe what was missing was the wind, scorching in summer, often freezing in winter. But as I say, I kept losing its context when I tried to paint it. What I wanted to portray was an image that was borderless, an image that seemed both battered and hearty, an image, in fact, whose raw level of dryness was an affront to anyone's desire for comfort. At the same time—and I had experienced this myself—there was a severe dimension of beauty in the image that was even lyrical in spite of the fact that sometimes only a pickaxe could break the ground where we lived.

It was not a death image I was trying to capture. Not at all. The earth and the wind here were full of vitality, but they were not necessarily friendly, but then neither were we. That may have helped us, that hardness. Maybe I should have concentrated on mesquites. I painted them for awhile, but I don't think I understood them then, and when I did understand them—the laciness of them that modified their disorderliness—I—who knows why?—did not come back to them. How could I? Trees and grass were not what had given me grief.

Let me make something clear before I go on, and in all the talks we've had I've never mentioned this. I know I haven't, but I want to make sure you don't draw the wrong conclusion. So mark this: I do not think that Buster's death meant that he was too sensitive or too fair of spirit to survive in a place like this. The place itself—the atmosphere of the city—that was not what killed him. The two courts got it right. In their own ways, both of my parents killed him; and I'll add this, though it hurts: I don't think his death had a meaning; I don't think it had a purpose. Nothing good came from it—*nothing*. And I know that's what I'll continue to think. Nothing good came from his death, but the thought does not undermine me. What happened was simply this: I lost someone I loved, and no amount of pretending that there was somehow a purpose in the fact would lessen my grief or change the truth of what happened.

In varying degrees of clarity, I've known that, in fact, since that terrible night, and I have never seen anything to change my mind. And though I was able to love again, and love deeply, I will keep thinking—I'm helpless to do anything else—that Buster's death had no meaning, no purpose at all. Thinking otherwise would demand that I go blind and deaf to the memory of him and his mother, a little woman who was broken by his death. I will not turn my back on her because her goodness demands honor, not neglect.

I was young then, and a lot about me was careless; but that was not the case with her. She knew exactly how valuable Buster was. She loved him completely, and he knew that. She loved him and so did I, but I will also admit—and I've thought about this a thousand times—Annie Lopreis had depths that I, at that point, never came close to fathoming.

I see again those scraggly runners of grass. There was not and there is not anything unusual about the image. Whatever time of year I see them, they appear to me to be in winter. Grass then is supposed to be strawlike, and the poverty of rain in those years meant that the greening that would come again in the spring would be short-lived, but the grass would stay alive nonetheless. That was not the case with Buster, except in memory, and there I see myself almost as clearly as I see him, but those two figures whose images sometimes still sing to me are vastly different from what they have become, or what I have become. Buster's still young.

There's another image, too. The grass that covers Buster's grave—and Grover's grave as well—and Ima Jean's—will be—and has been for a long time—thicker than the grass in most of the yards in the city. Few lawns got watered back then, except for the cemeteries. That, of course, has changed. So what we see around us is another thing that in several ways is different from what we used to see.

I have to say this directly. My parents did not, after their pardons, live tortured lives. In fact, not long after he came home from prison, my father began working for the city Parks department. After a few years he was named superintendent of Parks and kept the position for the rest of his career. His retirement party was big, the celebration in May, a month before he was actually due to retire. Those organizing the party wanted as many people there as possible, so they held the big event before people started going away on summer vacations. The sendoff was good, then two weeks before his official final day on the job arrived, he died in his sleep. In his obituary—newspaper people like yourself wrote them then, not the family—he was celebrated as the popular long-time Parks superintendent and former mayor and faithful Elder at the First Presbyterian Church. Nothing was mentioned about the shooting or the conviction or the fact that he had spent time in prison; and the same was true four years later when Mother died. A part of the past had simply disappeared.

I don't exactly know why, but this morning I got out my old scrapbook. I had no intention of reminiscing, not about that distant time. There was just one thing I wanted, and it was, curiously enough, one of the only things I kept from the papers back then: a clipping that quoted my father's letter of resignation as mayor. He had issued it on Thursday morning, after having killed Buster on Saturday night. When I pulled it out and read it, I knew why I had been drawn to it. I knew why I had cut it out and why I had kept it, though I confess I could not have said so back then. Addressed to the "Honorable Aldermen," the note said:

> *Please accept my resignation as mayor of the City of Kiowa Falls, effective immediately. I am in such a torn up mental condition and worry on account of recent events and family troubles that I am in no condition to attend to the important duties as mayor.*
> *I regret—*

I quit reading it. I had seen what I needed to see: confirmation that my father had actually been upset, distraught enough to come close to incoherence—at least awkwardness—in his note. I hope I didn't invent that. I find at least a gesture of relief in the thought that he was not altogether hard, that he was decent enough to be bothered by what he had done. Not everyone is. There are thousands of ways to buffer oneself from the truth.

I will not pretend I was full of suffering when I retrieved the clipping. All I wanted to confirm was that, in however minor a way, my father had been bothered by what he had done. I had not—at least consciously—seen *any* dimension of suffering in him, except for some odd phrasing in the pitifully inadequate note. I know, too, that the awkwardness might have been due to fear more than guilt. After all, in his first statement to the press, the young District Attorney had mentioned the possibility of the death penalty. My father, of course, managed to escape that. He might well have also had the notion that his world, his life—whatever happened—was ruined. At best it would become vastly different from what it would have been. That's what I assumed, too. But now I think I was wrong.

I don't think his world really did change, not after his conviction, not after he weathered the next two-thirds or so of a single year. That's the irony, and I sometimes feel bad about it, and at other times confused. My point is this: I don't think my parents suffered, not for what they did to Buster, not for what they did to me. Maybe—and I'll confess this if I should—I was and am complicit with them. That, I think, once frightened me. And maybe it still frightens me that there *is* a time for everything, even if one thing cancels out another. But the most troubling part of the mystery is this: my father and my mother killed my husband, a young man I loved. They did it coldbloodedly, and neither guilt nor regret seemed to touch them.

What happened did not occur on the spur of a moment. They had threatened to kill him months before they actually committed the crime. Their story—hell with Dad's note, I was trying to read too much into it—their story, as I see it, had nothing to do with sin and redemption; and as far as I know, they never even had the impulse to ask for forgiveness. They lived their lives as if what they had done had never occurred; and I and the church and the city allowed them to do that.

Although my father never ran for public office again, he moved back into the community. No one seemed troubled by what had happened. No one, in fact, seemed to remember what had happened. All stayed, as we say, normal, though years later I did overhear someone say that, years back, a certain attorney here—he, too, has been gone for some time—used to tell the young ones in his firm about what once happened long ago: a mayor of our place shot his son-in-law to death before witnesses, and he suffered no harm.

I knew of that attorney, but I don't know what his purpose was, other than perhaps to warn his novices about how fragile justice is. And if that's what he had in mind, he was right. My father and my mother died peacefully, unstained, untortured, and unbruised, while Buster's story disappeared. That's what I can't accept.

But I will also confess that, however much I don't want to admit it, what is personal sometimes seems sufficiently meaningful in itself, though it might die with me. I can say that, but I have never been able to stay comfortable with that, in spite of the fact that in the random outbursts of that miracle called memory, *then* often supplants *now;* but *now* just as often supplants *then;* and through it all, through tears and joy and rage and spans of mindlessness even, the strangeness of the world endures, sometimes even wondrously—and I admit that, too—in spite of what so many so easily forget.

About the Author

James Hoggard's work in multiple genres has routinely been called "brilliant." A poet, short story writer, novelist, playwright, essayist and translator, he is the author of twenty books and the recipient of numerous awards, including, in 2006, the Lon Tinkle Award for Excellence Sustained Throughout a Career. He has also been Poet Laureate of Texas and twice president of the Texas Institute of Letters.

His novel *Trotter Ross* (Wings, 1999) was called "far and away the finest novel about masculine coming of age in current American literature" by Leonard Randolph, former director of the National Endowment for the Arts Literature Program. Writing about *Patterns of Illusion: Short Stories & A Novella*, the novelist John Nichols said, "Hoggard knows as much as anyone on earth about the small tender mercies and brutalities of people ... a truly wonderful writer." His collection of poems, *Wearing The River* (Wings, 2005), received the PEN Southwest Poetry Award. His most recent book is *Triangles of Light: The Edward Hopper Poems* (Wings, 2009).

In addition to appearing in periodicals such as *Harvard Review, Southwest Review, Words Without Borders, Manoa, TriQuarterly, Arts & Letters, Image, Massachusetts Review, Partisan Review,* and many other journals and anthologies, his work has also appeared in India, England, Canada, and the Czech Republic. He's given readings and lectures at universities throughout the U.S. as well as in Mexico, Cuba, and Iraq. A noted literary translator, Hoggard was chosen to give the University Professors Lecture On Literary Translation and Theory at Boston University.

Hoggard is the Perkins-Prothro Distinguished Professor of English at Midwestern State University in Wichita Falls, Texas.

Critical Praise for Other Works by James Hoggard

Make no bones about it: *Trotter Ross* is far and away, the finest novel about masculine "coming of age" in current American literature.... The author has given us the most fully-realized and interesting protagonist since – well, yes, since Holden Caulfield.

    — Leonard Randolph, former director
       NEA Literature Program

Trotter Ross ... comes to life as a smart and troubled young man trying to establish himself even as he hurtles toward a dangerous climatic confrontation.

    — *Publishers Weekly*

On one level there emerges in *Trotter Ross* a tight, powerful narrative and clear picture of the towns and highways and sheltered places of a real and literal Texas and New Mexico, for Hoggard has a poet's eye for detail and an ability to call on the language to crack and pop as he needs it to. The deeper dimension is mythic.

    — Marshall Terry, author of *Tom Northway,*
      Dallas Stories and *Angels Prostate Fall*

In *Patterns of Illusion,* James Hoggard's terrain is the human heart, especially its boundaries, the shadowy edges where everything that really matters happens. Conflict, in the classical sense, is not what these stories are about. They're quiet stories about the beginning of conflict, the literary equivalent of a storm warning. The author catches his characters at the edge of crisis. And the weight of what may happen is what makes these stories matter.

    — Brent Spencer, *Dallas Morning News*

In *Triangles of Light,* the voice is Hopper's, the poetic craft is Hoggard's. For anyone who is fascinated by Hopper's images, reading this book is like encountering one possible version of Hopper's "primary imagination"—that part of him that was compelled, by what he saw in the world, to respond passionately and deeply.

> — Reginald Gibbons, author of *Creatures of a Day;* finalist 2008 National Book Award

James Hoggard's account of his long fascination with Hopper is so finely tuned that it's as if Hopper, ever the skeptic, resonates in response, and channels himself through Hoggard's poems to recreate the psychic matrices of his own creations. Drawn from language as sparse and telling as the painter's gestures, these poems provide "a local habitation" for Hopper's scenarios and personae, with a consanguine authenticity that is utterly convincing.

> — William Pitt Root, author of *White Boots* and *Faultdancing*

In 1962 the painter Edward Hopper said, "Maybe I am not very human. What I wanted to do was paint sunlight on the side of a house." With spare, sure strokes, in a passionate and graceful series of poems written in Hopper's imagined voice, James Hoggard takes the risk of rendering the painter startlingly more human. *Triangles of Light* deepens our experience of Hopper's haunting work and the visionary spirit that created it. Your own light and shadows may change indelibly.

> — Naomi Shihab Nye, author of *19 Varieties of Gazelle* and *I'll Ask You Three Times, Are You OK?*

This collection *[Patterns of Illusion]* of always-original stories and a novella is fascinating, deeply moving, often lyrical, and occasionally brilliantly bizarre. Hoggard knows as much as anyone on earth about the small tender mercies and brutalities of people, whether intimately together or breaking apart. He describes the human heart with a poignant lyricism and sometimes brutal hurting — and he understands well the demon soul. I have seldom read anyone so well-tuned to the rhythms of children and fractured families. It is as if John Cheever had morphed with Raymond Chandler and Carson McCullers somewhere in that vast land of Texas. The writing is simple, occasionally almost delicate, yet layered with interpretive possibilities. Always the stories are affecting for the depth of love revealed, and for the raw emotion that grows out of Hoggard's quiet approach that eventually explodes with power, or with surprising bursts of hilarious laughter. Herein also lies the best dialogue I have read in a long long time. Hoggard is a poet, a seer, an astute psychologist, and a truly wonderful writer.

— John Nichols, author of *The Milagro Beanfield War, Nirvana Blues,* and other works.

Wings Press was founded in 1975 by Joanie Whitebird and Joseph F. Lomax, both deceased, as "an informal association of artists and cultural mythologists dedicated to the preservation of the literature of the nation of Texas." Publisher, editor and designer since 1995, Bryce Milligan is honored to carry on and expand that mission to include the finest in American writing—meaning all of the Americas, without commercial considerations clouding the choice to publish or not to publish.

Wings Press attempts to produce multicultural books, chapbooks, CDs, DVDs and broadsides that, we hope, enlighten the human spirit and enliven the mind. Everyone ever associated with Wings has been or is a writer, and we know well that writing is a transformational art form capable of changing the world, primarily by allowing us to glimpse something of each other's souls. Good writing is innovative, insightful, and interesting. But most of all it is honest.

Likewise, Wings Press is committed to treating the planet itself as a partner. Thus the press uses as much recycled material as possible, from the paper on which the books are printed to the boxes in which they are shipped.

As Robert Dana wrote in *Against the Grain,* "Small press publishing is personal publishing. In essence, it's a matter of personal vision, personal taste and courage, and personal friendships." Welcome to our world.

Colophon

This first edition of *The Mahyor's Daughter*, by James Hoggard, has been printed on 55 pound Edwards Brothers Natural paper containing fifty percent recycled fiber. Titles have been set in Parisian type, the text is in Adobe Caslon type. All Wings Press books are designed and produced by Bryce Milligan.

On-line catalogue and ordering:
www.wingspress.com

Wings Press titles are distributed
to the trade by the
Independent Publishers Group
www.ipgbook.com
and in Europe by
www.gazellebookservices.co.uk